Other DI

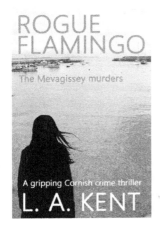

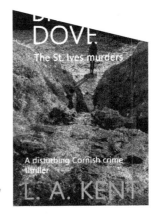

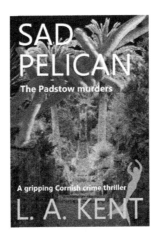

FOR ROBERT

SILENT GULL

L A Kent

Published by WillowOrchard Publishing

www.lakent.co.uk

Silent Gull

First published in Great Britain in 2017 by WillowOrchard Publishing

Published by WillowOrchard Publishing.

978-0-9575109-5-1

A CIP catalogue record for this book is available from the British Library.

For information about the Treloar series, the characters and the authors, and beautiful photographs of Cornwall where the series is set:
www.lakent.co.uk.

Map of Fowey Bodinnick Polruan and The Valley of the Tides

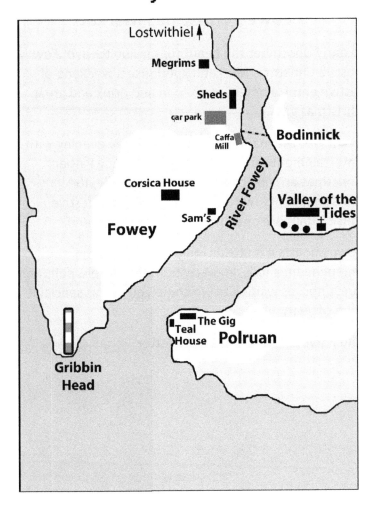

Celebrate Christmas in Cornwall at Fowey Christmas Market

In early December the beautiful seaside town of Fowey hosts a Christmas Market. Experience a weekend of festive entertainment, with food and drink and great Christmas gifts.

Events for the market start on the Friday evening with entertainment through the town including Father Christmas arriving by tug, a lantern parade, the Christmas lights switch on, a hog roast and festive music. Stalls are open throughout the weekend.

Fowey boasts a fantastic range of unique little independent shops, great restaurants, hotels, pubs and guest houses waiting to welcome you at this special time of year.

The Fowey at Christmas Newsletter

One

It was cold on the water. It was late November in Cornwall. It was late evening. A figure clad in a wetsuit, in a navy blue kayak, was pulling against the inflowing waters of the tide across the River Fowey from the Fowey side. A bright intermittent moon was shining off the water then disappearing behind sweeping clouds. The kayaker moved silently and expertly between the boats moored in the channel, then hugged the far side of the river which was uninhabited and safe from prying eyes. It steered into a tributary, where the going was easier, and glided up to a small jetty where a second figure clad in jeans and a dark hoodie was waiting, breath misting in the cold air.

A large tanned hand reached down to grab the prow and secured the kayak to a ring before moving to repeat the action at the stern. The paddle was handed up and then the paddler raised its arms and was lifted onto the jetty and into a passionate

1

embrace. The paddler pulled a beanie off its head and a mass of red curls fell down its shoulders.

'Hey Babe,' said the lifter, smiling to reveal perfect white teeth in a tanned handsome face with piercing sapphire eyes. He was a good-looking boy.

'Hey Hitch,' said the girl returning his smile.

Her name was Georgiana Spargo and her father, Christian, was one of the most feared and despised men in Cornwall. If he had known the purpose of her crossing and who she was visiting, he would have killed her with his bare hands.

At the end of the jetty was a series of old terraced buildings and thatched roundhouses, all entirely in darkness. The lovers should have been alone. But someone was watching and listening. A man was standing inside the nearest roundhouse in the darkness having just emerged from the flotation tank. He should not have been there at night. What psychologist Dr Ivan Speer, ever on the lookout for an opportunity for blackmail and betrayal, with all his experience of troubled minds, should have remembered, was that secrets are dangerous, and even other people's can get you killed.

Christian Spargo resented Jackson Power. How could anyone leave California for Cornwall; abandon the weather, the space, the money, the opportunities? Christian's greatest regret in life was that he hadn't left for the US years ago. Opportunity lost. His dreams had been limited to the narrow grey horizons of the UK.

The US would have understood him; appreciated him; valued him; Christ, honoured him! Here he was treated with civil contempt. Oh, they respected his money and feared his assumed violence, but they didn't like him. They bridled at his uncouth presence in their riverside idyll. Just like his hero, Napoleon Bonaparte, he was misunderstood and despised. They had a stereotypical image of a gangster and they had pinned it on him.

But the real reason for his hatred of Jackson Power was a bitter, festering obsession with a commercial defeat. Christian had been about to exchange contracts on the purchase of Seal Hall when he was outbid by a ridiculously higher offer by Power, the Hollywood superstar, much to the delight of the local community. Everyday, Christian could stare from the upstairs windows of his substantial home, Corsica House, set among the evergreen trees above the narrow streets of Fowey, across the Fowey River to the domain of his enemy on the top of the opposite wooded slope. He tried not to, but sometimes it was irresistible.

Power, a Minnesota farm boy whose real name was Rolf Lindström, had shot to fame in the nineties when he had been cast as an unknown Hollywood newcomer to play the hero in the first of a phenomenally successful series of movies about a fictional medieval kingdom. Twenty years later he was a multi-millionaire with a beautiful wife, Erin, a family home on Mulholland Drive in Los Angeles and millions of devoted fans. He had gained great fame and fortune, but he had lost his eldest son.

Jackson and Erin had named their four children for their Hollywood favourites. The eldest, a boy, Ford after director John Ford; then daughter, Davis, after actress Bette Davis; son Hitchcock, known as Hitch, after director Alfred Hitchcock; and finally daughter Gardner, known as Posy, after actress Ava Gardner. All had been wonderful in their Camelot life until Ford fell in with the wrong crowd, took to drugs, escalating to heroin, and despite his parent's frantic efforts and copious cash, died of a massive overdose in a seedy motel on Hollywood Boulevard the previous year.

Erin had turned to her therapist, but bereft and inconsolable, Jackson Power had left for Europe. He had toured the continent fleeing his pain and eventually found himself in London. Sitting in the bar of the Savoy hotel, he had been leafing aimlessly through a back copy of Country Life magazine when he had come across an estate agent's details of a property for sale in Cornwall: Seal Hall. He knew it was perfect for a project that had been ripening in his mind. He phoned the agent and secured the property sight unseen. Over the course of the following eighteen months he had created 'The Valley of the Tides: a therapeutic centre for traumatized young addictive personalities and their families'.

Seal Hall, originally a Tudor manor, had served over the years as a boys' boarding school, a TB sanatorium and a hotel. Consequently there were a number of existing buildings beyond the main hall which were turned into facilities from therapy and treatment rooms to swimming pool, gym and flotation tanks. The interior of the hall had been gutted and transformed into the equivalent of a luxury hotel and spa to accommodate residents and a stable block transformed into en suite rooms for families and friends. Steps led from Seal Hall's gardens down to the water's edge on a tributary of the Fowey River. Here were the chapel and graveyard of the original Tudor estate, the seaweed pool, boat storage and a small jetty and a flotation tank in a thatched roundhouse.

The following morning Christian Spargo's thoughts were for once not turned toward his nemesis across the water, but to his youngest daughter, Georgie. She had come home very late the previous night, in fact, it must have been the early hours of the morning. Since the summer she had been unusually quiet. Normally the girl was full of life and laughter but for the past few months she had been distracted and distant. Of course what he didn't and couldn't know was that Georgie was constantly thinking about Hitch Lindström, and obviously unable to share her thoughts with her father. Christian's loathing and resentment encompassed the entire Lindström family.

Georgie Spargo had met Hitch Lindström that summer on 20 June at 21:37. He was attending the 21st birthday celebration of his best friend, Kit Penrose, at Sam's in Fowey and she was waiting on tables. The attraction between them had been instant and electric. Even Kit, who by that time had visited several pubs and bars and consumed a substantial number of beers, noticed. Kit worked at The Valley of the Tides as a gardener/handyman and lived in a small terraced house in Fowey which he had inherited from his grandmother. When Hitch wanted to overnight in Fowey, this is where he stayed.

Christian stood on the patio outside his drawing room in the pale early morning light gazing at the river where a mist was creeping along the water towards the sea like a predatory ghost. The air was still and silent. Threads of smoke drifted from an occasional chimney. He was pondering what to do about Georgie; whether he should speak to her mother or to his wife, Lana, who was nearer in age to his children. His elder daughter, Josephine, was of no use. She was living in London and wasn't close to Georgie anyway, and his son, Leon, he was a boy and therefore useless when it came to emotional issues.

One of the many myths surrounding Christian was that he had dumped his first wife, Lizzie, for a newer, younger model: Lana. In reality Lizzie had left him. She had gone off 'to find herself' and he had little contact with her. He smiled to himself as he recalled one of Napoleon's sayings which he thought entirely appropriate to his relationship with his first wife and her quest: 'Never interrupt your enemy when he's making a mistake.' As he chuckled softly the silence was broken by a piercing scream coming from low across the water. Hopefully that's Power dead, he thought. He was half right; it wasn't Power.

Two

Ducking away from the smoke, which was building strongly, then running down towards the river he had been smiling, happy, seriously pleased with himself, it had all come together. Jumping over rocks and jagging round trees and bushes, eyes accustomed to the dark, he had slowed as he got close to the creek. Still smiling he could smell the smoke, it seemed to be getting stronger, or was it just the breeze swirling more of it in his direction?

He had laughed as he slowed down at the creek bank and turned right and jogged along the path towards the river where he saw the boat moving slowly towards the bank, and the lights of Fowey above the opposite bank. 'This is what it's all about,' he said to himself and he couldn't stop smiling as he had jogged towards the boat.

He jogged carefully, watching the lights jumping up and down with him as he ran, thinking back, 'star dies suddenly. How and why?' Ha, that's what they said in the paper,' he thought, 'and now here we all are. Bloody stars, who needs the bastards?' remembering what had brought him to The Valley of the Tides; 'couldn't have worked out better, shame it took so bloody long.' The boat was closing in even more slowly and he saw that he needed to speed up to be able to grab the rope when it was thrown, and he had laughed when the boat turned sharply away to go round again.

He was late, only a couple of minutes, and Mad Cam hadn't seen him waiting where he should have been, by the rusting old bollard at the top of the bank. At that time of the cloudy morning there was no light to help. He was supposed to flash the small green torch light to show Mad Cam that he was there and ready.

He needed Mad Cam to get back quickly. He needed to get on, and as he watched the boat turning to come back it was much too slow. He couldn't smell the smoke anymore, maybe the breeze had changed direction, maybe the fire had gone out , 'I don't think so,' he had thought and laughed again. He looked at the boat and shouted quietly, 'hurry up ….. come on man.' Standing still and looking over the top of the boat he could see the lights of Fowey stretching up from the road along the bank opposite; up to the straight string line of lights

9

running along the Readymoney road near the top of the hill before they disappeared behind houses on their way down to the cove.

It had taken ages working out how to escape, how to move on. Starting out, he hadn't really wanted to hurt anyone, but in the end he had to, and it had all worked out.

It had been great to start with, he was his own boss, could do what he wanted, which had been bloody brilliant, he knew, everyone said so, and they kept coming back. There was even a waiting list, growing and getting longer all the time. The list had disappeared overnight, he'd read about it in the papers. Perfect.

'No-one knew, really knew,' he thought, 'a few people thought they did but no-one could prove it'. He smiled again and looked down the river towards Polruan, not much to see, just the vague outline of the hill on the left in the distance as it dropped down to the estuary, a different shade of dark, and the Christmas lights on the quay. He smelled the smoke again and laughed. Shouted under his breath again at the boat. He had to hurry.

Standing at last by the old bollard and noticing his breath white in the chill air, he pointed the torch at the slowly burbling boat and flashed it on and off until its engine tone changed slightly and moved slowly towards him. He only stopped flashing when the boat swung against the high outgoing tide and was side-on to the bank, two metres off, prow pointing upstream, and holding its position. 'Oi boy, where you bloody been?!' growled Mad Cam, 'we need to get off, quick, not get stuck by 'ere. Right.' …….Then Mad Cam curtly barked, 'looking!'

A dark rectangular crate was suddenly swinging past, to the right of his head, and was quickly lowered to the ground next to him. He reached down, freed the holding loops from underneath, said 'OK Cam go,' and the winch was swinging the rope back and up to the deck. Less than a minute later another crate was swinging its way to the bank and he stacked it on top of the first, then a third arrived and after freeing the loops said, 'right go, thanks man, appreciate it …. call you again soon.' The engine was already increasing its pitch and moving forward; turning back out into the river even as the rope was winding back to the deck. Cam said nothing. He stood and watched as the boat, still without lights, faded quietly down the river, back towards the sea.

The smoke was suddenly there again, on the breeze, just for a second, and he smiled and looked down at the crates before walking over to the sack trolley he had left close to the bollard earlier and wheeled it over to the crates. He wheeled its base under the bottom crate and shoved hard, twisting the handles as he pushed, then kicking the base with his right foot as it got too hard to push alone, until the crates were hard up against the uprights of the trolley. Pausing for breath for a minute he smiled as he remembered how it had fallen off the back of a lorry in Mevagissey - at least that is what the driver he had given the fifty pounds to had told him he would tell his boss when he asked for a new one. He had got a bargain; it was brilliant. With three wheels arranged in a kind of triangle on each side and made for getting heavy boxes up and down stairs, it was perfect for getting precious and delicate cargo safely around the rough paths and over the occasional logs it found itself dealing with these days.

He laughed out loud, pulled the handles towards him keeping his right foot against the base, tilting the trolley, then he carefully lowered it until he was holding the handles at arm's length, said, 'right let's get on,' and set off, back towards the smoke, wheeling the crates up the slope and away from the river.

Three

If Christian Spargo was one of the most feared men in Cornwall, his younger brother, Gideon, was one of the most feared in Europe. Were a seagull to fly westwards some 40 miles from The Valley of the Tides it would reach Newlyn, where it could fly over the fish market to land on the roof of a terrace of stone cottages, home to Abraham Spargo, Christian's father, and son, Gideon.

Here, at his bedroom window, for hours on end, sat Abraham Spargo watching the world go by like a beady-eyed, silent gull. Long gone were the days when he had ruled his boys with an iron rod. Now he was marooned in this cold room, at the mercies of his depraved son Gideon. It was Gideon who now ran Gwavas Fish, the family fishing fleet, supposedly his main occupation. But Abraham knew that the boy had inherited his grandfather's taste for smuggling and had expanded it into darker realms. Gideon had no boundaries. If there was money in it, Gideon would smuggle it: alcohol, cigarettes, drugs, weapons, people ... Abraham was scared of his son Gideon, although he would never admit it. So, he remained silent.

Christian on the other hand was a 'legitimate businessman'. Sneering at his brother he would often say; 'If I'd wanted to profit from human misery, I'd have become a dentist.' But Abraham remembered that in his youth, his elder son's hands had not been so squeaky clean. And Christian was the only person Abraham knew who was not frightened of Gideon. Well, apart from his granddaughter Georgiana, but then she was frightened of nobody and nothing. He adored her. And he didn't see enough of her since Christian had moved them all to Fowey. All his grandchildren ... gone away.

Christian Spargo had never been involved in the Gwavas Fish business. He had worked on the boats during school holidays but he had always hated the smells and the mess: fish, guts, oil, diesel, wet ropes, bloody sea water. Whilst Gideon was eyeing the illegal possibilities in Europe, Christian was eyeing the legal opportunities in the West Country, and his gaze fell on leisure and tourism. He had started with two rather seedy night clubs in Union Street in Plymouth, a fact which some of his Fowey neighbours loved to fling in his face. They had enjoyed a reputation for trouble, rough doormen, dodgy dealings and lax application of the licensing laws. They were known as the places to go to source anything from female company to weapons. But his business interests had moved upmarket; had developed to include cafés, bars, holiday camps and hotels and his empire stretched from Bristol to Penzance. Seal Hall was to have been the jewel in his crown. Was to have been.

Gideon had never married; never given him grandchildren. Abraham knew why, but didn't dare speak of it. So, in his silence he brooded, and the thing he dwelled on the most, was not the knowledge of his son's many terrible deeds, but the fact that he had cost Abraham his dearest, oldest friend: Jago Treloar.

Further back along the coast towards Fowey is the port of Falmouth, one of the world's deepest natural harbours, set in one of Cornwall's larger extended wooded valleys. Home to dockyards, boatyards, and a healthy tourist trade, Falmouth is a larger version of Fowey. Here on a bluff overlooking the estuary, a former hotel had been converted into a hospice for police officers. It was into this building on that cold late November morning that Detective Inspector Félipe Treloar, son of Jago, walked with a heavy heart. Treloar hated these places. For a man who saw more than his fair share of death and suffering, he had a morbid dread of serious illness and the natural end of life.

Treloar was the son of a Spanish mother and a Cornish father, with blonde blue-eyed good looks which made him a favourite of the media and hence the Chief Constable. He was the head of a small team in Devon & Cornwall Police which handled serious crime and he had a reputation for getting results.

He had come to visit his former boss and mentor, a retired Detective Chief Superintendent, Joe Thwaite. Every visit he was reminded of the man he had worked with, a big booming Yorkshireman who instilled terror into the ranks; now much diminished. As Treloar crossed the polished wood floor towards the reception desk he glanced around at the soothing primrose walls and the bold seascapes. He recognised some new additions as the work of his near neighbour and friend Ochre Pengelly.

Having signed in, he slowly climbed the stairs to the first floor like a reluctant schoolboy on his way to the headmaster's office. He walked along the plush carpeted hallway to the end and knocked on a door before opening it. He entered the room to be met by the customary stuffiness: a mixture of too much heat and too much cleaning product.

Joe Thwaite, now a frail wraithlike figure, was sitting in a reclining armchair in the bay window facing out over the dockyard. Treloar felt his spirits lift; the last time he had visited Joe had been confined to bed but as he approached Treloar could see the man looked much improved.

'Morning Boss,' Treloar said, laying a hand on the older man's shoulder.

'Hello there lad,' Thwaite replied. 'Good of thee

to come so quick.'

Treloar smiled as he reflected on how his former boss's accent seemed to get more pronounced with every visit. Probably too much time spent alone with his past.

'I got your message.' The younger man said, sitting in the second chair in the window.

'Aye, well. I wanted to tell thee something whilst there's time. It's been weighing on me of late.'

'What is it Boss? Something from one of our cases?'

'Nay lad, not exactly. More like the one that got away. A right bastard I never nailed. More like a right bastard and his spawn ...' he broke off, coughing and reached for a box of tissues. Treloar poured and handed him a glass of water.

'Ta lad,' he said recovering, 'where was I?'

'A bastard and his spawn?'

'Aye a right bastard if ever there were one. And we never got the bugger, not for 'owt major.'

'OK ... how can I help?'

'I want you to nail him. And I'll give you cause. His youngest's an evil shite who likes to hurt people and loves nowt but money. He has no soul, none lad.'

'Who are we talking about?'

'Gideon Spargo. He's the worst of 'em, but they're all rotten them Spargos.'

Treloar looked surprised. There had been Spargos in Cornwall forever; they were an ancient clan. Some said the giant Corineus, founder of the county, was a Spargo. Of course Treloar knew of the Spargo family and the many lurid stories that surrounded them, but nobody had ever been able to convict them of anything that sent them away for any serious time.

Thwaite noticed the look on his protégé's face.

'Aye, I know, many 'ave tried. But none 'ave had thy reason.'

'My reason?'

Thwaite fell silent for a while, gazing out to sea and then sighed deeply.

'Spargos, one or all of the bastards, are responsible for what happened to thy father.'

Treloar started in his chair. His father had gone missing, presumed drowned, whilst swimming in a cove near the family farm on the north Cornish coast some years previously. Despite himself he raised his voice. 'What? You're saying the Spargo family made my father kill himself, drown himself?'

'Nay lad ... They made him disappear but thy father's not drowned. He's alive and well.'

Four

He got the idea after Alan in Seattle sent the email warning him not to use the crabs, with a credit note attached, last year in November. They were putting on a week of "holiday specials", just before Thanksgiving and it was sold out. He had ordered twenty five kilos of flash-frozen Dungeness crab from the fish market in Seattle, Pike Place. The food fundies said that they didn't quite have the flavour and texture of live crabs but he knew they were flash frozen straight out of the sea; Alan had taken him on the boats, he'd seen them do it, and they were normally guaranteed superb.

Reliable guy, great supplier, but Alan had been caught out like everyone else by the epidemic caused by algae off the northeast Pacific coast. It had affected most shellfish, especially crabs, and no-one was allowed to catch them or sell them once the problem had been identified. A big chunk of the shellfish industry in the western USA had been seriously screwed, including restaurants, and especially the fishermen.

They tasted great but made people violently ill, causing vomiting and worse, almost immediately after eating them. Alan had sent him an email with a warning and an apology and a credit note. Amazing, he'd sent it the day the crabs arrived. A bright red sticker from the United States Fish and Wildlife Service had been stuck onto the credit note before it had been scanned, talking about severe illness and even death and brain damage, and the crabs were taken off the menu. But even then he thought they might come in useful and after throwing most out he had locked three kilos in his personal freezer; being head chef at The Rock in Brighton was driving him nuts.

When he had taken the job it was great. The new owners had sold shares in a software company they had founded in Johannesburg, South Africa, and had some serious money. They had spent a lot on refurbishment, had an ambition to run a top restaurant in England and had hired him to help them achieve it. The pay was good and the flat on the top floor above the restaurant had been nicely done out and he had been able to move miles away from his bitch of an ex who still lived in Solihull.

They pretty much left him to get on with it, but had to approve the menus and taste the food before they were printed up, and to meet new staff before they agreed contracts. The specials were different. They depended on the often unplanned fish, meat and game that turned up in the morning or that he had been called about the night before. He did what he wanted with the specials menu, had to, there wasn't enough time for "trials" and they weren't always around anyway. He had always been creative and was a good chef; truth be told he was a bloody great chef, and he really enjoyed thinking about food and inventing new dishes and cooking them, himself, personally.

Making it to the top in Brighton had not really been that hard, it had even been interesting at first although he did miss being hands-on. Always the supervisor, keeping his eye on what everyone else was doing, what supplies were coming in, that they were on time and top quality when they arrived, stored properly, checking what was on order and who from and when it was due in, walking round the kitchen seeing what was being done and how, making sure everything was properly cooked and ready on time, looking at the plates before they went out, making sure the presentations matched the pictures that he used for training in the morning menu meetings with the kitchen crew before they got going. So much to do and not much of it was cooking.

There was a meat chef, a fish chef, a pastry chef and a pudding chef; and sous chefs and commis chefs and trainee chefs and assistants and apprentices coming out of his ears, but it was all still down to him, his responsibility to make sure it all worked, that the customers would keep coming back, that the waiting list kept growing.

The experimenting and dish development was for the afternoons, or the seriously early mornings, and it wasn't unusual for him to pull an all-nighter to finish off an idea, when there was no-one else in the kitchen. The sousies helped, couldn't have done it without them. Most of the time though from when he got out of bed in the morning to whenever he crashed, he was nothing more than a bloody supervisor, a foreman, a teacher, an inspector; he was seriously stressed, and he hated it with a passion.

Five

Abraham Spargo's father, Abel, had been a monstrously cruel man; a sea captain; a bully and a tyrant. When Abraham was twelve and on his maiden voyage aboard the trawler St Cecilia, then the largest vessel in the Spargo fleet, Abel, drunk, had tied his son's arm into the net and thrown him overboard, threatening to keelhaul the boy. The horrified crew had hauled the net back in quickly, too quickly, causing a fracture which the terrified boy had hidden. Untreated, it had healed badly and left Abraham with a damaged left arm. The experience had left him with deep psychological scars.

When Gideon had been a child, abused and tormented by his older brother Christian, Abraham had turned a blind eye; the abused tolerating the abuser. Now as an old man, just as he had once been terrorised and humiliated by his father, so he was by his younger son. The wheel had come full circle.

Only in his youth, before his marriage, after his father had drowned when he was fourteen, had Abraham been truly happy. His schoolmate and pal Jago Treloar had been big and brave and fearless and he had protected Abraham from bullies. Jago had included him, made him feel valued. He had taken Abraham along on the famed Brittany Ferries' trip to Santander. Thinking back to that night brought a smile to his face. They had been a bunch of lads on a night out in Plymouth. After a few too many beers, they had ended up on this ferry thinking they would dock in Roscoff and get back the next day. However, they ended up in Santander in northern Spain, Jago had met his future wife Inés and the rest was history. Abraham had been at Jago's wedding, at his children's christenings.

And on the one occasion that Abraham had stood up to Gideon, it had been for Jago Treloar. He had warned Jago that Gideon had put a price on his head, a contract out for his death. He had told Jago to disappear to save his farm and his family, and in doing so he had lost his best friend.

It was as 1 Timothy 6:10 in the King James Bible states: "For the love of money is the root of all evil." Abraham knew that was true of his son Gideon. Whilst there had always been an element of smuggling alongside the fishing in the family business

Gideon had moved into the dark but profitable areas of drugs, weapons and people trafficking. And when Abraham thought he could fall no lower, he had discovered there was no depth to which Gideon would not sink for his precious gold.

Of course, when you're bringing in high risk cargo, you can't just sail into port. Not always. So that had been the problem. Jago Treloar owned a farm on the north Cornish coast near Zennor with access to the sea: Cove Farm. Gideon wanted that access and temporary use of farm buildings for storage. Jago refused and threatened to go to the police. The next thing Abraham knew he got word in the port of Newlyn that the contract was out. He warned Jago. Jago went swimming and never returned. In eight years he had heard no word. He had lost his best friend and it was all down to Gideon. Abraham hated his son.

Six

'Great' he said to himself when he was nearly there and could see that the flames had almost completely died, that the coals were beginning to glow red and that their glow was spreading. It was still dark, the breeze was coming and going, and he heard the hoots of two owls calling to each other in the woods as he looked at the coals and thought. He could see that he had around half an hour before the coals would be full on and ready for the first of the smoking boxes; plenty of time to fillet two of the special haddock that would be inside one of the crates. They were special because they shouldn't be landing haddock, not here, not now.

There was a local ban on and inspectors were turning up and going through the markets and harbour cold stores all along the south Cornwall coast to enforce it. Ha! It was to stop juveniles being caught, to conserve the stocks. "Bloody rubbish," Mad Cam had said. He had told him there were plenty of the bigger fish around, you just needed to know where they were, and how to catch them, and that the fisheries people were a waste of space. He wouldn't take the juveniles anyway, it wasn't worth it, didn't get much for them and he hadn't caught any since he had resized his nets and square meshed them years ago, never mind about throwing them back. "Idiots," he had said. Running dark might be risky, but it helped Mad Cam keep his good customers happy, and his catches away from prying eyes. And where he was catching them, hidden from the eyes of the competition.

Not that many would have tried to follow him anyway. At the right time of night, at the right state of the tide, the haddock shoaled next to the Hole, the Gribbin Hole the fishermen called it. Three miles out, south of Gribbin Head at the mouth of the Fowey estuary, it was a deep basin two hundred metres across and with steep walls formed below the floor of the seabed. The tide pushed the water down into it and circulated the water round it and when it swirled back out it brought with it the best fish food in Cornwall, whichever way the tide was flowing.

The faster the water, the more the food and the

bigger the shoaling fish. But the faster the water, the more dangerous it was and the more difficult to keep the nets away from the wrecked boats already around the Hole. With nets caught, the fast circulating water and bad weather could be lethal, for men as well as their boats.

Cam had mapped the wrecks, and studied the way the water worked them as it flowed around and over the Hole for years; he was in his element. A few thought they knew that he fished there and thought it must have been why people called him Mad. No-one knew that he knew the Hole was the second in a line of holes, all the same size, fifteen kilometres apart. It stretched from the hole that Bodmin Moor's Colliford Lake reservoir was built around, ran across the English Channel and surfaced again in France, ending with the hole that was part of the Reservoir de St Michel in Brittany, not far from Roscoff. No-one knew that he was sure when and how it had been made and why the holes were there, in a line.

Harry wheeled the trolley into the outdoor preparation area that was part of his covered smoking and barbecue kitchen, switched on the light and laughed when he saw FAL FISH stencilled onto the sides of the crates, then braced himself and heaved the top one onto the counter. Then he lugged the other two crates up and lifted their lids to see what he had scored, then he laughed again and said, "fuck me Cam you're brilliant, if anyone can, Cam can," before lifting two eighty centimetre haddock out of the second crate. He saw four massive red gurnard and more haddock in the ice underneath. The first crate was full of big crabs - spider and brown - and the third had a mix of large cod and more red gurnard.

He looked across at the smoker grill then back at the two haddock and lifted one back into its crate before heaving all three crates back onto the trolley and wheeling it across to the cold-room where he would count and weigh the score in a few hours time. He carefully wrote what he could see of what was in each crate onto freezer-proof labels and peeled and stuck them to the crates to save time later.

He had nine breakfast specials this morning - six freshly smoked haddock with poached eggs and three herbed and poached gurnard with poached eggs. He would wait until the haddock were on the smoker before picking the chervil and chopping it; it was just around the corner against the wall of the herb garden for protection from the elements. He sowed a fresh batch of seeds in the greenhouse every six weeks and asked the gardener to plant them out after four weeks. It was easy to grow but the stems were fragile and easily flattened by the rain and blown over by the wind.

The gurnard fillets were already skinned, and sitting in the fridge waiting for the olive oil rub, salt, and a good sprinkling of chopped chervil before being bagged and vacuum packed before poaching. He had been awake and out of bed early to prep, no need for sousies today. The fish took six minutes, so he would wait for the guests to arrive before starting to cook them; the haddock was a different story.

He threatened the guests, they needed it, even enjoyed it, quietly amongst themselves. "I'm not going to spend time cooking great food if they can't be arsed to eat it when it's ready," he had told the restaurant manager, then the facilities manager when he had been hauled up to the office after the first time. They had to be at their tables by eight o'clock at the latest or their breakfast would be auctioned to the highest bidder, by him. At eight o'clock the fish would be off the smoker, golden brown, the skin deliciously crispy and the flesh deliciously creamy, and the eggs would have just been carefully lifted from the salmon poacher and precisely positioned on the plates. Too late meant soggy skin and hard eggs, but everyone knew the rules so that was OK. The hot-smoked haddock was legendary and the auction had only taken place three times so far, each time to a crowded breakfast room as the meal-missers had entered and cringed.

He smiled and looked around as he automatically reached for a filleting knife. It was his place, his space and the Chef hated him for it. The sous chefs and assistants in the main kitchen were intrigued and impressed with it, and the Chef was seriously jealous. His smoking and barbeque kitchen had been built onto the side of his specials kitchen, at the end of the main kitchen serving The Valley of the Tides.

Jackson Power had quickly agreed to the extension only two months after he had equally quickly agreed to Harry's suggestion for the conversion of unused space at the back of the main kitchen to make it into the specials kitchen. To be his, for preparing and cooking up to ten meals twice a day, five days a week, in exchange for free board and lodging ….. and therapy at no cost whenever he wanted it, which he didn't, he didn't need it anymore ….. and forty five thousand pounds a year ….. and a variable payment per private meal cooked depending on how long it took …. and a variable payment per cooking therapy session depending on how many people attended and how long the session was. He had quickly discovered how sessions could be built around herbs, and that chervil was a favourite, and that nearly everyone was amazed to learn how they could use simple freezer bags with the air squeezed out before being tightly tied, if they didn't happen to have a vacuum pack machine at home for prepping fish for poaching.

Seven

Bella pushed open a faded sea-green wooden gate and found herself in a small courtyard garden with uneven steps leading down to an open door in a two storey white washed house. She was in Polruan across the river from Fowey. She leaned the bike against a wall and stepped inside. She was about to call out when a strong arm grabbed her from behind and a hand clamped across her mouth. She twisted away from the grip and spoke.

'I take it that's a gun in your pocket.'

'Well of course, but that doesn't mean I'm not pleased to see you.'

A muscular man with steel gray hair and deep blue eyes stood grinning broadly at her.

'I thought you said it was a blue gate,' Bella said.

'It is.'

'Really Dico; it's teal like the duck, like the name of the house for fuck's sake. Have you got something to drink? I could murder a large malt. It's miserable out there.'

'Come this way my lovely,' he whispered leading her down a short staircase and turning into an open plan kitchen and sitting area with a beamed ceiling, a quarry tiled floor and old pine furniture. He took a Glock 26 pistol from his pocket and put it in the microwave. She walked through the room to stand in the small bay window looking out over the river to the tower of Fowey parish church. To her right a french door would open onto a patio with cast iron table and chairs overlooking the river. Dico came up behind her and handed her a tumbler of Laphroaig.

'Thanks. Very nice,' she gestured around the room, 'not unlike your place.'

'Well it's damned quiet. Does anybody actually live here?'

'Of course, but it's largely rentals and second homes, and it's totally out of season now, and too early for the Christmas gangs. Show me around. I want the tour.'

They headed out of the kitchen and along a short hallway into a large white painted bedroom with a pine four poster, a wall of fitted wardrobes and jute carpeting. A red leather Chesterfield was slotted into a bay window overlooking the patio she had seen from the kitchen. A door led into a bathroom with a walk-in monsoon shower.

'The main living area is upstairs,' said Dico leaving the bedroom.

Bella followed him back up the staircase turning up a second flight into a large room with wooden floors, scattered bright modern carpets and perfectly mismatched modern sofas. But the main feature was floor to ceiling windows the length of two walls overlooking the river.

'Wow. I see you're really slumming it,' Bella exclaimed.

Dico grinned. 'Someone has to do it. Anyway, I don't suppose your accommodation is a hovel, is it?'

'No. Indeed it's very luxurious, much smarter than home.'

'I wish I could get inside to check it out for myself.'

'Yeah, like you could have passed for a new age therapist.'

'Rather like you could have passed for a biker gang leader in that Serbian op.'

'Well, at least my tattoo is real. As I recall, your cover was nearly blown when one of yours started to wash off!'

'A tattoo? Really? Do show.'

'Christ Dico, if you weren't such a great fuck I'd have shot you myself by now for sure.'

He grinned at her and turned to head back down the stairs.

'What are you supposed to be doing today anyway?' he asked over his shoulder.

'It's my day off and I'm on my usual bike ride of course.'

'Well, we can have *some* kind of ride. Follow me.'

'Really Sir, and you my superior officer and all.'

'Well, to redress that, you can go on top.'

Eight

The specials breakfast service had gone well and he had enjoyed himself even though the haddocks had all arrived on time and there were no auctions; Sous Carole had been borrowed from Chef for the morning and she was a delight. As always. She was first choice, and she had only had to pick the chervil leaves from the stems, after first cutting the stems from the plants while he watched on carefully to make sure she cut enough, and then finely chop them. She was eager, nearly always knew what to do before he told her, and was a quick learner. Today she had asked if she could poach and plate-up the eggs, and he had agreed. She had done well.

Stepping out of his lift onto the second floor veranda, on the way back to his room, he turned to his right and saw a woman walking quickly, almost trotting, not dressed for the cold morning air, her breath misting around her head and trailing behind her, her shoulder length black hair looked slept in and uncombed. Her high heeled yellow shoes clacked on the hardwood veranda decking and her short black skirt with vertical yellow stripes was creased and it swished from side to side with each step. He could see a black bra strap through her thin yellow blouse and he wondered where she had been, and where she was going. The breeze gusted and her hair flew to the left and she reached back with her left hand to stop her skirt floating any higher than the stocking top that he had glimpsed and he was suddenly back there, in Brighton, even earlier in the morning, in the summer, and he smiled, then frowned, then without thinking checked that his key ring was in his pocket, and smiled again.

*

It was three thirty in the morning in mid June, warm and dry, no clouds, sunrise was still nearly an hour and a half away and he was on his way to see what the boats had landed overnight at the Hove lagoon fish market just outside Shoreham. He remembered especially wanting to know if he had any monkfish cheeks waiting for him; they were ordered for the specials menu, but you could never be sure. He had been working on the July menus and was pulling an all-nighter and was knackered. "Fuck, that stuff's shit," he said as he opened the van door. It was new, it gleamed even in the gloom of the multi-storey lighting, but you wouldn't know it was Jupiter Red and most people wouldn't recognise it as a Mercedes unless they saw the Merc star on the front grill.

They would just see a stylish looking panel van with dark windows, and the Rock Restaurant name stencilled on the side in white, in serious capital letters, made it even more so. In a ride looking that cool at that time of the morning he couldn't afford to be carrying so he had topped up before leaving the restaurant on the way to The Lanes multi-storey car park where the council had convinced the owners they were getting a good deal on two permanent parking bays. Yeah right.

But the top up hadn't worked and he was still knackered, and moaning as he drove too quickly out of the car park into Black Lion Street before screeching right at the lights onto Kings road then slowing down quickly when he realised what he was doing just as Kings road turned into the Kingsway dual carriageway.

He had been using Amphetamine Sulphate off the street and the quality was so up and down he never knew how much he needed, or was even safe. "Bastards don't care, don't fucking work for a living and don't give a shit," he had muttered. Sometimes the crystal had been cut so many times you needed loads and got fucked with the chalk or glucose or salts or whatever else they put in it and sometimes it was so pure you could OD if you weren't careful and the bastards didn't care. 'Pay more and die! Don't know and don't care, doesn't matter where you score or what you paid for the fucking wraps,' he was thinking as he slowed down, 'got to stay lucky … bastards,' as he reached for his phone to call the fish market to find out which door to park at.

Driving along Kingsway, carefully, his eyes flicking from side to side, there was no traffic, the beach huts were silhouetted against the moon-lit sea, it had only just risen and was still low in the sky, and he was about to dial the fish market when his eye was drawn to the other side of the dual carriageway, to a couple leaving The Salt Room restaurant, well, drawn to the top of the woman's legs really, well, to the stocking tops and the bare flesh underneath the short swishing skirt. Instead of dialling he switched on the video and pointed it at the couple, and slowed down.

The guy looked middle aged, familiar even from the back, and then the side as he drew nearer. His right hand held a jacket that casually hung over his right shoulder. She didn't seem to mind as his left hand held up her skirt and slowly rubbed one cheek, then the other, and he slowed down even more and did his best to keep them in frame as he drove past.

He had looked back at them in the door mirror as he was passing The Hilton and was surprised to realise that he was right and he had recognised the guy. He was middle aged, and he was a doctor, local, one of the great and the good, and he had met him last week, at the restaurant. The owners had called him up to be congratulated personally by a party celebrating the mayor's birthday, and the doctor had been sitting to the right of the mayor's wife. He had particularly enjoyed the turbot and told him it was excellent, and his wife had agreed, saying that it had been steamed to perfection and asked with a flirtatious smile if he would give her the recipe for the shellfish sauce. She was also middle aged, and good looking, and also not the lady that was naked under her skirt that the good doctor was fondling as they approached the front doors of The Hilton.

He had just driven past the ghostly doughnut shape of the Brighton i360 viewing platform at the bottom of its tower and the dual carriageway was about to run out as the road turned back to single carriageway, and he remembered thinking quickly, 'OK maybe this shit's not so bad', as he slowed and swung round in front of The Holiday Inn and back along the other side of the Kingsway dual carriageway instead of carrying on towards

Shoreham. He had been driving slowly and the video was still running and he saw, now holding the phone steady on the top of the dashboard and zooming slowly out as they got bigger on the screen as he closed on them, that they were perfectly framed, the doctor's arm still behind the short skirted lady, the lady's right hand rubbing up and down the front of the doctor's trousers, and they kissed just before they turned and walked through the front doors of the hotel.

At the traffic lights in front of The Salt Room he had swung back round again, back towards Shoreham, laughing now, and this time stayed on Kingsway until turning to the left down Wharf Road at the sign to Shoreham Port just past the model boating lake. He drew up outside an open double door with the number 3 above it and was still smiling as he opened the van door and stepped down. A tall bulky older man with flyaway salt and pepper hair and what looked like three days of thick red stubble on his chin, swinging a square black crate in one hand, walked out of one of the double doors. He was wearing blue overalls over a black T shirt, and yellow wellington boots and he said, 'Mornin' Harry, thought that was you on the camera … Christ, you look like you just been serviced … or you already thinking 'bout what you goin' to do with them cheeks?'

Nine

In life, as in politics, perception is everything, reality nothing. Gideon knew this well. Much as people believed he could not feel pain, they believed he liked to inflict it. Neither was true. Gideon knew that perception was everything, reality nothing, and with fear this was truest of all. People feared Gideon Spargo for things he was believed to have done, things he was believed to be capable of doing. He was a bogeyman; a mythical fiend. In truth, Gideon was an 'a' man: amoral, asexual, apolitical.

People thought that Gideon could feel no physical pain, that he had a form of congenital analgesia. But this wasn't the case. However, it suited Gideon that they believe it. If people think they can't hurt you they don't try to. Gideon actually bruised easily. He had known that since childhood, a victim of brother Christian's casual cruelty. It suited him that people feared him and kept their distance. He needed his personal space. As a child, Christian would delight in locking his younger brother in confined spaces: cupboards, fish boxes, storage lockers. Dark, dirty, smelly places. In adulthood Gideon craved cleanliness, space and light. His room in the house in Newlyn was on the ground floor opening onto the rear garden and it was painted ice white. He wore white, cream and pale pastel yellows and blues. Unlike Christian he was tall and very thin, as if etiolated from all that time spent in the dark, yearning for the light.

Across Mount's Bay from Newlyn towards Porthleven was a headland south of the South West Coastal Path. On this promontory stood a 19th century sea captain's house, with land access via an unmade road and sea access via stone steps cut into the cliffs above a small cove. This was Gideon Spargo's secret lair, his private escape and home to his fortune.

Gideon had always loved gold. From childhood, stories of pirates and local folklore of Cornish wreckers and smugglers had enthralled him. They hunted, fought over and died for gold. Now he was a smuggler, a pirate and he coveted gold. He never thought of himself as a trafficker.

In a cellar excavated in the foundations of the house to store wine and comestibles Gideon stored gold, a treasure trove of sovereigns, Britannias, krugerands and ingots. He loved to sit amongst it, to touch and to feel it, and to calculate its worth. And then of course there was the cash: US dollars, sterling, euros. Bank accounts were not for him; too traceable and too intangible. Cash was king and gold was God to Gideon Spargo.

Occasionally his sanctuary also housed some of his most precious merchandize. Special orders, high value goods needed to be kept safe, unsullied and in pristine condition. Top product commanded top dollar. There were strict rules: no touching, no photographs. Piteous girls were kept well fed, no alcohol, no drugs. Gideon tolerated no abuse by his people, it was a threat to business and Gideon tolerated no threat, no insubordination. Gideon craved control. He had grown up powerless and fearful and he despised both states. He now had power and control and he suffered no mistakes.

Except for Jago Treloar. That had been a mistake. It had been stupid to push it with the bastard but he hadn't been able to resist the opportunity to exert his power and get at the old man by fucking with his childhood friend. But Treloar wouldn't give in to his demands despite his threats and when he had drowned it brought too much attention to Cove Farm so Gideon had been forced to back off, move down the coast and find easier prey. It was a rare defeat and it still smarted. But the fucker's death, and his role in it, had still been a victory over the old man and they both knew it. Gideon hated his father.

Then there was that old copper. Joe Thwaite had been after his family for years. It was a total obsession with the man. Bloody self-righteous bastard; must have been his Methodist chapel upbringing in the Yorkshire Dales. Gideon had long since turned his back on God and despised all church-goers and do-gooders. Thwaite had been trying to put him away for years until the old fucker had been forced to retire through ill health. Rumour had it he was now on his death bed. Gideon would definitely be sending flowers to that funeral. Jesus, he remembered when he was a child one day down at the fish market in Penryn, minding his own business, Thwaite had accosted him, bending down to breathe tobacco fumes in his face: "I'm watching thee lad and I shan't stop." Well at least the old bastard had proved true to his word.

When Gideon had first decided that his future lay in developing the smuggling side rather than the fishing side of the family business he realised that he would need to lay down a marker to stamp out any thought of insubordination or anyone dipping their sticky fingers in his tills. He may have been making his fortune illegally, but it was his fortune; the contacts were his contacts; the routes his routes.

Very early in his smuggling days one of Gwavas Fish's trawler captain's had appropriated a sizeable haul of cigarettes. This became common knowledge among the men and had reached Gideon. On that boat's next trip Gideon had presented himself on the quay intent on joining the crew. He was nineteen, a pale skinny young man. The captain was forty five, a hulking 15 stone giant with thirty years at sea.

At the end of the last trawl when the catch was being hauled aboard, Gideon had grabbed the captain's arm and shoved it into the winch mechanism, crushing bone and tearing flesh. His hand emerged looking like pulped octopus. "Now you won't have to worry about light fingers," Gideon said softly as the horrified crew looked on, "nobody steals from me."

The incident was explained as an unfortunate industrial accident. The captain moved away. Gideon had chosen well; not only was the man a senior captain and a thief, he was also a bully much disliked by the men. Gideon had secured his reputation and Abraham knew that his time had passed. Over the years, others who dared to cross Gideon had simply disappeared, but that first demonstration of power and ruthlessness had been highly effective. Gideon was a feared man.

But of all the apocryphal stories that were to cement Gideon's fearful reputation, it was that of the crucified child which held the most power. And as with all such stories it was founded in an element of truth.

One night a large and fractious group of people had been brought across to the cove below the Captain's House. On landing they had been herded up the beach towards the steps, quarrelling, pushing and shoving. Suddenly a powerful light illuminated a horrifying scene at the base of the cliff: the crucified body of a young girl. Silence fell and the difficult group were instantly subdued, docile and malleable. And the legend of Gideon Spargo was secured.

The reality was actually different from the image. On a rough crossing from France to the cove below the Captain's House a young girl had died. Her body had been brought ashore after the other cargo and placed in a cave at the foot of the steps. Hearing that the following group were proving troublesome, Gideon had seen the opportunity to impose order by instilling terror. A makeshift cross had been erected from two pieces of driftwood and the dead child nailed to it.

Over time the story had morphed into multiple crucifixions, the sounds of hammering, piteous cries and the stench of death. All from one contrived event on one evening. Power.

Gideon's reputation brought him business opportunities and where people couldn't be intimidated they could always be bribed, blackmailed or, as a last resort, bought. His network of contacts spread over time as he betrayed and bullied his competition and whilst the authorities knew all about him, nothing could be made to stick, nobody would speak against him.

Ten

When DI Treloar received the call from DS Colin Matthews that the body of a child had been found floating in the river Fowey near The Valley of the Tides he had just left a meeting with his new boss, Detective Chief Superintendent Nicholas 'Nicky' Chamberlain at the Devon & Cornwall Police hub in Bodmin.

Chamberlain was already displaying a refreshingly different attitude from his predecessor Detective Superintendent Suzanne Winters, 'Frosty' to the troops. She would have been stressing the extreme importance of discretion; how they were dealing with important, rich celebrated people here; how the media would be all over the story and they would all be under the spotlight. Luckily she had been transferred to Lincolnshire and was now dealing with turnip rustlers in the fenlands.

Chamberlain had come to Cornwall from the Greater Manchester force on a promotion. He had a plain speaking, hands-on reputation and already his approach was going down well with the troops. Winters had been a politician, reluctant to get her hands dirty; loath to leave her office; Chamberlain was more concerned with "action to get the job done" than with how that action would be reflected in the media. He was a short wiry man with tight curly black hair, greying at the temples, and a pair of large red framed spectacles. He had no interest in his personal image or that of his teams as long as they were honest, effective and accountable. He was happy for Treloar's team to get on with the job and he would be there for any help or support they needed. Treloar thought: so far, so good.

The focus of the discussion had been upon the structure of the major crime team. Chamberlain had kicked off:

'I've been looking at the makeup of your team. Besides you as inspector, you have two sergeants in Colin Matthews and Samantha Scott - though I appreciate Scott is currently seconded to Interpol – a constable in Luke Calloway and an acting detective constable in Fiona Sinclair.'

'Yes that's right.'

'Well I think we need to alter the balance. I want to keep Sinclair or at least get a permanent second constable. What do you think of Sinclair?'

'She's good. She fits in well and she's smart; self-motivating; shows initiative and she handles sensitive situations with discretion.'

'Fine. Have a word with her. Sound her out.'

'Will do, Sir.'

'I have heard excellent things about DS Scott, not least of which is glowing feedback from Lyon. They have expressed an interest in extending her secondment but my understanding is that she would prefer to resume her role on your team. Irrespective of her decision she is to be offered promotion to Inspector in the New Year. I would expect her to accept. Your thoughts?'

'She is absolutely due promotion Sir and I would welcome her back but I do appreciate that Interpol is a great experience and opportunity for her.'

'Well I'll speak with her and get a decision. Now you are also up for DCI and long overdue from what I can see in your file. Least said about some of my predecessor's ... recommendations the better I feel. Agreed?'

'Yes Sir.'

'Please call me Nicky, at least when we're alone. So DCI from January 1st.'

'Thank you Nicky.'

'Which leaves us with Colin Matthews. He's been a sergeant for a very long time. Showed great promise initially but seems to have stalled.'

'Detective Superintendent Winters valued him in the role of sergeant.'

'You mean she used him as a glorified PA from what I can see. He clearly has impressive technology skills but I'm not so sure he fits the profile I want for your team. Especially now you have Calloway with credentials in that area and potential to progress.'

'Colin's always contributed Sir ... Nicky. He brings a measured, considered perspective. He may be a little ... cautious, but he is respected by the others.'

'Mmmm ... let me think on. So Sinclair to stay, Scott to return with promotion, you for DCI and Matthews to be decided. Agreed?'

'Yes Nicky and thank you.'

'Credit it where it's due. I'll give you my decision on Matthews within the next couple of weeks and confirm with Scott. I'll be in touch Phil.' And with that he rose to his feet.

It was one of those perfect early winter days; still and breathless. A perfect soft washed blue sky, painfully bluish yellow at the horizon. A day for death: a perfect day for a funeral. No wind. Choir voices and church bells drifting mournfully through the air. Plumes of smoke rising up from chimneys like the souls of the virtuous dead.

As he drove down from Bodmin, Treloar was mulling over the call he had had from Colin Matthews, especially one strange tirade from the normally reserved sergeant, a long standing member of his major crime team:

'This is Cornwall; people drown here. They go into the water when they shouldn't; after children, after dogs, when they're drunk. They don't respect the currents or the tides or the power of the sea. They go out on power boats and sit-on canoes that they can't handle; they get into trouble and wreak havoc. They cost a fortune in search and rescues missions. Just ask those boys over there,' he said pointing across the river towards the Fowey lifeboat. 'If the odd one drowns perhaps it'll serve to teach the others a lesson. But I doubt it.'

As Treloar headed for Fowey Chamberlain was reflecting on the man. It was abundantly clear from his file that he was an extremely capable officer, exceptional even, but he had stalled at the rank of Detective Inspector. He had also heard rumours of over enthusiastic methods, the bending, if not breaking of rules and scant regard for authority. But he had also heard that the Chief Constable thought very highly of Treloar with his photogenic looks and his Cornish heritage spiced with that Spanish maternal element. The media and the public rated the Inspector.

Clearly there had been a strong antagonism between the man and Chamberlain's predecessor Detective Superintendent Suzanne Winters. She had been a stickler for the rules with an obsessive concern for appearance and image. She had also carried a chip on her shoulder as a woman progressing through the ranks. She had been little liked or admired but she was highly competent and highly skilled in administrative management if lacking in team leadership. She would be better suited to her new role.

First impressions? He liked the man. He was obviously intelligent and he clearly inspired respect and loyalty in his team. People wanted to work with him and that was critical in a major crime team. Chamberlain would need to keep a watching brief for a while but the vibes were positive. So far, so good.

Treloar had cut down to the join the A390 at Lostwithiel and headed west to take the B3269 down to Fowey. Although this meant heading west to then turn back east, it was easier than threading his way through minor roads and single track lanes. At Caffa Mill in Fowey as he waited for the ferry to Bodinnick his mobile phone rang. It was DS Colin Matthews again.

'Hi Phil. Where are you?'

'Col. I'm waiting for the ferry. What have we got?'

'Young girl, maybe six or seven. Nobody has reported a child missing. Could have fallen from a boat or been swept out but the weather's been very quiet recently and she's not been in the water long. I reckon she was washed down from Seal Creek by the last tide and caught in the channel by pure chance: her hair tangled in a mooring chain,' Treloar respected Colin's opinion: the man kept a boat in Fowey and had been sailing the local waters for years.

'Where is she now?'

'Well they brought her over to the jetty here below Seal Hall because it was the nearest land and offers far more privacy than Town Quay over in Fowey. We've got her by one of the roundhouses down by the water.'

'Roundhouses?'

'Yeah. They've got these new build round thatched therapy and treatment rooms with flotation tanks and mediation rooms whatever. All very yummy mummy, new age.' Colin was an old-fashioned traditional sailor.

'Any idea at all on ID?'

'Well, Dr Forbes reckons ...'

'John's there?' Treloar asked in surprise. Dr John Forbes was the Senior Home Office pathologist and was not often called out to a crime scene.'

'Oh yes. Orders from on high, what with the Jackson Power connection, and apparently there are "sensitive issues" around some of the residents here; the rich and the famous, so it's all "need to know" basis, fewer people involved the better.'

'Yeah, yeah. Like that's going to make any difference. Something always gets out, they know that. So what does John think?'

'First impression: ligature strangulation. And ...'

'Hang on Col, I've got to move. Look I'll be there in a few minutes. I'll meet you down by the creek.

A few minutes turned out to be more like an hour. After crossing the river and heading up past The Old Ferry Inn, Treloar crested the hill and turned right down a lane towards Seal Hall. He had only travelled a few hundred yards when he came across a young man trying to herd a flock of sheep along the road. Treloar switched on his hazard warning lights and climbed from the car to help. Having grown up on a farm he knew how to behave around livestock.

'Need a hand?'

'Oh yeah please. I'm trying to get them into the next field. The gate's about 200 yards along, but they keep running past and some are trying to get through the hedge.'

'Right. You go ahead and direct them in through the gate. Stop them moving further down the lane. I'll round up the stragglers and drive them towards you.'

'Thanks mate you're a life saver.'

When they had finally got all the sheep into the field and secured the gate Treloar spoke.

'What happened? You can't have been trying to move them on your own.'

'No way. I just came across them in the road. Some idiot has cut out a length of barbed wire from their field. Just nicked it and left a fucking great gap!'

Rural crime was on the increase but this was

probably more likely to be mindless vandalism. He handed the lad a business card. 'Call it in. Take some photos with your phone and send them in. You'll need a report for the insurance.'

'I didn't know the police were trained in shepherding,' the young man said with a smile.

'Misspent youth,' Treloar called over his shoulder as he headed back to his Land Rover.

When he finally reached the entrance to Seal Hall he turned in from the lane onto what amounted to a farm track. The only indication that he had reached his destination was a discreet slate sign on a pole reading Seal Hall. No mention of The Valley of the Tides. After a few hundred yards the track forked and he could see that the left hand fork led down to the water. He took it. Soon he came across a cluster of vehicles pulled off onto the grass verge. He recognised Colin's Audi estate and pulled up beside it. Grabbing his waxed jacket from the back seat he headed down towards the creek.

Eleven

Cornwall is a different country. The traveller can sense the change as they journey out beyond the Tamar Bridge into a landscape of wooded valleys and granite outcrops. And to Treloar, south east Cornwall was a very different country from his homelands on the north west coast. This was an alien terrain, a land of wooded valleys, fingers of water probing inland from the sea; the rivers Looe, Fowey, Helford and the Fal, daddy of them all. It was a sheltered, confined, shaded and enclosed land. He was a man of the high windswept moorland, exposed, exhilarating endless horizons, fingers of land poking out into the sea; Cape Cornwall, Gurnard's Head, Zennor Head. He was a foreigner here. He felt unsettled.

So Sam was coming home. Well, back to Cornwall, her home, her Georgian house in Truro was sold. She had fallen out of love with it when she suffered a vicious physical assault there some years back, then with the move to Lyon ... He had not seen her since she had left after the business in London, scarcely spoken to her. Christ was it only the previous year. That summer she had met his sister Lucia at the family farm and the two had kept in touch. Lucia lived in Barcelona and it was only a short flight to Lyon. She had told him of fun weekends staying at Sam's apartment on the Boulevard des Belges, meals in Café Sillon and le Neuvième Art, walks along the banks of the Rhône. But from Sam herself, not a word. Perhaps she had moved on; put her feelings for him behind her. Perhaps that chance had passed. Lucia would know; he would talk with her over Christmas.

It was in sombre, reflective mood that Treloar trod the path down into the dappled light along the banks of Seal Creek. As he made his way down the track to the water he surveyed his surroundings. To his left was a small chapel, very old and dilapidated, set in an overgrown graveyard. Below it on the creekside was a row of old fishermen's cottages in the process of renovation. Straight ahead he could see the jetty with a few grounded rowing boats, the creek itself and the wooded bank on the other side. To his right were three newly constructed thatched roundhouses and beyond, the widening creek leading out to the river Fowey. At the creek's entrance boats and yachts of various sizes were moored and further out he could see across the river to Fowey and Town Quay.

Most of the activity was straight ahead by the jetty. He could see pathologist Dr John Forbes, Detective Sergeant Colin Matthews and Detective Constable Fiona Matthews. A police photographer was working further out on the jetty and a number of uniforms were moving along the creek's bank, searching.

'Sorry, sorry!' Treloar called as he reached the jetty, 'sheep in the road; had to help clear them.'

'Good morning Félipe,' said Dr Forbes.

The grim faced group were standing around the body of a little girl lying on a body bag that was much too large for her small frame. She had obviously been pulled from water: she was still dripping. Her long dark hair was fanned out around her head to reveal an ugly red wheal around her neck. She was dressed in jeans and pink polka dot sweatshirt. One foot was shod in a dirty tennis shoe, one was bare. Treloar stared at the tiny white foot. It seemed the most pitiful element of the scene in front of him. He leaned in more closely and stared at a mark on the bare ankle.

'What can you tell me?' Treloar asked.

'Not much really,' said Forbes. 'Young girl; somewhere between five and eight; very slight build. Not been in the water long. Died within the last twenty four hours. Looks like strangulation, but could have drowned; caught in the mooring chain accidentally. Fully clothed; no obvious injuries; no obvious signs of sexual assault.'

'Is that a bruise or a tattoo?' he asked pointing at the little foot.

'Can't tell yet. I'll let you know.'

Dr Forbes was not keen on giving an opinion before he had made a thorough inspection of a body and he was certainly not happy at being called out. Somebody here had clout.

'I'm finished here; just waiting for you really. May I take her now?' Forbes was tetchy and anxious to leave.

'Of course John. Call me when you have something.'

Forbes nodded and smiled sadly, beckoning to two men who had been standing quietly by the graveyard gate with a collapsible stretcher. The group watched in silence as the little girl was lifted and wheeled away.

'Right,' said Treloar rubbing his hands together, 'what do we know about this place? Colin, you're local, what's the word?'

Colin Matthews, who lived in a Fowey terrace and had been first at the scene, told them what he knew of The Valley of the Tides, the latest incarnation of Seal Hall.

'So the locals are alright with this incomer?' asked Fiona whose parents were from Argyll.

'Yeah. He's glamorous, he's famous, he's rich,

he's brought employment and his guests spend money in the community. What's not to like? And they mostly feel sorry for him, what with his son dying like that.'

'And you think the girl went into the water in this creek, not the main river?' asked Treloar.

'Put money on it. She would have been taken out by the tide but her long hair caught in the mooring chain and she held fast,' said Colin. As he was both a local sailor and known to be tight with his money this carried weight with the assembled group.

'What are those?' asked Treloar pointing at the roundhouses.

'Therapy rooms,' said Colin.

'Oh yeah, you already told me that, what are they for again?' Treloar was preoccupied with his father. He needed to focus.

'One houses a flotation tank and the other two are for some sort of meditation stroke contemplation stroke yoga stroke massage sessions.'

'And that?' asked Treloar pointing to a long low shed he had just noticed beyond the roundhouses.

'Boat storage. Kayaks and sit-on canoes. That sort of thing. I looked,' said Fiona when Colin raised a questioning eyebrow.

Twelve

He was buzzing when he got back to the Brighton restaurant. Six o'clock and two sous chefs and an assistant were in early, sitting around eating bacon butties. He asked them to unload the van when they had finished, and sort out who would take it back round the corner to the multi-storey and park it, then ran upstairs to his flat where he went to the his desk and opened and switched on his laptop, took his phone from his jacket pocket and switched it on, turned it over and looked at the bottom and said, 'oh shit! Where the fuck is it?"

He hadn't connected it up to the computer before and couldn't remember where the cable was, or if there ever had been one, or what colour it had been if there had been one, or whether maybe he had ever actually used it, maybe when he had taken those pictures out on the trawler for the PR for the new menu, fuck, no, he had picked the best and emailed them straight to the designers, what about the pics of Phyllis with the before and after pheasants, shit, he'd emailed them straight to the IT guy to get up on the web site, couldn't email this file to the PC, must be too big, would take forever, maybe get lost, like the video of the Gloucester Old Spots up at Old Wood Farm, Christ must have had it then, when was it, what did he do with it, fuck, look in the filing cabinet, must be with the manuals, 'YES! Thank fuck for that'.

Concentrating hard he spent the next two hours getting the video onto the laptop and using the basic video processing software that he had had to download from the phone company web site to cut out the useless sections, where the camera was pointing anywhere other than at the good doctor, his lady friend, or their surroundings, making sure that the date and time stamp was showing. Christ what a hassle! Then he realised he needed a DVD disc or memory stick.

He realised he was knackered again. Went to his shoulder bag on the kitchen table and took out a wrap, couldn't be arsed to smoke it, just balled it up and swallowed it, then some orange juice from the fridge, it would take longer but get there in the end, then he needed to go down to the restaurant office, shit. They would be over him like a rash, 'where's this? What does that mean? Can we use this instead? Have we got any of this? Where did you put that? We haven't got enough of this', Christ.

He was right, but didn't get caught by as many as he thought he would, told them to look at the to-do-today lists and work sheets and photographs and instead-of sheets and stock print-outs and inside the fridges and start thinking for them fucking selves for a change and left the office with three memory sticks. Before long he had the video on the memory sticks and was buzzing again, and it was nine thirty and he knew he ought to be down in the kitchen. After checking that the video ran perfectly from each of the memory sticks he looked at the blown up grainy black and white picture on the wall of himself and a fisherman on a trawler and thought, 'fuck it, let's see how they got on on there own ... in a minute. Delegation right?'

He got some more orange juice from the fridge and went back to the laptop and set about making sure he knew the doctor's name and finding out where he lived and worked. The name and the working parts were easy, then so was the living part because it turned out he lived at one of the work places and loads of people, including The Argus, thought he was a hero because of it. Montpelier Villas, one of the poshest parts of Brighton, and he carried out private practice and occasional but urgently needed pro bono work from his private surgery on the ground floor of his house, which was behind big iron gates, a tall wall and old established trees.

When he wasn't working at his Montpelier Villa surgery, patients and prospective patients could see him at either the private Montefiore Hospital in Brighton or the equally private Hove Clinic where he was a regular consultant and able to make use of their first class rooms and other facilities if more than simple diagnostics and treatments were thought to be necessary. The receptionist at the Montpelier Villa surgery was an experienced nurse and a fully trained and practising pharmacist and would be pleased to help refer patients to the most appropriate facility, according to the Doctor Raymond J Sykes web site.

The web site had also told him that the Montpelier Villa facility was able to provide prescription medicines meeting the needs of most ailments on initial diagnosis and repeat prescriptions when necessary for those patients not having a convenient pharmacy close to their home or place of work. There was also a fully equipped treatment room for patients needing massage or physiotherapy including chiropractic treatments for which practitioner partners were available by arrangement although urgent cases could be referred to the Hove Clinic by the practice nurse after an initial discussion.

'Right, on with the show,' he said to the picture on the wall, 'we'll go and visit the good doctor tomorrow,' and went down to the restaurant to see what today's crisis was and what he would need to sort out.

'I said it's about a surprise for his wife,' he had to repeat, 'I'm sure he'll understand, it won't take long, but I can't stay away from the kitchen for more than half an hour today,' he said to the experienced nurse receptionist when he rang the Montpelier Villa surgery at eight thirty the next morning. He'd had two hours sleep eventually, he thought, couldn't get off after trialling minted cod dishes until two o'clock and was knackered even though he had smoked two wraps and just swallowed a third. 'Nine fifteen would be great for me,' he had said, and listened, then, 'OK, ten o'clock, but it'll have to be quick because I've got to get back for lunch,' and after a few more seconds, 'NO, not eating it, cooking it!'

He was wearing light blue jeans, a pale yellow short-sleeved cotton shirt with an open neck underneath a grey linen sports jacket, and grey trainers, and was feeling good as he waited for the taxi to arrive. Confident, businesslike. One of the memory sticks was in the breast pocket of his jacket and his shades were folded in one of the inside pockets.

At nine fifty five the London-cab-style blue and white taxi stopped outside the Montpelier Villa gates and Harry told the driver he wouldn't be that long and asked him to wait, maybe fifteen or twenty minutes and had walked straight to the intercom in the wall, pressed the button and announced himself and the gates opened and just before ten o'clock he was sitting looking at the nurse who was younger than he expected and wore a light blue just above the knee dress with a dark blue pinstripe and white buttons all the way up the front, the bottom three of which were unfastened. It looked as though there was a watch on the end of a chain that was clipped to the collar of her dress and snaked into a breast pocket. She wore white plimsolls without socks and had long blonde hair tied back in a pony tail and was sitting back behind her reception desk after greeting him and letting him in through a side door to the Villa.

A modesty panel was stopping him knowing for sure that her legs were well on display behind it as her dress draped open on either side of her crossed legs. He could see that she had only one foot on the ground and she could see him wishing the modesty panel wasn't there and looked down at her legs and at the same time took the watch out of her pocket and then smiled at him and said, 'it won't be long now'.

At ten o'clock the good Doctor Sykes opened his polished and dark mahogany door and invited him in, after first shaking his hand and introducing himself. As they walked in he could see that the room was just like any other doctor's surgery he had ever been in, but a lot more up-market, with armed leather chairs for patients, abstract paintings on the walls, and the computer at the end of the doctors desk was a folded Mac Book .'This shouldn't take long,' he had said to the doctor, smiling as he passed the memory stick across the desk, saying, 'maybe you'd like to have a quick look before giving it to your wife.'

'Ah yes, Harry, I remember now, I couldn't be sure it was you, out of uniform,' the doctor said and he laughed before reaching over and pulling across the Mac Book and then opening it and plugging in the memory stick. The Mac Book was quick, very, and it was only a few seconds before the doctor tapped the mouse-pad and the video began playing, and only two seconds before the doctor scowled and then only a few more before his neck reddened and he looked at Harry and said, 'bastard,' and after another ten seconds when his face had reddened completely he said, 'Jesus ... what do you want, money?'

'Well Doctor Sykes, that's not a very nice way to be speaking to someone who's looking to help you out … or maybe you'd like your wife to get her surprise … give me the stick back.' With the stick back in his pocket he said, 'it's like this, very simple. Speed is what I want, not money, a regular supply of it, good quality. I reckon Dexies will do it, that's probably Dextroamphetamine to you, ten milligram tabs or twenty mills in the caps if you can get them, five a day of the twenties or ten of the tens, for as long as you don't want your wife surprised. Easy, what do you reckon? I'm sick of the crap on the street and you can help keep me happy and safe and your favourite restaurant turning out great food.'

'Bastard … how do I know you won't show this to my wife anyway? What guarantee do I have? How can I trust you?' Sykes asked.

'Well you won't know for sure until we're down the track a long way will you, so the only guarantee you can have for now is the certainty that if you don't oblige, your wife will definitely be receiving more information than she would probably like … maybe via the Argus, or the mayor's wife, maybe she could see it first? What do you think?'

Sykes looked at his watch and said, 'Christ! … How will I get them to you? I'll have to see. That's a lot of Amphetamine'.

'Post it to me at the flat,' he said and handed

over a post-it he had written on earlier, 'here, I'll expect the first package by next Tuesday, a week should be long enough, then keep it coming on a weekly basis. If it doesn't turn up you and yours will be hearing from me, or The Argus … or the mayor's wife.' He took the memory stick back out of his pocket and placed it on the desk in front of the doctor and said, 'keep that as a reminder,' and got up to leave, turning before he did, saying, 'don't get any funny ideas, there are three more copies of that, one is with my solicitor in an envelope waiting to be opened if anything strange should happen to me, one is in a safety deposit box and I'll keep the third at home to remind myself how lucky we both are.'

As he left the doctor's room he smiled at the receptionist and said, 'thanks, told you it wouldn't take long,' then he looked at the blue haired old dear waiting to go in and smiled again, then strode out of the door, down the path and through the black iron gate and got back into the taxi.

Thirteen

Originally a timbered Tudor manor, Seal Hall had been largely rebuilt in the 1700s after a disastrous fire. As Treloar and DC Fiona Sinclair drove into the courtyard they found themselves on a circular gravel drive facing a large stuccoed stone three storey house with an ironwork veranda at the first storey. In the centre of the gravel stood a stunning modern fountain featuring water running from the sleek skin coats of three dark metal intertwined seals into a rock pool. The ground floor windows were large paned sash evenly located either side of a stucco pillared portico covering the huge oak entrance door. The first floor windows opened onto the veranda. The second storey had smaller paned sash windows and the chimnied roof was of Delabole slate. Treloar, who had completed his own double barn conversion the previous year, admired the elegant balance of the building.

The main house faced south and was set in

parkland of lawns and mature trees including a number of giant cedars. Set back to the right of the property was a converted stable block with a central clock tower. There would be tremendous views of Seal Creek, the wider river Fowey and out to sea, particularly from the upper stories. The aura was peaceful and harmonious. He could see why Power had chosen it for his project.

'I could do with a fortnight here,' said Fiona as they climbed from the Land Rover.

'You are not sufficiently troubled Constable Sinclair. Not yet anyway.'

'Families can stay here too Sir not just troubled young people.'

'Fiona. It's Phil.'

'Sorry. I will get the hang of it, I promise.'

DC Fiona Sinclair had recently joined the serious crime team when DS Samantha Scott had been seconded to Interpol in Lyon following a difficult case in which Treloar had been personally involved and Fiona had proved herself to be highly competent and discreet. Treloar missed Sam in many ways. He valued a female presence on the team finding that a woman brought different insights and worked well in eliciting information from some people. Sam had faced the wrath and censure of Superintendent Winters.

Before her transfer, with the last vengeful slash of a dying dragon's tail she had attempted to have

Sam demoted and had blocked Treloar's promotion for a second time. Winters resented Treloar's "golden boy" standing with the Chief Constable, and Sam Scott had rebuffed her misguided drunken pass at a party. But a colleague with influence who had worked with them on the case in London had intervened and arranged for Sam's placement in France. And now Winters herself was gone under questionable circumstances leaving behind rumours of dubious behaviour. The remaining member of the team, DC Luke Callaway, was on leave, away in Jamaica visiting his grandmother.

As they crunched across the gravel the front door opened and a woman stepped out to stand between two potted topiaried bay trees. She was in her late thirties with expensively shaggy cut brown hair, bright hazel eyes and full lips. She was slim and maybe five foot three, dressed in a pair of black Capri pants and a cream loose-fitting silk blouse. Curiously, given that it was late November, her scarlet toe-painted feet were bare. She smiled as they reached her, checked her Tag Heuer watch and spoke in a soft voice with the faintest Cornish lilt:

'Good morning. You are the police? We were told you would be coming. I am Sindy Cardrew and I am the Chief Operating Officer at The Valley of the Tides. Welcome.'

Told by whom? Treloar wondered.

Without waiting for a reply, she turned and

walked back inside. She exuded authority. They followed.

Through the huge oak door they found themselves inside a surprisingly light hall. The original wood panelling had been washed the palest yellow and cleverly concealed lighting brightened corners and highlighted the ornate stucco barrel vault ceiling. At the rear of the hall, beneath the mahogany staircase, a water feature echoed the design of the seal fountain in the courtyard.

The furniture was modern: expensive blond wood and primary coloured upholstery. The single antique was a grandfather clock with a deep resonant tick. The eye was drawn up to the only decorative piece in the space: an enormous sculpted chandelier in steel and glass which resembled drifting seaweed. *No IKEA in here* thought Fiona.

'Would you mind registering with Caitlin?' Ms Cardrew indicated an open archway to the left of the front door.

They walked through into a smaller space, presumably a former footman or butler's room. Standing beside a high blond wood table was an impossibly Californian girl in true Beach Boys' tradition: impeccable white teeth, cornflower blue eyes, an even soft tan and the requisite long blond hair. She smiled and spoke with a sunny American accent. She was clad in tight faded jeans and a black Weird Fish t-shirt. Unlike her boss she was shod in black leather ballet shoes.

'How y'all doing this fine morning?'

'Caitlin. These police officers need to sign in. Will you help them with that?'

'I surely will,' Caitlin replied lifting an iPad from behind the table, 'if y'all will give me your names?'

They completed the formalities, left their coats and walked out duly badged as visitors.

'Perhaps we should speak in the library,' said Ms Cardrew padding softly across the stone floor to enter a room to the left of the front door.

They entered the room, stepping back in time. She closed the door behind them. Original dark wooden floor to ceiling bookcases lined the walls stretching up to meet ornate white plasterwork. A large colourful modern carpet in pastel sea shades covered most of the floor. Scattered through the room were an assortment of old writing desks and modern sofas with low blond wood coffee tables. And everywhere: books. Sunlight streamed through the windows bathing the room in soft golden light. There were internal wooden shutters. The atmosphere was welcoming and peaceful but the room was deserted.

Sindy Cardrew led them to an arrangement of two sofas and a low table at the far end of the room beside a window. She sat down and indicated they should do likewise. They did.

'We won't be disturbed in here. I've taken the liberty of ordering coffee.'

'Where is everyone?' asked Fiona.

Cardrew glanced at her watch again. 'Well there are sessions and activities until lunch and again until four. The library is normally quiet until the evening during the week.'

At that moment the door opened and the lovely Caitlin strolled across the room carrying a tray.

'Here y'all go.' She said placing the tray on the table. Fiona resisted the urge to call out "Have a nice day!" to her retreating back. There was a cafetière, four rustic white pottery mugs with matching milk jug, a glass bowl of dark crystalline sugar lumps, teaspoons and a plate of tiny Florentine biscuits. They all helped themselves. The Florentines were excellent.

'I understand that you have heard about ...'

'Do forgive me Inspector, said Cardrew raising her hand palm out, 'before we start, I have asked our House Director to join us. It will save you critical time, and avoid repetition and confusion to speak with us both at the same time. And to answer your question, yes, we have been told about the unfortunate child. The Assistant Chief Constable rang.'

Name dropping already. "House Director" well that explains the fourth mug, thought Fiona as the door opened again and a figure straight out of Hollywood casting advanced towards them. He was tall and thin, dressed in baggy brown corduroys, scuffed deck shoes and a checked flannel shirt. He could have been anything from forty to sixty, his hair grey and unkempt, his small wired glasses perched on his nose.

'Ah,' said Cardrew standing. The others followed suit. 'Dr Beckermann. Let me introduce Detective Inspector Treloar and Detective Constable Sinclair. Dr Johann Beckermann is our Principal Psychologist and House Director. He leads in all matters concerning health and therapy; I lead in all other matters. Let me ask him to tell you about The Valley of the Tides.'

Beckermann nodded sharply at Treloar and Sinclair in turn, extending his hand.

'Our residents are suffering from behavioural issues: addiction to drugs, alcohol, the Internet; eating disorders, depression anxiety; terrible stresses in their daily existence,' said Beckermann.

'Are they violent, or dangerous in any way?' asked Treloar.

'No, not in the way you mean. Only to themselves, in some cases. They are not the profile of a person who would murder a child. We are more like …'

'The Priory?' Fiona interjected.

'Well yes. But we focus on younger people.'

'So that is what your residents have in common: their age?' said Treloar.

'Well yes.'

'Their money?' asked Treloar.

'This is not an NHS facility but neither is it a profit making enterprise. It was established by Mr Power to help young people who risk suffering the same dreadful fate as his son Ford. His motives are honourable and we are benefitting troubled young people,' said Sindy Cardrew with some annoyance

'And, I might add,' said Beckermann, 'none of our residents have ever been committed under any mental health legislation. We are not a psychiatric hospital. However we do take referrals from the criminal justice system when therapy is seen as a constructive alternative to incarceration. But we are not a prison.'

'Of course not,' said Treloar soothingly, 'and we appreciate your cooperation,' he paused. 'Is there any CCTV coverage of the grounds as part of the security here?'

'This is a sanctuary not a penitentiary. We do not monitor or record our residents or their visitors Inspector,' Beckermann blustered.

'Really Johan,' said Sindy Cardrew in a tone full of warm honey, 'I'm sure the Inspector is only asking a reasonable question under the circumstances.' She turned her calm gaze to Treloar. 'But no, I'm afraid we cannot help in that regard. Johan is absolutely correct.'

The doctor nodded his head sharply in satisfaction at the vindication.

'Can you tell us who was staying here last night?'

asked Treloar.

'Really!' Beckermann exploded, 'our residents are effectively patients and as such they are entitled to absolute privacy.'

'We aren't asking for their records, just their names. We will want to talk to them. We are looking into the unlawful death of a young child and we believe all reasonable people will be more than happy to assist us in that. Your staff, residents, or visitors, may have seen something invaluable.'

'Quite, quite, Inspector,' said Ms Cardrew soothingly, 'I'm sure we can accommodate your needs. Everyone will be pleased to cooperate. I'm certain of that.'

Everyone? Treloar wondered.

'I shall speak to Rolf about this matter,' said Beckermann standing and storming from the library.

'Rolf?' asked Fiona.

'Rolf Lindström. Jackson. Jackson Power is a stage name,' said Ms Cardrew with her inscrutable smile. 'Now where were we?'

Sindy Cardrew left the library to organise more coffee, returning with an iPad. She sat and scrolled through a few pages. The door opened and Caitlin brought in a tray, placed in on the table offering them one of her perfect smiles, and withdrew with the empties.

'Right,' said Cardrew, 'well obviously there's the family: Rolf Lindström or Jackson Power if you prefer – although he's away in London at present, his son

Hitchcock who's known as Hitch, and elder daughter Davis. Then the residential staff: myself and Caitlin Lee who you've met and the therapists: Dr Beckermann, Dr Ivan Speer and Bella Dean. There are other staff members, catering, cleaning and gardening, but they don't live on the premises and weren't here last night.

'At what time would they have left?' asked Fiona.

'Oh, everyone's gone by eight. We're fairly quiet at the moment, with Christmas approaching.'

'So, residents and guests?' asked Treloar.

'Well, firstly there's a hybrid: Harry Forrester.'

'A hybrid?' asked Fiona, 'wait, do you mean the chef?'

'Yes. Harry came to us for therapy and has stayed on as a specialist chef. He provides some meals and teaching for residents and guests in return for board and lodgings and ongoing therapy. It has proven a great success. He's very popular.'

Fiona looked at Treloar with a roll of her eyes indicating she had more to say on the subject, but later when they were alone.

Currently we have fourteen residents. The guests are resident Tom Palmer's mother Gloria and her sister Jane Sharpe. I should perhaps mention that Guy Masterson is the son of Gregory Masterson ..,'

'The media tycoon?' Treloar interjected.

'Indeed. And Juliet Morrow is the daughter of

Flora Morrow,' Treloar was nodding as she continued, 'the MP and junior minister.'

'I see,' said Treloar thinking that this explained the high level intervention and the presence of John Forbes: celebrity, politics and press.

'We believe the child's body went into the water in Seal Creek. The opposite bank of the creek is uninhabited farmland and your grounds are not open to the public. If a stranger *were* wandering around here yesterday he, or she, would have been noticed; your upper windows overlook the water; some of your facilities are right on the water. We will need to speak to everyone. People are often not aware that they have seen something of interest until they are prompted.'

'Yes well I'm not sure where they all are at the moment. Certainly several are off site; I saw a party heading to Fowey after breakfast. Perhaps, to save your time, I could speak to everyone during the day and arrange a schedule for ... tomorrow morning?'

Treloar considered. He needed to go carefully with this lot, and yet he didn't want anyone absconding. He made this point to Sindy and she assured him that she would make it abundantly clear that attendance the following day was not optional. And after all the body had been found in the river not on the grounds of Seal Hall, it could well have nothing to do with this lot. With a sense of unease Treloar agreed to her suggestion. It concerned him further that she seemed pleased at his concession.

'I take it that you have no objection if we take a look around the grounds whilst we're here?' he was sure she would be happy with that given his acceptance of her plan.

'Absolutely. Would you like me to be your guide?'

'No. Thank you, but we'll be fine on our own,' he stated.

They had left Seal Hall and were looking around the other buildings that made up The Valley of the Tides. Ms Cardrew had repeated her offer to escort them but Treloar insisted that they had taken enough of her time. She had agreed that they would come back the following morning to talk to the staff, residents and guests who had been around on the day they believed the girl had gone into the water. She would prepare a list of appointments. All very cooperative and efficient.

At the side of the house was a newly constructed kitchen area with stairs and lift access to the upper floors on the outside of the original building. They could see into a brightly lit well equipped kitchen and preparation area. A number of people were seated on stools at a long work surface. It was some kind of lesson or demonstration. They were all watching a handsome man wielding a pestle and mortar.

'That,' said Fiona, 'is the famous Harry Forrester,' pointing at the man.

'Who is Harry Forrester?' asked Treloar.

'Really Sir ... Phil, and you with a chef for a sister' – Treloar's youngest sister Beatriz was training at Seafood on Stilts, a restaurant in St Ives – 'she'll know all about him. Famous. Michelin stars, celebrity clientele, books, the lot. Then, total crash. Burn out or something. Lots of rumours. Totally fell off the radar. So this is where he's hiding out.'

'Any rumours about issues with children?'

'No. Absolutely not. Drugs and women was the word.'

'Well, that would explain the therapy here.'

'Yeah. Good fit.'

Fourteen

They had turned up in the post on the Friday morning before he went down to the restaurant for the THIRD fucking time. He had already been called down once by the night bell at five o'clock to see a tired and scruffy looking young guy wearing damp and still sandy bottomed waders who pulled two strings of good sized sea bass out of the back of a van, seven altogether, and again at six thirty by one of the assistants on the internal phone to see a forager who had brought in three carrier bags full of wild sorrel. He had written a note on the kitchen office board to remind him to see the restaurant manager for a petty cash top-up later in the day before going back up to the flat.

'Bloody brilliant!' he had thought, 'four days early, Sykes must be wetting himself.' He saw when he quickly thumbed the top off the white plastic tub and pulled the orange plug of sponge packing out of the top that the good doctor had even managed to get hold of the capsules. He was surprised to see an official looking printed label on the side of the tub that specified taking no more than one capsule in a six hour period and that no more should be taken than two per day with a warning in capital orange letters that they were high dosage. He counted forty two of the bright orange capsules after tipping them from the tub onto an unopened IntraFish report about fish eating trends in Japan.

'Well, he had better not be bloody well thinking that this is going to last for three weeks,' he had thought as he held up the tub and re-read the label. He had been thinking that three or four capsules or five or six tablets at a time for an all-nighter should cover it, a couple more occasionally for a friend if he was lucky and she was up for it. So, if the good doctor sends forty two EVERY week we'll be well happy … with a few left for a rainy day, and all legal!' Smiling, he had folded the report carefully and used it to pour the very first of his little helpers, to keep him sane, to keep him going through the nights, his little sousies, back into the tub, and hid it at the back of the sweater shelf in his wardrobe.

*

When he stopped day dreaming he was still on the veranda. It was still chilly. He looked round and she was no longer there. He had his hands on the rail and was looking out over the gardens towards the woods. The floating skirt woman had gone, and he laughed to himself as he thought back and wondered who she was and where she had gone to, and where she had been.

He went back to his room to change into his cooking therapy kit. Sindy Cardrew, Jackson Power's Chief Operating Officer had been clear. 'If we're going to do this, you are going to do it properly! No half measures Harry,' he had been told when he had pitched his therapy idea. 'A clean outfit at the beginning of every session for you, a clean fresh apron for the people every time, even if they've had one before, they can sell them on eBay if they want! Make it last at least an hour, make them DO something - don't just show them - and make it physical.' Johan Beckermann, the House Director and the consultant psychiatrist with them in the meeting had looked at him sternly, nodding, and his head had swivelled slowly, looking at each of them in turn as he replied in a serious tone, 'right, of course … physical,' before standing up and leaving the meeting.

So, this morning there would be seven, one female visitor, and six residents - three male and three female. Their ages ranged from late teens for one of the male residents to the forties for the female visitor, and there were no disabilities. He didn't differentiate between the way he treated the residents and the visitors in the sessions. Not often anyway, sometimes just having a quiet word on the side with a resident if he thought they needed it, just got them all involved and following his lead.

Everyone had introduced themselves, most of them nervously, and they were standing at his end of the kitchen at the long preparation counter. It overhung cupboards and had tall stools pushed underneath the overhang. Like a breakfast bar, which it often was for kitchen staff arriving early in the morning. There were four on one side and three on the other, and in front of each of them there was a large stone mortar and pestle standing on a wooden chopping board. Next to each mortar and pestle was a mezzaluna and two teaspoons, a clove of garlic, a half-teaspoon to full-tablespoon measuring set and a glass measuring jar, and a folded apron was to the side of each chopping board. Behind each chopping board was a bottle of extra virgin olive oil, a small bowl of sea salt, a tea strainer, and an empty Kilner jar. In the middle of the counter, down its length, were three rolls of kitchen towel, standing upright on holders, and next to each, a bottle of white wine vinegar.

He was at the end of the counter, with the same

things in front of him but with two extras. A pile of recipe sheets was turned upside down so the top one could not be seen, and a tea towel was covering the second. In the middle of the counter, to warn anyone that might have been thinking about leaving a delivery or anything else on it, or having a late breakfast, was a long rectangular sign mounted on top of a pole half a metre high that had been pushed into a drilled rectangle of planed and varnished wood, saying HARRY'S BAR in red capital letters on a black background. He reached for it, said, 'Welcome', and placed it on the floor next to him. He was embarrassed because he should have removed it before the introductions but had been distracted by the female visitor, who had black shoulder length hair and had smiled at him and raised her eyebrows quizzically when he took his place at the end of the counter.

'Right, thanks for that everyone, let's get going. First,' and he lifted the tea towel, revealing two jars, labelled A and C, 'this is what you're going to be making this morning. It's called salsa verde by a lot of people and green sauce by a lot of others, and these are two different versions of it and they both go really well with fish. It's harder work than tartare sauce, especially with the mortar and pestle instead of a blender that you might want to use at home, so you'll be getting a bit of a work-out. It's very different from tartare, but I think you'll find that the extra effort is well worth it. I'm going to pass the jars around for you to taste each one so that you can see which you prefer and that is the one you'll be making. I'll be interested to know if you can tell me what you think is different about them.'

He passed the C jar to his right and the A to his left and they went down the sides of the counter, crossed at the end and came back to him. 'Right, who liked the A jar best?' he asked and three people raised their hands, 'so the rest of you preferred the C jar?'

'No', said the smiling lady with the eyebrows and shoulder length black hair that he now knew was Jane, the forty something female visitor who was looking more and more familiar to him, and then Jimmy, the teenage resident quietly agreed, 'yeah me too, they're both really great.'

'Well trust you two! What about you, Jane, going for C and you Jimmy making the A then, just so we get a good amount of each one made this morning?'

'OK by me,' Jane replied, and Jimmy agreed.

'Brilliant, right, does anyone know what's making the difference between them?' He asked. There was a lot of shaking of heads, then one of the female residents said, 'well I thought A was more creamy, soft, and C was a bit kind of sour, and ...

well, not soft ... not hard though, no, that's not right it doesn't make sense ... can't be cream though can it because it's not white? ... Dunno what I mean do I?' There were a few chuckles and a lot of nodding of heads.

'Yep you're heading in the right direction Luce,' he said, 'it's anchovies that makes the A creamy, and I guess that's the more traditional recipe. C has got capers instead. Not everyone likes the flavour or texture of anchovies though, you know on pizza, or anything else, so we do both here. So, just make sure you select the ingredients for the one you prefer. You could try both if you really must, to see what happens!' He laughed and handed round the recipe sheets.

'Right, first we need to get the water on for the eggs, then we'll go outside to pick the parsley,' and he pointed them over to the sinks and a large pan underneath one of the taps.

'Glad to see you're back with us,' Jane said, turning her head over her shoulder as she walked towards the sinks, forcing him to raise his eyes from her backside as it swayed and jiggled, even in the faded blue overalls she was wearing over a tatty looking orange blouse.

'Ah, thought that might have been you ... a bit warmer now are we?' He said quietly, and smiled at her, touching the outside of his jeans pocket as he did, checking for his keyring without thinking. 'Right, someone fill the pan please. Cold water, then put it on the stove, and everyone get two eggs and place them in the pan. Once the water is boiling we'll give them eight minutes. So, while that's happening we'll go and get the parsley. Pick up a pair of scissors each from that basket next to the eggs and let's go,' he said and led them outside.

'So, parsley grows all year round but we keep some in the poly tunnel because when it rains or hails really hard, or snows, which it does every winter here of course,' he said laughing, 'it sometimes gets completely flattened and can take time to grow back. Sometimes we even have to start again from scratch so we keep some under the poly just in case, to make sure we've always got some to keep us going. We'll get today's from the garden, let me show you.

This is Italian, a giant variety, we get the seeds from Heligan, only about ten miles that way as the seagull flies', he said, pointing over the river, and he bent and snipped three long, very bushy sprigs of the flat leafed parsley from one plant, then three from another, and turned and held up his green bouquet. 'It looks like a lot but you're only going to be using the leaves then bashing them so it reduces in volume quite a lot. Cut six to eight sprigs each, a couple from each of three or four plants, so that you're not completely using up any of the individual plants, that way they'll keep growing. They'll replace the stems we've cut with new shoots. They last longer that way. So, you'll end up with a bunch that looks like this.'

'Right, I'm going to pop back to the kitchen to see if the water's up yet and put the timer on. Come on back when you've finished here. Oh, don't forget to give your bunches a good shake before you come in, like this.' He held up his own, turned it upside down and shook it vigorously for three or four seconds. 'Just in case there is any protein you don't want lurking in there, you don't want it running or sliding around on the chopping board.'

Fifteen

Behind the main house was an old glasshouse largely given over to rows of salads, herbs and tender vegetables. A small walled garden reminded Treloar of his mother's precious vegetable garden at Cove Farm. Almost hidden behind the far garden wall were two poly tunnels for soft summer fruits and herbs. Across a wide lawn stood a second glasshouse, a modern replica but larger in scale which housed a swimming pool. They skirted the rear of the hall crossing a covered patio with ironwork tables and chairs and large potted palms, emerging beside the stable block. This apparently had been converted to accommodation for visiting families. They did not see a soul. Time to go. Back down to the creekside to see how the search was going. They climbed back into Treloar's venerable Land Rover.

'Weird. Did you notice she wasn't wearing shoes?' said Fiona.

'Yes. Unusual. It was warm in there but even so

...'

'I think she was trying to ... I don't know, distract us somehow?'

'By being helpful and cooperative.'

'Well, yes. I suppose when you put it that way. And do you buy that about security? I mean I didn't see anything, but a Hollywood megastar and other rich celebrities, with no CCTV?'

'Yes I thought that. Perhaps there's something Ms Cardrew isn't telling us. At least, not in front of the good doctor. Or perhaps ... perhaps there's something Ms Cardrew doesn't know?'

Treloar drove out into the lane with a last backward glance at the splendid seal fountain.

'And that arsehole!' Fiona continued. 'Do you think he really speaks like that or are the name and the accent just a Freudian thing? What a pompous prick.'

'Yes, he is rather full of himself. Perhaps he's a great therapist?'

'You bet? I can't imagine him actually listening to anyone long enough,' she spat.

'You clearly didn't like him Fiona.'

'It's Fi. I hate Fiona. It makes me think of kilts and shortbread and those poxy little dogs on biscuit tins, you know like Tintin's mutt .... Snowy. If you're going to be Phil, I'm going to be Fi,' she said vehemently.

'Right. Fi it is Ma'am, and by the way Snowy is a

94

wire fox terrier not a Highland terrier.'

'Sorry Sir,' she said her face flushing beetroot.

They exchanged a look and both burst into laughter as his phone rang.

'Treloar.'

'Phil, it's John Forbes. I've just started the post mortem and ...'

'OK John. What have you got?' he sensed the man's uneasiness.

'Well it's that mark on her ankle. You remember. We thought it might be a tattoo.'

'Yes.'

'I've cleaned it up and it's recent and it's not a tattoo. It's a brand in the shape of a fish.'

'A brand? You mean hot irons and cattle?'

'I do Phil, and of course, slaves.'

'Christ. Let's keep that quiet.'

'Agreed. The speculation ...'

'Quite John, quite.'

'There's something I forgot to ask,' said Treloar reversing into a gateway and turning back the way they had come, back to Seal Hall.

Shit he thought to himself. Branded children. What the hell were they looking at here? And he had forgotten to mention the family. This business with his father was distracting him. He needed to focus; compartmentalize. There was nothing he could do, nothing he felt he could do at that moment about his father. He needed to talk it through. He would do that tonight. Until then ... focus. Ask the estimable Ms Cardrew to include the family on the interview list and to use the 'restrooms'.

Sixteen

Situated down beside the water of Seal Creek was a medieval chapel and graveyard, built at the time of the construction of the original Seal Hall, and preserved in its original state, untouched by the subsequent years of disaster and development.

Juliet Morrow had discovered the overgrown graves, crosses and stone angels on one of her first explorations of the grounds and woodland around The Valley of the Tides. She liked to conjure images, shades of the people buried there; illegitimate children of the lord of the manor, drowned sailors washed ashore and lonely schoolboys abandoned and forgotten by their families when Seal Hall had been a boarding school.

The day before the body was discovered and her private, secret place invaded, Juliet had been visiting Jenna Mellin. Both girls were sixteen years old; they shared the same initials and the same birth month, June. The main difference between them was that

Jenna Mellin was dead and had been for more than 300 years.

Jenna Mellin had in a massive fire at the hall at the turn of the 18th century. Juliet felt an affinity with her beyond the coincidence of their names and birthdays. Juliet was also familiar with fires; she liked to start them.

Juliet Morrow was a small mousey girl with flat brown eyes and a forgettable face, so unlike her mother Flora Morrow, Member of Parliament for Redhill South, the junior minister, 'Foxy Flora' to the tabloid press for her glossy good looks, shapely figure and sharp wit.

Juliet had learnt at an early age, something that most learn eventually, other people's disappointment can be excoriating. She had grown up knowing she didn't pass muster. She was not beautiful like her mother; she was not brilliant like her father the eminent plastic surgeon Mr Michael Morrow. She was handed over to a series of nannies and au pairs at an early age and had grown up the victim of her mother's consequential guilt, an endless escalating cycle of neglect and indulgence which had left her isolated and confused. Her father had largely ignored her.

For her tenth birthday her parents had a fairy castle garden tree house built at their Surrey home. She had loved it of course. She had burned it to the ground.

"But we thought you'd adore it," cried her

anguished mother.

"Oh I did, I did," protested an uncomprehending Juliet. "That's why I burned it."

After that there were no more combustible presents, no pets and certainly no second child.

To Juliet fire was the most marvellous element in life. Imagine the thrill at its invention. Where there was cold and dark suddenly there was heat and light. She loved the light, the heat, the smell, the noise and most of all the devastating destructive power. And she had been learning to master it, to control it.

And then calamity.

That summer they had been staying at her grandmother's holiday cottage in Porthtowan on the north Cornish coast. Her mother called it a cottage but in reality it was a 1930s wooden chalet set up on the cliff overlooking the beach. At the top of the steeply sloping back garden was a shed where beach paraphernalia was stored: surfboards, decrepit windbreaks, old deckchairs, cricket and croquet gear dating back to her Uncle Henry's childhood. And the petrol for the outboard for the small boat. Everything went up with a whoosh, but the flames didn't spread to the house so what was the big deal?

And then disaster.

She would have got away with the shed incident but then, at the end of the summer holidays, she had been experimenting with barbecue fluid in her father's study fireplace. What was she supposed to do;

it was pouring with rain? A freak gust of wind from the window deliberately opened for the draught had blown a pile of papers and caught a curtain and in her surprise she had dropped the fluid and ... well there had been a small conflagration. Even the firemen had agreed it was an accident. But her father was incandescent. He had consulted colleagues, identified the newly opened, highly expensive, highly confidential Valley of the Tides, and here she was. Bummer.

Juliet had been sitting beside Jenna's listing gravestone of the overgrown grave talking to its occupant.

'Have you seen that new "guest"? He's supposed to be here to kick a cocaine habit, but I don't believe it. I think he's got TFPS: Total Fucking Prick Syndrome.'

She was referring to the latest arrival at The Valley of the Tides, the twenty year old Guy Masterson. He was good looking and could be charming, but he was arrogant and could be mean. Juliet could picture him pulling the wings off butterflies. He was also filthy, stinking rich. His father, Gregory, owned half the Internet and a shitload of publications and unfortunately he was a constituent of her mother who had recommended this place to him.

Juliet had taken an instant dislike to him. She'd seen him creeping to the very creepy Dr Ivan Speer, psychologist, and letching after the impossibly beautiful, incredibly fey and dopey Bella Dean, some kind of sensory therapist who drifted about in layers of silk and cashmere in subtle blending shades of blue and grey looking awfully like the actress Sienna Miller. Bitch.

But. But he did have one redeeming feature. He was in possession of a splendid Armor Antique Silver Zippo lighter deep carved with the American flag. Guy was a Gauloises cigarette smoker. And where there's smoke.......

Seventeen

As Treloar walked back from the cloakroom he saw Caitlin heading away from the library carrying a tray, heading, presumably for the kitchen. As he neared the front door he could hear a voice coming from Caitlin's lair. It was deep and throaty and female and very sexy.

'Yeah. I've just heard. I've just got back.' Something made Treloar hang back to listen. It was obviously one side of a phone call.

'About the right age and word is it's some kind of strangulation.'

'I don't fucking know.'

'Oh yeah. I reckon it's our boy. See what you can find out.'

'Ciao Dico.'

The conversation ended and Treloar waited a minute before clearing his throat and walking nonchalantly into the room, checking his watch. He looked up and stammered.

'Oh h..hello. No Caitlin?'

Standing at the table was the most gorgeous tall slender blonde in a floor length dress which looked like moulded seaweed. Her thick hair cascaded over her shoulders and down her back to her waist. Her eyes matched the sea green dress. He looked down expecting a tail. She had to be a mermaid.

'No, sorry she's just run to the kitchen She won't be a moment. May I be of help?' she asked in a voice so totally different from the one he had heard that he looked around to see if somebody else was there. The voice was light and breathless and lisping. He was speechless. She spoke again.

'You must be one of the policemen. Caitlin told me you were here. Your colleague just left. Oh do forgive silly me,' she extended her hand for the briefest of glancing handshakes, 'I'm Bella Dean. I'm one of the therapists.'

'Félipe Treloar. Detective Inspector,' he replied. At that moment Caitlin returned.

'Have y'all met?'

'Yes and I was just coming to tell you that we were leaving,' Treloar blustered.

'All taken care of. Thank you Inspector.' Caitlin tapped her iPad and smiled.

'Right. Well goodbye then ladies,' Treloar turned on his heel.

'Goodbye Inspector,' he heard Caitlin call, 'and have a nice day!'

Treloar hurried to his Land Rover. Fiona was waiting, scanning her phone.

'Did you see that girl?' he asked.

'Oh yes. Something eh? How does she move in that dress? Bella Dean – sensory mood therapist – all to do with colours, scents, sounds apparently,' she indicated The Valley of the Tides website on her phone, 'like aromatherapy with bells and whistles. Well probably more likely with whale calls.'

'There's something up with her. I overheard her talking to someone called Dico.'

'Well that's a bit of a poxy name but still?'

'No Fi that's not the point. She was talking about our drowned girl and she was asking what this Dico could find out?'

'You thinking press?'

'Not necessarily. She was talking in a totally different voice from the one she used when we actually met. I don't know what I'm thinking, but something's off. Look into her.'

'No problemo.'

Eighteen

'Great, the eggs will beep in a couple of minutes and then I want a couple of you to take them out and put them in that bowl full of cold water,' he said, pointing to the other side of the kitchen next to a sink, 'it will stop them cooking. So, for now you need to pinch the leaves off fifty grams of parsley, which will give most of you around two good handfuls. Some of you, especially the ladies, might get three, if you do, no problem. I suggest weighing it first then testing how many handfuls you have so that you know for next time. First pinny up though, this stuff's great to taste but I'm reliably informed that it's a bugger for getting stains out. The scales are over there,' and he pointed to three sets of scales on the opposite side of the kitchen. He only had to remind two of them that they needed to weigh the parsley BEFORE they started picking the leaves from the stems, then began picking the leaves from his own sprigs. When he had finished they were all still carefully picking and he went over to collect two of the eggs.

As he turned to walk back to his place at the counter he suddenly became aware that the main kitchen was getting into swing for lunch; it was noisy and the heat was drifting from the ovens over to his side. The chef was staring at him, frowning, and one of the sous, it was sous Carole he realised, was saying, 'Chef, hello ... Chef?' There was the noise of knives hitting chopping boards as two sous-chefs sliced carrots and leeks. 'Morning Chef,' he shouted breezily to the other side. When he got back to his place he picked up the A and C jars and held them up, labels towards the chef, and the two choppers stopped for a second, looked up and smiled and wiggled their fingers at him just before the chef turned round again. The chopping restarted, and he saw sous Carole looking at him, standing to the side of the chef. She looked at him smiling, holding up two bellies of pork, one was about twice the size of the other, and she dropped her arms and shrugged her shoulders. She suddenly looked back at the chef, grimaced, held up the bellies again and said, 'Chef? Which one Chef please?'

'Right, great. Well done, that always takes

longer than you expect it to but the result is well worth it. It doesn't matter if there's still a bit of stalk. Now, watch me, then using the recipe sheets if you need to,' and he handed them round, 'just do what I am going to do.' After drying the eggs with kitchen towel he peeled them, first rolling them on the board to crack the shells, and told the group to make sure the skinny membrane was also taken off, then walked over to the sink and rinsed them, came back to his place and dried them with a piece of kitchen towel. 'You need to make sure you don't have any small pieces of eggshell on the egg surface, so a light rinse will help. Not that we're going to use the whites now, but if you're thinking of having the smoked salmon with egg mayonnaise salad at lunch-time you won't be thanking yourself if you or your mates find yourselves crunching on small pieces of egg shell.'

Then he used the mezzaluna to gently cut the eggs in half, removed the yolks using one of the spoons and put the whites on one side. Then he poured two hundred millilitres of the oil into the jar. 'Right, I'm making the caper version so I need to wash the capers,' he said and picked up the tea strainer and tablespoon measure and went to a large bottle of capers, took out three tablespoons of capers and put them into the tea strainer and washed them under a cold tap.

'If you're making the anchovy version, you need

to rinse them too. In cold water, then dry them as well. They're over there next to the capers. Right. So, the garlic gets chopped into six pieces, the capers or anchovies get chopped roughly and put into the mortar with the garlic, then a sprinkle of the sea-salt and they are crushed together using the pestle. Like this. Can be tricky if you've not done it before, don't worry though, you'll soon get the hang of it. It's quite a lot of fun really.' And after a few seconds he stopped, picked up the mortar and walked round the counter showing everyone the result.

'Easy so far, even I can do that,' said Jimmy.

'Hmmm, right,' he said suspiciously, 'now, all you've got to do is add the parsley and eggs like this and pound it and scrunch it and grind it with the pestle until you've got a fine green paste,' and he added his parsley and eggs and began pounding. After a few seconds he theatrically bent and sniffed the bowl and said, 'Wow, just smell that, fresh parsley and garlic, amazing. See, it's easy. No problem. You'll need to slide the mixture off the pestle with your fingers and back into the bowl once in a while. Just watch as it builds up and drop it back into the mix when you need to. Off you go.'

After a few minutes of noisy and rapidly whirling wrist action he had finished his own and was left with a slightly dry looking dull green paste. He nodded at it and then looked round the table. They were concentrating hard and raising their heads occasionally to look at the others and were beginning to tire already. The wrist actions were slowing and beads of perspiration were beginning to appear on foreheads. 'How are you doing Jimmy?' he asked.

'Getting on fine here Chef,' Jimmy grunted, his wrist working the pestle slowly up out of the bowl of the mortar then back down with a twist of the wrist when it reached the bottom, up and back down again, and again, with determination showing in his face.

He got up and went over to Jimmy, 'May I?' he asked and Jimmy passed the pestle and moved over and he put the pestle into the mortar and began very quickly running it around the inside of the mortar in a circular motion. After twenty seconds he stopped and tipped it so that Jimmy could see the result. 'Now, push the mixture on the sides back to the bottom and begin pounding again, then try the side-rub, crush-roll yourself, see how you get on,' he said. The others had been looking and before long they were all getting on well with the side-rub, crush-roll and looking a lot happier. He walked back to his own spot and waited for them to begin looking up questioningly before he walked slowly round the counter, suggesting to some that theirs needed a bit more work and to others, 'well done, that looks great,' and, 'brilliant, that's just right.'

Jane had been one of those needing a bit more work and when she had raised her head and looked at him as though she thought she might have finished he could see that she was red in the face and she wiped her forehead with the back of her hand. He walked over to her, looked into her bowl and nodded then reached into the pocket in front of his apron and pulled something out and handed it to her and said, 'great, well done Jane.' She looked puzzled and took it from him before opening it up and seeing it was a brand new, very fluffy, black head-band, with HARRY'S BAR in capital red letters on the front.

'Bastard,' she laughed at him, and everyone laughed along, and he walked round handing out head-bands to everyone.

'Right, now just add the vinegar and mix it in, just a tablespoon, like this,' he said, mixing it in with a teaspoon. They copied him. 'Now put 200 mils of the oil into the measuring jug and add it, around a quarter at a time, to the paste and mix it up before adding the next bit. Like this.'

'Et voila,' ready for tasting! Brilliant everybody, well done. Have a taste and tell us what you think. They all loved it, and enjoyed tasting everyone else's, even the A likers liking the Cs' and the C likers liking the As'.

'Now, you just need to pour it into the Kilner jar and you're good to go. No washing up for you today,' and he laughed. 'Now, here's the important part. This will last for two or three weeks in the fridge, so take it home if you're going that way soon, but feel absolutely free to bring your jar along to lunch or dinner here if you like, no-one will mind and if you want to share it with others no-one will mind that either. BUT, no-one is going to be offended if you don't want to keep it. Just say so now, or let me know discreetly later. I can tell you that The Gig down by Polruan harbour will always find a space on the menu for it and put a two pound donation into their RNLI box for every portion served.' No-one said anything.

Then Jane said, 'brilliant, that was really good, thanks Harry,' and started clapping, and suddenly everyone else was clapping and saying things like, 'RIGHT ON', and 'brilliant,' and Yeah, thanks.' Then they began drifting off clutching their hard-earned Kilner jars and the chef and staff on the other side looked on jealously.

'About The Gig?,' Jane asked when everyone else had gone; they were about to leave his end of the kitchen via his specials restaurant door and she reached down and rubbed the top of his thigh, through the outside front of his left jeans pocket where the fabric had been well worn and faded by the frequent and unconscious patting of the keyring, then a little lower until she was pressing the keys themselves and he could feel a sharp edge biting into his skin. 'Are you up for it tonight?'

Nineteen

As Treloar and Fiona Sinclair were leaving The Valley of the Tides, Tulip Khan was checking in at The Old Custom House Hotel across the river in Fowey. Tulip Khan was a freelance journalist based in Bath. She had taken the call from her Cornish contact mid morning and headed straight down the M5 motorway. Dead girl in river in suspicious circumstances on doorstep of Hollywood superstar's pet clinic full of teenage nutjobs? No brainer.

Several years previously she had written a controversial article for a national tabloid about a series of grisly murders that took place in Porthaven along the coast west of Fowey. She had championed the cause of the perpetrator and this had brought her much notoriety, not least amongst the police who had worked the case. However this had brought about an email exchange with one team member, which had led to a grudging respect and an ongoing relationship. Thus Tulip Khan, given the head's up, was the first media representative to arrive to cover the story of the dead girl. A mixture of death and stardust was highly sellable, an editor's wet dream, and the chance for a desk on a London major had brought Tulip to the sea-facing room at the boutique hotel.

Tulip didn't really get Cornwall. She was an urban girl. She had grown up in Cheltenham and studied Sociology at the University of Bath. She had fallen in love with Bath and had stayed on after graduation. She loved the ease of life; everything you could want to hand: history, architecture, shops, restaurants, takeaways, theatre, museums, gyms.

If you weren't fussed about the sea what was the point of Cornwall? Everything was so far away! There were no shops to speak of unless you wanted to buy poxy wooden fish or ornamental lighthouses probably made in China! The food was all right if you liked fish or the nasty pasties and the place was open. OK, it wasn't exactly cold, but it was so awfully damp. Like walking through fog. And did the wind ever stop blowing? Winter in Cornwall: ghastly. Grey skies, grey water, grey woods.

Last time she'd been here was no better; different but no better. High summer: hordes of kids, traffic jams, same bloody wind but blowing sand rather than rain, coach parties traipsing the streets eating fish and chips and dodging seagulls: nightmare. She agreed with a colleague, who had told her before her first visit, that civilisation ended in

Exeter. However, she had to admit that the hotel was good. Her room was decent sized and comfortable and she grudgingly accepted that it was pleasing and calming to look out over the river. If she wasn't careful she would find herself forced to consider that she might be enjoying her stay.

What she knew so far was that the body of the young girl found in the river was still unidentified and unclaimed. She also knew that the girl had not drowned but was dead when she went into the water; she also knew that the body had been brought ashore at the jetty below The Valley of the Tides.

Tulip knew The Valley of the Tides. When it had first opened its doors she had been among a small group of journalists who had been invited and given a tour. A colleague on the West Briton had owed her a favour and offered her his place. The event had been hosted by the Director Sindy Cardrew. Tulip had been impressed by the woman who carried a calm air of authority and competence. Tulip's piece for the newspaper had been complimentary about the setup and the staff, especially Ms Cardrew. You never knew when a friendly contact might prove useful.

Sadly, Jackson Power had not been present but Tulip thought that he was staying there when the girl had been found and she had heard a rumour that there were two residents who would be of great interest to editors: an MP's daughter and the youngest son of Gregory Masterson. Guy Masterson being in residential therapy was pay dirt for Tulip but she would need to tread carefully and choose her target publication with care. Masterson senior was not a man to cross. But Tulip had discovered that there was to be a friends and family evening before Christmas and she wanted in.

On the second floor of Seal Hall was a beautiful corner room with dual aspects looking over the creek and across the river towards Fowey. When he had first arrived at The Valley of the Tides, Dr Ivan Speer, Chief Psychologist, had commandeered this to be his office and consulting room. It was a large room with french windows opening onto the veranda which ran the length of the second floor. The walls were painted the palest blue, the wooden floor polished. There were high backed wing chairs upholstered in canary yellow and a chocolate leather sofa. The furniture was old pine: freestanding cupboards, a chest of drawers and a battered kitchen table with two chairs which served as a desk.

The wall facing the creek held a huge mirror. On the remaining walls was a series of Magritte prints: *Empire of Light*: a blue sky with cumulus clouds above a darkened street with lit windows and a single illuminated street-lamp. *The Castle of the Pyrenees*: a blue sky scudded with clouds over a dark rough sea, a large rock topped with a medieval castle floating in mid air above the breaking waves. *Sixteenth of September*: a large deciduous tree against a blue sky with a crescent moon near its crown. The room smelled of warm citrus, the scent drifting from a mosaic oil burner on the chest of drawers.

When he had taken the post, Speer had arrived with great plans. This was a dream position; unrestricted funding, open-minded management, hands-off ownership. Speer had spent most of his career in the treatment of troubled children, adolescents and young people. He had arrived with exemplary testimonials and a lauded reputation. Dr Ivan Speer loved children. This had been the obvious place for one of his long-standing patients, Guy Masterson. Such a troubled boy.

Speer was experimenting with a new approach to obsessive behaviour. He believed that rather than preventing it one should indulge it with a view to satiating the compulsion. Guy Masterson was his first guinea pig.

Speer stood at the window watching as his pet patient headed out along the coastal path to Bodinnick ... The good doctor was worried.

Twenty

Whilst an inveterate urban girl, Tulip was a devotee of the countryside for exercise and relaxation; most weekends would find her hiking on Cotswold Edge or paddling Chew Valley Lake. So after checking in, she returned to her room to dress for the great outdoors. She pulled on the Oboz Sawtooth boots she had bought that summer in Montana when trekking the Bighorn Canyon; best ever vacation. She picked up her stuff pack and loaded it with two small water bottles, a muesli bar, an apple and her iPhone. She grabbed her down jacket, her Canon PowerShot camera and her beanie hat and headed out. She had checked the ordnance survey map and expected to be gone no longer than three hours. Out of habit, she told the receptionist this and added her intended route.

Tulip was fit. Bath, like Rome, was a city of seven hills and she lived at the top of one of them. She was a seasoned walker. As a child she had spent holidays in Wales exploring the Brecon Beacons and the Black Mountains. Today's walk took her to Caffa Mill and across the river Fowey on the chain ferry to Bodinnick, then up the hill past the Ferry Boat Inn before bearing right off the road onto the footpath heading seawards. From here it was uphill passing between the overhanging leaf-shedding trees and spiky shrubs. Through gaps in the hedge to her left she could make out small fields of grazing sheep, to her right glimpses of the river.

Suddenly she emerged from the gloom onto an open section of path overlooking the river to Readymoney Cove, the Tudor fort of St Catherine's Castle and the daymark on Gribbin Head and out across Seal Creek towards the sea. She uncapped her camera: it was a great view and would make a brilliant location shot for her piece. The sun was getting low in the sky. She needed to get a move on.

She turned and headed eastwards following the path along the hilltop high above the creek. She could make out the rooves of Seal Hall ahead. She was entering a tunnel of twisted windblown trees blocking the light from the sky; it was suddenly cold. Tripping over an exposed root she swore and stumbled clutching the camera to her chest.

'Mind your footing,' said a soft voice.

Tulip gasped and looked up to find herself face to face with a young man. She had neither seen nor heard his approach. He looked familiar somehow but she couldn't place him. He was good looking with large long-lashed grey eyes and a broad white-toothed smile. There was nothing remotely sinister about him but Tulip was instinctively if irrationally afraid. She wanted to turn and run but something held her.

'You're heading onto private property I'm afraid. If you proceed on this path you'll need to cut up over the hill that leads back to the Bodinnick road. It's getting dark and there are no streetlamps and precious few houses; pitch black, total darkness.' He closed on her grinning. He was trying to scare her and succeeding. Time to get out of there. It was completely still and silent and the darkness was seeping along the path.

Then a sound: heavy breathing and muttering followed by footsteps coming towards them from behind the man. A middle aged man in a battered Barbour waxed jacket appeared.

'Guy, Guy where are you off to? We have ... Oh, you have a companion.'

'No, no,' Tulip gabbled, 'just a chance encounter. I must get back. It's getting dark.'

The young man made no move to acknowledge the interloper, keeping his gaze fixed upon Tulip. Before she dragged her eyes from his and turned to retrace her steps she caught the look on his face: fury. And at that moment she recalled his name: Guy Masterson. So here he was. Of course, she remembered him from the extensive coverage of his various escapades in the media, though not that owned by his father Gregory of course. Then, as if a switch had been thrown, his face resumed the guileless smile,

'Enchanté,' he whispered, bowed and turned to the new arrival. 'Come along then my dear Speer'.

And with that he brushed past the other man and headed back the way he had come, the older man trailing in his wake. Tulip felt a wave of relief flood across her. As she turned and made her way back along the path a late ray of sunshine burst through a gap in the trees ahead of her and a blackbird burst into song. The last canto of Dante's *Inferno* came to mind: the ascent from hell.

Twenty One

Back in his room he was wondering what the evening would hold and whether or not it would turn into a night when he found himself suddenly in front of his desk, and stood there thinking, looking down to the river, wondering. 'What kind of girl is she? What does she like? What will we do? First thing this morning she didn't look exactly like she'd fancy the quad bike at night on the footpath over to Polruan, maybe a taxi? Long way round … safe though.' Then the Fowey pilot boat moved slowly into view, past the frame of the window, going down the river, slowly, then it was dwarfed by the massive and slowly appearing blue bow of a china clay transporter. It looked as though it was chasing the smaller boat down and was about to catch it. He flashed to thinking about a mouse leading an elephant down a quiet street by its trunk and laughed.

'Ah! Great idea, don't want one that big

though, ha! Wonder what the tide will be like later,' he thought, thinking about a special hire of one of the ferry boats. 'If one of them can't do it one of the lads from the shipyard would help. The weather's good and it's not that far so she should be OK with it. Great.' He checked the small yellow tide table book that was mandatory in that part of the world and lived on top of his desk and saw that it wouldn't be too low for The Valley of the Tides slipway so he reached over and grabbed the phone off the desk and quick-dialled the ferry office and organised their small boat to pick them up at six o'clock and to bring them back at nine thirty. They charged an arm and two legs after nine thirty and had to be dragged out kicking and screaming, if at all, after ten thirty, so that would have to do. 'Brilliant, sorted.'

Before he knew it, he had taken the keyring from his pocket, unlocked the top right desk drawer and opened it and retrieved a square black plastic box, lidded and locked. It wasn't big, around a foot square and eight inches high, and he reached into the back of the drawer for another key, longer and thinner, and opened the box and lifted the lid and saw all the tubs and could see without counting them that they were all still there and knew exactly how many caps there were because he'd been adding a new line on his five bar gate counting sheet every week for the last ten months and after every new line he had multiplied the total number of lines, first by forty two, then after two and a half months by sixty three because Sykes had missed two weeks and he had started shitting himself thinking that Sykes must have died or got caught or something but then found out he'd gone to fucking Leeds to see his mother who was fucking ill and hadn't had the fucking sense to let him know so when he had eventually rung up he had said he wanted more, half as much again, and if they didn't start fucking arriving soon, including what he had fucking missed, he would send the fucking video to the fucking Argus.

'Wow. Cool. Still more than two thousand five hundred. More than two thousand six hundred by New Year. Party on that!' He said to himself. He could see from the five bar gates and notes that it would have been two thousand five hundred and sixty two if he hadn't had the occasional extra stay-up fun ... or helped out, only when absolutely necessary of course. 'Sixty down in ten months, not too bad,' he thought, 'ha, great investment.' He locked and closed the box and put it back in the drawer, dropped the key on top of the box, pushed the drawer to and locked it and dropped the keyring back into his pocket.

Lunchtime. The coals were nearly grey, 'About ten minutes go now ... Oh ... Christ!' he was thinking, and he looked to the table on his right to check that the membrane on the monkfish cheeks had been knife-skimmed properly. It had. 'Brilliant … that Carole's amazing … worth her weight in reliable oysters ... bloody brilliant.' Six monkfish cheek burgers had been ordered for the one thirty specials sitting and he needed to make sure they were on the table on time. Four with the caper sauce and two with the anchovy. He had had small green flags made, mounted on wooden toothpicks, with As and Cs drawn carefully on each side in black, which would be planted into the assembled burgers to hold them together and let the table know which were which.

He could see sous Carole through the window at the cooker range, next to a steaming pan and next to it on the counter he could see a bowl of thinly sliced chips. She looked at him and smiled and waved, and he smiled back. He looked back at the monkfish cheeks and took in for the first time the jars of salsa verde, mayonnaise, thinly sliced red onions and tomatoes, lettuce leaves, and the stack of plates next to them and the split brioche burger buns on a board next to them, and the A and C flags in a pot next to the board, and turned back to sous Carole to say thanks but she was too busy checking the oil temperature to notice.

He looked back at the grill, then at the monkfish cheeks … and grimaced and shook his head. He could never forget the first time, should have been easy ... Brighton ... The Rock .... Christ, what a mess. He had used the cheeks in curries, soups, and finely chopped in omelettes, on their own and with crab, all sorts of crab, and prawns, and deep fried and served with chips, and they had always gone down well.

*

In early July, after collecting a load of cheeks that were larger than expected from the Hove marina fish market, as soon as he had seen them, and thinking that they were the size of good homemade beef burgers, he had wondered what they would be like in a bun and what they would go with. He had asked the fish chef, after putting four aside in his fridge for trial work, to get them properly prepared and individually vacuum-packed and stored in the freezer where they would stay until he had decided what to do with them over the next couple of days.

After he had double-checked that the crew had cleaned and tidied the kitchen that night, he had gone up to his flat to wait until he was sure that they had all gone home and dropped five sousies and was bloody well determined to enjoy himself and bloody well make the most of the next few hours.

His idea for the burgers had been spot-on and

the four he had cooked had all worked well but he quickly decided that he wouldn't offer the regular burger buns, only the brioche buns with a choice of caper or anchovy salsa verde and it had only taken a single bite of each to be sure that he was right and which ones would be going on the specials menu, and then he had gone to the kitchen office for the kitchen camera so that he could disassemble one of the burgers and rebuild it in stages with a photo of each stage so that the chefs and sous chefs and assistants could see exactly what needed to be done, and that was all finished by ten past one, when he went upstairs to the flat and got out the laptop to type up the recipe and paste the photos into place in the recipe as he was typing it up. By two o'clock it was all done, printed and checked, and then he emailed the fish chef asking him to make sure twelve of the monkfish cheeks were taken out of the freezer as soon as he got in so that they could defrost naturally before lunch service opened and that monkfish cheek burgers were written up on the specials board and printed out fully on the specials menu, and he was still seriously buzzed and needed something to do.

After swapping his chef jacket for a plain light blue T-shirt and still wearing the faded and antique-torn-and-worn Wranglers and red trainers he had been wearing in the kitchen, he had gone to his desk and taken out his black box and unlocked it and taken out a pot and shaken a handful of caps into a small plastic freezer bag just in case, and grabbed his yellow bomber jacket off the coat stand and put in on then dropped the plastic bag into his right jacket pocket and gone back to the desk and put the pot back into the box and the box back into the desk and locked them all away and was outside heading round the corner into The Lanes towards The Brighton Dive on auto pilot before he knew it.

It would be open until at least three o'clock, which would give him some company if he wanted it when he saw who was in, and time to think about what next. The early sous chefs and assistants were an independent and pretty competent lot and the chefs got in pretty early anyway, so he didn't need to be back in the kitchen until mid-morning. Great.

Not ... OK, it was fairly busy so there was plenty to see, it wasn't too dark down there and the music was soul tonight, and a few friendly gays that he recognised had drifted in because the gay bars closed at two o'clock and three had stopped to talk which was sometimes good fun but not what he wanted tonight and there was no-one he knew in so he had had three double malts on the rocks and decided he would go and see Tamsin. At home at Roedean. She was a teacher and shared a neat cottage near the school in Roedean Crescent with two other teachers, female, just over a wall and behind a gate, he smiled, thinking about the good doctor, but this was a small wall and an unlocked gate, not far out of town, only just up the hill really, but too far to walk, but maybe not, maybe, the weather was good, so he was going to start walking and see how he got on and flag a taxi if he needed it.

'Mornin' 'Arry,' a deep gravelly voice said just before he walked bang into the guy, his forehead stopping sharply against his chin. He had just drained the last malt and turned to walk towards the door and BANG, he wasn't going anywhere, just as far as the closest he had ever been to the sometimes smoky and sometimes sweaty smelling, and tonight it was smoky, Big Malc, Mitch's minder. 'How are we today then? You're feeling good I see,' Big Malc said, 'eyes are like black fuckin' saucers man, where you been getting it? We know where you ain't been getting it, where you goin' man? Stay and talk, come over and have a chat with me and Mitch, sit, let me get you another drink, what is it 'Arry?'

'Hi Malc, I'm good yeah, just off now, got to go or I'll be late, to the girlfriend's, how are you doing?' He had asked. 'Great,' and tried to step round Malc but Malc had just stepped over and blocked his path so he looked up and said, 'yeah, scotch please, rocks' and moved back to the bar.

'Go sit over with Mitch, he's resting his ankle, I'll bring the drinks over, just getting a round in, sitting over there under the stairs,' Big Malc said.

He didn't remember making an actual decision, just didn't want to spend time with Mitch, or Big Malc, and had veered towards the bottom of the stairs instead of pulling out a chair at the table underneath the stairs and was suddenly yanked back as the handle of Mitch's crutch caught in his jacket pocket. 'Shit,' he said, feeling for his pocket which was now ripped, to Mitch, turning, he said, 'What the fuck's up man? And he yanked the crutch out of Mitch's hand and swung it over his head down towards Mitch but it hit the side of the stairs above the table and broke in two, where the top half joined the bottom half with a height adjuster screw. 'Do that again and I'll fucking kill you, you stupid bastard, who the fuck do you think you are!?'

Mitch had his hands up in a protective gesture, and he had been about to bring the broken half of the crutch that was still in his hand down onto the top of Mitch's neatly combed black haired head when the forward momentum was suddenly stopped when Big Malc grabbed the end of it. He swirled round pushing the bottom half of the crutch away from himself forcing Big Malc's arm back which pushed Big Malc over while he was still off-balance and then he stared wide-eyed at Big Malc lying heaped and looking surprised on the floor and then he turned round to Mitch, 'what the fuck are you cunts playing at? Piss off,' he said. Then he saw Big Malc reach over and pick up the bag of caps that had fallen to the floor when his pocket had been ripped.

'Sit, sit, here, just for a minute,' Mitch said, 'for fuck's sake Harry sit down, I just want a quiet word'.

'Look Boss, look what the twat's got here,' Big Malc said as he stood up, throwing the bag with the caps onto the table as he moved in close, towering and crowding, too close for him to do anything useful with the bottom half of the crutch that he still held in his right hand.

'So,' Mitch said after he had looked inside the bag, 'moving up in the world yeah? Look man I just want to talk, sit down.'

He turned back towards Mitch, 'you fucking maniac, call off your gorilla and give me those back and fuck off, I'm going, I've got a fucking date and if I ever need shit gear from you again I'll call you right!' He leaned over and snatched the bag from Mitch's hand and stuffed it into his right jeans pocket, threw the crutch at Mitch and it bounced off the table, knocking over a half full glass of something that was probably lager and an empty shorts glass before hitting Mitch sideways on in the chest, shouted, 'just fucking cool it and stay away from me!' and turned and strode two at a time up the stairs.

He didn't know that he had just missed being strongly invited to leave the bar by a very wide bouncer who was six inches taller than Big Malc, but he was still well-excited and seriously buzzed. He had just come on to the seafront at Marine Parade and was about to go steaming past the pier, still well-up for walking to Roedean, when he saw the clock tower at the end of the pier telling him that it was almost three o'clock. Time with Tamsin was running out. There had been little traffic and when he heard a car behind him he turned and saw that it was a taxi, so he waved it to stop.

The taxi driver was less than impressed when he said he wanted to go Roedean, but looked happier when he had said that he'd pay twenty pounds for what would probably be a five minute ride at that time of the morning and sure enough five minutes later they had picked up Marina Way after some iffy and complicated driving from Marine Parade near the marina, turned right onto Roedean Road and after the golf course taken the left into Roedean Crescent where Tamsin lived, down at the school end, behind a two feet high brick wall, and stopped and he handed over a twenty pound note and got out and quietly closed the door.

It was warm and the weather was fine and still dark but there was enough light from a street light up the road for him to see and to vault the wall and land between two rose bushes with white flowers. He bent and scrabbled together in his hand some pebbles from the flower bed and looked at the upstairs window that he knew was Tamsin's then took his mobile phone from the jacket pocket that was still intact and speed-dialled Tamsin's mobile and it went to voice mail and he said, 'Shit,' and hung up without leaving a message and moved closer to the window and threw up a pebble that hit the window with a sharp pinging sound and waited but the bedroom light didn't come on and the curtain didn't open. Nothing happened.

He chose two pebbles next time, one larger than the first, the other about the same size, and threw them both at the window and they both hit it and there was a sharp pinging and then a solid rapping sound close together and he waited and the bedroom light still didn't come on and the curtain still didn't open. Nothing happened.

'Come on Tammy, wake up, open up, what's up?' he whispered loudly up to the window, then bent down to pick up two larger pebbles, small stones really, and he threw them at the window, harder, and they both hit it with solid rapping sounds very close together and the light still didn't come on and the curtains still didn't open. 'Shit,' he said and tried the mobile again and it was still going to voice mail. Then a light at the other end of the house came on and the curtain opened and he saw a woman with long hair looking at him so he had walked across the lawn, gesticulating with his hands and arms for her to open a window until she did and he said, 'Oops, hi, I'm after Tamsin, could you let her know please. Thanks. Yeah, I'm Harry, she'll know, just ask her to come down and let me in. Thanks, yeah that would be great.'

'Tamsin doesn't want to see you, she isn't going anywhere you stupid man,' the woman said sharply, 'so go away.'

'What do you mean? Where is she, she must be, she said call any time, any time, she'd love to see me.' Harry said.

'For goodness sake Mr Forrester, she doesn't want to see you again, ever, she's not interested any more now than the last three times you've been here so please leave, now, or I'll call the police. Don't come back.' The woman banged the window shut, the curtain quickly drew closed but the light stayed on. He stood staring at the woman's window for a while and turned as he heard a window open across the street, and turned back to the woman's window, and looked again at Tamsin's window which still showed no light and no open curtains.

'Fuck, now what?' he said to himself after he had vaulted back over the wall, and then he looked at his watch but couldn't see the time because it was too dark, so he walked thirty metres up to the street light where he could see that it was still only quarter to four but beginning to get light so he decided to go back into town and find an open bar and set off walking back to the main road. 'What the fuck's she talking about, the last three times?' was the thought that kept buzzing round his head as he walked, looking straight through the small group of golfers just collecting in the car park that had arrived for what he knew from experience was an early brandy snifter before first tee off. 'She was well up for it before, I'm bloody sure, when I was here … what last three times? How did she know who I fucking well was? … How did she know my fucking name?'

He didn't find a taxi prepared to stop, a few went past with their roof signs switched off and had just ignored his waves and by four thirty he was pissed off … beginning to get bored, weary, it was light, and he was back on the seafront and the only place he could think of was Buddies, the twenty four hour place just along Kings Road, couldn't remember if you had to have food but could remember that they never closed and served alcohol, great. He dropped three more sousies and was soon drinking a pint of bitter, and half-looking at a menu, trying to decide whether to not eat a margherita pizza or burger and chips … 'what three times … how did she know my name … Tammy was really up for it … where was she?' were thoughts that were still pinging round his head when the waitress came over again, in her strong American accent, to ask if he was ready to order yet. 'I'm still deciding but can you bring a double malt on the rocks please while I make up my mind?' he asked.

'Well, I can, but you need to hurry up 'cos I'm going off soon and I'd like to serve you 'cos you look like a nice guy, in fact you look familiar, you been here before? Anyway ... or you could just pay for the drinks now ... I'll bring you two large malts if you like ... and give me your tip now.'

Four hours later he knew that her name was Sue, that she was from New York, that she had been at Buddies for two weeks, would be for the rest of the summer, well until the end of October at least, that she lived in a small but comfortable top floor flat in Marine Square in Kemptown just off Marine Parade and didn't know how she paid for it and didn't care because she was the best at sex he had ever met. 'Head to die for, deep or what, wow,' he had thought when he caught his breath for the third time, AND she had seriously gone for the "guess which way the tongue is moving now?" and the "early morning bristles" games. And she had a seriously dirty laugh and she had laughed a lot and said, 'well, I guess I'm a Susie too ... yeah I think that would be great, I know

I can give you a LOT of help if you give me some of YOUR little helpers!' when he had given her his tip. And she had ... helped a lot ... and his head wasn't buzzing at all as he walked back to his own flat.

Twenty Two

It hadn't lasted long. He arrived back in his flat above The Rock feeling great, the best for ages. The shower was good, came out fresh, he was looking forward to seeing Sue again, and he felt good, relaxed, happy, when he walked into the kitchen at quarter past eleven. 'Morning everyone,' he shouted as he walked in and he heard a few greetings above the noise of knives chopping and fans whirring and people shouting and pans banging. Normal.

He walked round the corner and into the restaurant and over to the manager so he could see the menus they were running for the day and discuss any special needs diners that the manager was aware may be coming in at lunch-time, there were none, everything was fine. Normal.

He walked back into the kitchen and over to the meats corner and said, 'morning Meat,' to the meat chef, 'how's things, everything all right?'

'Yeah, we're coping. The beef delivery was late but we're nearly butchered up now so we'll be fine for lunch, but you might need to check what's left for the dinner service. Doesn't look like there's enough sirloin there to me, you might need to give them a ring ... and the belly pork, you might need to have a look at that too.'

'Ah ... right, well Meat. Here's the thing. It's your job to make sure we've got enough of everything. Enough, not too much, or too little, enough! What I suggest is that you have a look at the fucking sirloin and the fucking belly pork and YOU find out if YOU need any fucking more and fucking get on the phone and order it if we do, because if there isn't and we have to take any of the sirloin or pork dishes off the menu you'll be down the fucking road. Why didn't you check them first thing after getting in like you're supposed to? For Christ's sake Meat, get a grip.' He heard himself saying not too calmly, growling but not quite shouting, through gritted teeth.

'Sorry Chef, I'll get on it Chef,' he heard Meat mutter as he walked over to the fish and seafood section. 'Hiya Fish, and how are WE doing today?' he asked sharply.

'We're all fine here Chef, thanks. Everything's on track, needed a bit more shellfish stock but that's sorted now and we've adjusted the menu for this morning's deliveries and told the restaurant. Oh, and your monkfish cheeks are out and should be ready to go by twelve o'clock.'

'Brilliant, thanks Fish,' he said and walked to check out puddings and pastries, and Milly and Molly, the "P Sisters" as nearly everyone called them were fine, just as usual. The girls arrived early, checked stocks, and made sure that their staff knew at the beginning of every shift what was going to be needed and that it was always delivered on time and to quality. No issues.

'Sorry Chef, got a problem,' said Meat three minutes after he had spoken to Milly and Molly, just as he was about to open the first of the monkfish cheek packs. 'We're short of sirloin I reckon. I'd ordered it three days ago but they didn't deliver yesterday because they haven't been paid and their accountant's put his foot down. Won't deliver again until they've been paid. Don't know why they haven't been paid. Shit, we're stuck Chef. Sorry.'

'Christ Meat,' You go and find OUR fucking accountant and find out why he hasn't paid them, tell him there's no problem from our end and get him to pay. I'LL find some fucking sirloin from somewhere.' He rang Old Beet Farm first, that had just refused to deliver, and no amount of pleading and grovelling would make them change their mind. They hadn't been paid for four weeks and they wouldn't even think about making a delivery until they had been paid in full, 'and that's that,' he was told by the old man. Even though he had reached a great agreement for the supply of their brilliant meat products not long after he came to Brighton, with the old man personally, the old man was not budging now. Couldn't even if he wanted to, which he said he did, because his daughter was looking after the finances now and she had said to stop deliveries until they'd been paid, then SHE would meet someone from the restaurant to negotiate a new agreement.

'Fuck! ... Fish, you got a minute please?' he shouted, and when Fish arrived, 'I've got a meat problem to sort out, can you take care of the monkfish cheek burger orders that come through please? You've got all the instructions you'll need on the recipe sheets so you'll be fine. '

'OK Chef, no problem,' said Fish, 'there's already a couple of orders in, I'll get on it'.

'Great, thanks mate,' he said and Fish walked over to begin unpacking a few more of the cheeks and he heard him start telling one of the assistant chefs to get out all the bits and pieces, and a sous chef to start preparing onions and tomatoes. He ran up to his flat, grabbed three sousies from the plastic bag that he had left on the table next to his wardrobe, dropped them and ran back down to the kitchen.

Twenty Three

They had two main beef suppliers, apart from the specialists in Italy for Chianina and Scotland for Aberdeen Angus, both up on the Sussex Weald. Old Beet Farm was by far their biggest and he hoped that their back-up, Grassington Farm, just outside Barcombe, had the right stock and would deliver urgently. Eventually he got through to Michael, the owner, 'Michael hello there, how are you ... great ... listen, got a bit of a problem here today ... Ah, Harry, Harry Forrester, down at The Rock ... Brighton ... great ... yeah we've hit a snag and I'm hoping you can help, can't go into details 'cos the meat chef wouldn't like it .... Ha Ha! Yeah probably ... Listen, is there any chance you could let us have three dry-aged sirloins this afternoon? I'd be really grateful if you could let us have them if you've got them. It would be great if you could deliver them as well, I know I'm not asking for much, but we're short staffed at the moment'.

Michael was not silly. He might be able to as it turned out, but it would be a lot easier to persuade his son, who had lots to do and was really very busy, to make the delivery this afternoon if he could have an order for a few sirloins a week for the next three months, and to sit down and have a discussion about other cuts as well, and a long-term agreement. 'Right, Michael, if you can help us out this afternoon that's the least we should do … thanks a lot, we'll see Joe a bit later on and I'll call you later in the week to set up a meeting to talk about an agreement. If you could send us another four sirloins on Friday that would be great … yep … dry aged, twenty one days at least … all of it, thanks.'

Meat was hovering, red-faced, having heard the end of the conversation and he got even redder as he explained that the main supplier hadn't been paid because Meat had stopped signing off invoices as approved, and had been passing them through to accounts without the usual OK, or corrections notes which he had always done in the past. The accountant had said that he had sent emails to Meat asking him to come to the office to go through old invoices that needed paying and Meat said he hadn't seen them so had not seen the accountant and didn't know that there was a problem. 'Christ!' Meat said, 'Why couldn't he come and see ME for fuck's sake?'

Before he could answer he noticed a tray full of food being brought back by a waiter who was placing it back onto the service counter as though it had the plague, and walked over to him and asked what the problem was, having noticed on the way over that it was four plates of monkfish cheek burgers and chips that had been sent back. 'The customers say they're terrible Chef, can't eat them. One said they're not what's on the menu Chef, talked about it being rubber'.

He had already seen that the brioche buns had not been finished on the grill and carefully lifted the untoasted top of one of the burgers that had had a bite taken out of it and removed the layers of onion and tomato underneath it and saw a shrivelled dark brown lump that looked disgusting and knew straight away that it was a monkfish cheek that had not only been burnt in butter in a frying pan and not grilled carefully over the kitchen coals, but also that it had not been properly knife-skimmed to remove the membrane. He could feel Fish looking over his shoulder, and knew that all the assistants and sous chefs were looking at the small group staring at the rejects, and he turned, 'Fish you're fucking toast ... what the fuck? ... How the fuck could that happen? ... Can't you fucking read? ... Didn't you look at the fucking things before you sent them out? Jesus man

… Christ! … unbelievable.'

He looked at the waiter, whose name he knew was Jason, shaking his head and said, 'Sorry Jace, not your fault, not at all, let's go out and apologise and see if we can persuade them to give us a second chance, or at least accept a voucher to come back with friends and eat on the house.' Out in the restaurant Jason came to a sudden halt as he saw the empty table, and his face went redder and redder when he realised that everyone in the restaurant was looking at them.

That had been it, 'fucking wallies, what's the fucking point? What a bastard. Fuck it!', he remembered thinking and then he had gone straight up to the flat, dropped three sousies, gone straight back downstairs and stormed outside, down Black Lion Street and past the car park, between moving cars and across Kings Road and onto the seafront and then turned right along the promenade above the beach. People had stared at him; he had glared at everybody that caught his eye. 'Poor sods,' he thought.

He had still been wearing his pink chef's trousers, the bright berry double breasted chef's jacket, pink baseball cap and red trainers and he had stormed past people sitting under canopies looking at the beach, past cyclists on the cycle path, past ice cream and postcard booths, past the Hilton that he thought looked miles away across on the other side of the road, and he had looked up and seen the Brighton i360 viewing platform doughnut in the sky at the top of its tower and stormed underneath and past it and glared at people sitting outside the cafés on the grass close to promenade and stormed past them and then crossed the grass in front of the bandstand to the pavement that ran along the side of Kings Road and stormed past the other side of the cafés and under the platform on the other side of the tower and back to the flat.

When everyone had left the kitchen and restaurant after dinner service and cleaning up that night he had gone back down and pulled an all-nighter preparing the seafood sauces. They were on the menu as gravies. The crabs had been unlocked from his personal deep freezer and defrosted, and carefully used with prawn shells to make a rich reduced stock and then he had decided on the smoked Pernod and smoked dry sherry as the alternatives before adding his final, smoke infused, ingredients and tasting.

It was five-thirty in the morning and the first commis chefs had arrived to start work before he had finished, but he was well pleased. They were seriously delicious sauces and he would keep them locked in his freezer until they were needed. He would tell the waiters on the day to let other diners know that the two special gravies had sold out to make sure there was plenty to go round for the inspectors. He had grunted 'Hi,' to the early arrivals and gone up to his flat with a bad headache and feeling nauseous, and that was after as little tasting as possible, using only small finger tip dips.

They already had one star and they were going for the second. The Michelin inspectors had been back once and he knew they would be back again in the next few days. Consistency was their thing, well, after sheer brilliance, invention and great flavours. Last time they had been hunting in pairs and had both had a fish with seafood sauce, one as a starter and the other as a main, with meat dishes as the other starter and main. They would do something similar again, the sauce was the key. Pictures of the inspector teams were on strategically placed notice boards, they couldn't be absolutely certain which team would turn up, and the waiters would let everyone know when they arrived. His network had told him it would be any day now.

It had been perfect. Two days later a smartly but casually dressed middle aged couple had turned up for lunch, using names that had been booked in four weeks earlier. Jason had rushed into the kitchen and up to him and nervously whispered, 'Chef they're here, it's them, two, and I've told them that the smoky seafood gravies are still available'.

Their starters were tempura fried cheeses with orange and lemon chilli dipping jam, and the five porks platter with mixed green mini leaves and another dish of the chilli dipping jam. The lady chose a main of Monkfish Wellington with green beans, petit pois and chervil mash, and the man went for half a chargrilled Florentine steak "with the other half doggy bagged please," roasted tomatoes and the Italian three bean salad. She went for the seafood gravy with the smoked Pernod notes and he had gone with the smoked sherry choice. Surf 'n' turf, Ha! Perfect.

All the staff were nervous and those serving were taking the extra special care with bells on that you would expect. He had carefully defrosted the sauces and decanted them into their warmed white porcelain sauce boats just before the mains were taken out and they looked seriously good. They had great colour and their aromas were out of this world.

He was standing next to the maître D and they were looking at the couple on one of the CCTV screens in the kitchen office. They seemed to be happy enough with the food, even smiling occasionally. Neither of them accidentally dropped any cutlery on the floor to see how the serving staff responded but the man had asked if there was any non-dairy butter when the mixed breads platter was taken to the table. There was, and he wanted the sheep's butter.

When the mains arrived, the man had the first cut, into the amazing thick steak that he had drizzled with extra virgin olive oil. He had a good look at the pinkness and juiciness in the middle and nodded at her. She had sliced the Wellington in half and raised her eyebrows when she saw the bright whiteness of the seared monkfish, the greenness of the "lashings of layered chervil" as it said in the menu, the pinkness of the "pancetta and scallop pâté jacket", the orange patches of the "scattering of seared scallop corals", and cream to golden brown colours of the "light summer coat of fluffy but crisp puff pastry".

When they were about three quarters of the way through their mains, the lady's head seemed to jerk when she suddenly coughed. She began raising her hand to her mouth but it didn't make it before a fountain of technicolour vomit spewed right across the table, centring on her companion's hand just as it was lifting a piece of steak up to his mouth. Then she did it again, this time downwards and hard onto the table before the fountain bounced spectacularly across it, showering her companion.

Her companion had at first looked shocked, then succeeded in raising a hand to his own mouth just as he began vomiting behind it. Then he stood, looked around frantically while leaking vomit between his fingers and down over his clothes and shoes and onto the floor, and then he rushed towards the toilets and disappeared round a corner.

He couldn't believe it. He had turned away from the PC screen managing to stifle a laugh, hide his smile and not pump the air, while all hell broke loose in the restaurant. Other diners had become ill because the man and woman had been ill, the woman had seemed to faint and had collapsed head first across the table, and the man had been found soon after disappearing round the corner, prone on the floor of the toilet by another diner who himself had visited the facilities to be ill. Two ambulance crews had arrived after what seemed to many of the staff like ages but which later would be shown to be just six minutes, and two first responders that had arrived before the ambulances had moved on from the man and woman. They had dealt with the other diners who had been ill and who were still in the restaurant while the ambulance crews worked with the man and woman before taking them out on stretchers. Neither appeared to be moving.

Two weeks later the man was still in hospital in a coma and no-one knew if he would recover, the woman was back at home recuperating, the second star had not arrived, the waiting list had disappeared, and he had agreed with the owners that he would leave with no fuss, with a six month pay cheque. The restaurant was still closed and the CCTV video of the full technicolour event was going viral across the internet courtesy of the social media sites. No-one was really sure what had happened that day, and when the food safety inspectors arrived for a close forensic investigation there was no trace of any of the seafood sauce or its ingredients, apart from the Pernod, sherry, and smoking coals, which were taken away for examination and were fine. The restaurant could re-open.

The hospital and the Food Standards Agency had issued statements to the media confirming that tests had been carried out on the man and woman as well as five other diners affected that day, and they had showed that the man and the woman had been the victims of domoic acid poisoning which is rare and sometimes caused by an algae that effects certain kinds of fish and shellfish, but no trace of any food poisoning or virus had affected anyone else. The papers were saying that there was no forensic link between the food poisoning and the events of that day in The Rock.

He had spent two weeks relaxing and thinking about taking a holiday, then booked himself into The Priory.

*

Sous Carole turned towards him and held up her thumb and he saw her mouth form the words, 'OK go'. He brushed the monkfish cheeks on each side with vegetable oil and crunched a pinch of sea salt onto one side, then carefully but quickly loaded them onto the grill, salt side down. After three minutes he crunched and sprinkled sea salt onto the upturned sides then turned them carefully using a fish slice and began placing the buns onto the grill, cut side down, in top and bottom pairs as they had been cut from the original whole buns.

After one minute he turned the bun halves and after another took them off and laid them back onto the board into two groups and began spreading the salsa verde onto the bases with a small plastic spatula, taking care that the bases in the bigger group were spread with the caper sauce and that those in the smaller group were spread with the anchovy sauce. Then he quickly took the monkfish cheeks from the grill and dropped a large dollop of sous Carole's mayonnaise onto the middle of each cheek using another spatula and then placed an onion slice on top of the mayonnaise and then a tomato slice on top of the onion and finally the top matching half of each bun was placed on top of the tomato before he planted the flags and secured all of the matching halves together.

He picked up the board and walked inside and

placed it on the counter next to sous Carole who lifted a wire basket full of golden brown chips from the pan and shook it, then spooned the chips into tall wide pots that had been warming in an oven and he shouted, 'service please,' before lifting the burgers off their board and placing them onto hot plates and then placing the chip pots next to them. Ten seconds later they were on their way, on trays carried by two waitrons, through the specials restaurant door.

'Different world, how great was that, easy' he said.

'Pardon Chef?' said sous Carole.

'What, oh nothing ... don't mind me ... er ... that was great, thanks Carole.'

'No, thank you,' she said, 'thanks a lot.'

Twenty Four

It was a long way home for Treloar. He lived in a barn conversion, high on the moors near Zennor. From the highest point on his property he could see both the north and the south coasts of Cornwall.

Luckily, one of his family's oldest friends, one of his most trusted colleagues, was former Police Doctor Anthony Tremayne, and luckier still, he lived in Lostwithiel, some eight miles from Fowey. That's where Treloar was staying that night whilst Fiona Sinclair stayed with a friend in St Austell rather than return to her home in Lelant near St Ives.

It would also give Treloar the opportunity to talk over the news about his father. Doc Tremayne's wife Molly had been around when Jago Treloar went missing. She had been teaching youngest sister Beatriz to play the piano, and she had witnessed the girl's meltdown. Only Treloar's neighbour, Ochre Pengelly, the famous artist, author and Cornish entrepreneur, had saved Bee's sanity. Treloar trusted the Tremaynes with all things. They were like family to him.

The Tremaynes lived in the centre of Lostwithiel, ancient capital of Cornwall on the River Fowey. Their beautiful old house stood behind a walled garden, its upper rooms overlooking the river. It was dark as Treloar pulled in through the gate and parked beside Doc Tremayne's treasured old Mercedes. From the house came the sounds of laughter and Chopin. Treloar sighed and smiled as he walked to the open back door. Scents of fresh bread and Christmas spices greeted him.

Molly Rackham, Tremayne's wife was standing by the open door of an ancient Aga in fits of laughter. She looked like a jolly Dickensian character with her buxom figure and bright chestnut curls, her face glowing with the heat. On the scrubbed pine kitchen table was a cooling tray of some blackened smoking unidentifiable blobs. Doctor Anthony Tremayne, 'Doc', was on his hands and knees in front of the Aga sweeping more blackened pieces into a dustpan.

'Bad timing?' asked Treloar.

'Phil darling of course not,' cried Molly rushing across the kitchen to embrace him. 'Just one of Tremayne's experiments failing. Temperature too high. I told him but would he listen?'

Doc rose to his feet and grinned at Treloar. 'Scarcely a failure my beloved. More of a setback.

Take Phil through for a drink whilst I put in another batch. At a lower temperature,' he added under his breath.

Molly led Treloar out of the kitchen along a hallway to the front of the house and into a warm sitting room with a roaring fire. The walls were painted the colour of washed faded brick, the furniture an assortment of old leather Chesterfields and modern comfortable armchairs; old oak and new pine tables and cupboards; a baby grand piano and a music stand by the french windows. A warm scent of lemon and orange filled the air. It was one of his favourite rooms on earth.

'Sit, my darling sit. What will you have? Before the current debacle Tremayne made some passable mulled wine.'

'That would be great Molly. Thank you.'

'I'll be right back. I just need to put some towels out. I've put you in Handel. Very seasonal I thought.'

The bedrooms in the Tremayne household were named after composers. Not by a name plaque on the door, but rather by a portrait on the wall.

Molly returned with a tray of glasses, a steaming jug of mulled wine, and a tray of homemade cheese biscuits shaped like angels. 'Here we go, sustenance. I've made a nut roast; a new recipe. It'll be ready in about 40 minutes. Hopefully. So sit by the fire and relax.'

At that moment Anthony Tremayne burst into

the room rubbing his hands on a tea-towel which he then draped over his shoulder. A rotund man in his mid sixties with a bushy grey beard, were it not for his bald head he could have played Father Christmas.

'Bloody bad business today Phil,' he said picking up a glass from the tray.

'Yes Doc, as bad as it gets.'

'Still you won't want to talk about it this evening.'

'No, but there is something else I'd like to talk with you about.'

Molly Rackham stood and went to take the tea-towel from her husband's shoulder. 'I'll leave you boys to it.'

'No Molly,' said Treloar, 'please stay. I want you to hear this.'

'Christ Phil,' she said seeing his serious expression, 'you're worrying me.'

Treloar smiled at her. 'It's nothing bad Molly I promise. In fact, you could say it's great news.'

The nut roast was excellent: a mixture of parsnip, chestnuts, hazelnuts and mushrooms with sage and Cornish blue cheese and breadcrumbs wrapped in cabbage leaves.

'This is very good Molly. You must give me the recipe for Mamá.' Treloar's Spanish mother Inés, was a lifelong vegetarian and brilliant cook.

'I wouldn't dare to offer your mother cooking tips my darling.'

Over dinner in the kitchen, Treloar had explained the extraordinary news from Joe Thwaite about his father. After the initial exclamations of shock, they had largely kept their own counsel whilst they ate, each considering the implications of the revelation. Now, with the plates cleared and coffee made, they moved back to the sitting room.

Tremayne poked the fire and threw on a new log.

Molly sipped her coffee and sighed. 'Phil, think. This is marvellous news. What has really changed? You still love your father. You may feel like killing him right now but that will pass. What I don't understand is the timing. Why now? Joe's been ill for years. I know he's dying, but that's been on the cards for months.'

'A final reckoning,' said Doc Tremayne, 'knowing Joe he thought he could bring about a resolution himself without involving you Phil. But he's run out of time. He needs you to take it forward.'

'He says he doesn't know where my father is. He hasn't heard from him in two months.'

'If Jago knows how ill Joe is, he'll be in touch surely?' said Molly.

'Shit. I don't know what to do,' Treloar rubbed his forehead with both hands, 'should I tell the girls?' The girls were his mother and three younger sisters: Eva, Lucia and Beatriz.

Doc Tremayne spoke softly. 'Think of this as an

investigation like any other. All you have now is Joe's statement. We all keep secrets to spare those we love. You know that. Let me see what I can find out from the hospice. As a doctor I may be able to get information they won't give you. There may have been an enquiry, a name or telephone number left. Let me check. I'll do it tomorrow. And I'll visit Joe myself.'

'Tremayne is right,' said Molly adamantly. 'You should say nothing to your family until you know more. It will be a terrible shock; eight years. I fear for how Beatriz will react. We all remember how terribly she reacted when he went missing. I truly feared for her sanity. If it hadn't been for Ochre ....'

'Yes. You must wait for firm news. I can picture Lucia being furious that he has been gone so long and then overjoyed. You know she never believed that he had drowned. But Beatriz and Eva? Eva is such a silent, still waters running deep girl. She has stayed at the farm whilst you and Lucia moved on with your lives. I know you turned down the Met. but Eva has never been off the farm. She may feel cheated ... Wait till you know more.'

'You didn't know?' Treloar asked.

'No Félipe I did not know. Your mother does not know, but as you are well aware, she never has believed your father is dead.'

'Sorry Doc. Of course you didn't know. But someone other than Joe must have known.'

Molly and Tremayne exchanged a glance.

Later that evening as they prepared for bed Molly expressed the unspoken thought behind that glance. It was as if their minds had run in parallel since bidding Treloar goodnight.

'Edmund Maddox.'

'Yes, that's would be my guess,' Doc Tremayne nodded as he pulled on a nightshirt.

'I've always known there was something about him, something hidden.'

'Yes, I know what you mean.'

Edmund Maddox was a longstanding friend and neighbouring farmer of the Treloar family. He owned the Lost Farm Estate between St Ives and Penzance. It was Maddox who had sold the land and old barns to Félipe Treloar at a below market price, which he had then converted to make his home. The Tremaynes had met him many times at Treloar social gatherings.

'Well he won't be happy when he finds out that Phil knows.'

'What do you mean?'

'Oh come on Tremayne, you must have noticed the way he looks at Inés.'

'She's a beautiful woman.'

'It's not just that. For eight years he's been relied upon, called upon, and he's grown to cherish that. He has stood in for Jago in some ways. Phil does a lot I know, but he's not there all the time like Edmund is. He needs to be needed. With his wife dead all these years ... what *was* her name?'

'Tegwen.'

'Right, Tegwen. Well anyway. You mark my words. It will be difficult. Do you really think it will be worst for Eva? She's always struck me as such a strong, capable girl. Beatriz is so much older and stronger now. She has changed utterly from that frightened, abandoned creature. God what a nightmare. Poor Phil. We must do everything we can to support him and you my dear must do everything you can to resolve this. Fast.'

'As ever, my beloved, light of my life, you are absolutely right. I'll call Falmouth tomorrow.'

Twenty Five

The Gig down on the harbour wall at Polruan that night had turned out to be great, Jane had turned out to be perfect fun and interesting, the food was good, and later was even better, but after that he had started to meet her family and that was when it began to get tricky.

They had met at the top of the old brick path that ran down to the slipway from the back patio of The Valley of the Tides at six twenty and it had been a fine evening, with clear skies and no rain or serious winds forecast. They had strolled side by side, talking about how lucky they were with the weather, about how chilly it could get out on the water, and how great the views were, down to the slipway in time to see the small ferry-boat that had cruised up from Polruan just before it turned to hold tight next to the slip so that they could board.

Over the top of the boat as it came in to berth

they could see across to Fowey. The street lights of North Street were only around two hundred metres away, running behind the cottages that were alongside and backed onto the river, and up to the street lights running along each side of the Readymoney road stretching along to the car park, bright, white. In a few weeks time he would know that what he saw was actually Hanson Drive and that it led to Readymoney Road, but Jane would always think back romantically and call it Readymoney Road. She would remember that it led to Readymoney Cove, and that it passed Daphne du Maurier's old place on the way, and that she had moved there because she had loved it and that was why she had left "Ferryside" at Bodinnick.

Looking down the river towards Polruan they could see the red and blue Christmas lights on the quay in the distance and the dark outline of the hill that rose steeply up from the harbour, some lights giving it more shape. The glow of distant house lights marked some of the streets and some of the crazy tangle of narrow passages running down to and away from and alongside the river. The lights of the boatyard were on and there was an occasional low pitched dull metallically ringing thump from that direction. They had both smiled when they noticed the small Christmas tree with its own lights, including a star on the top that was tied to a vertical grab-pole at the edge of the boat, and laughed when they realised that they had each pointed to it at the same time.

They had both gone for a starter of mussels, which were delicious, steamed in white wine with shallots and cream, for just long enough they agreed, then sprinkled with freshly chopped parsley at the end, and a rib-eye steak on the rare side of medium with chips. Jane had insisted on buying her share of the drinks, and he had noticed on both of her trips to the bar that with her dark blue boots, wooden Folsom heeled Levi's, her rear end was swinging even more than it had been that afternoon. He noticed that this time it was even shapelier too, in mid-blue, skinny, very skinny, Levi jeans.

He also noticed other men in the bar noticing, some taking the opportunity to smile at her as she made her way through them to the bar, and commenting on the bright yellow Weird Fish Sgt Kipper's Lonely Hearts Club Band sweat-shirt she was wearing. Just after serving Jane the first time, the barman had looked over at him behind Jane's back after watching her depart, and raised his eyebrows and winked at him. The barman's wife had flicked a tea towel at his shoulder and said 'Oi you!' Jane had heard, guessed, and he had seen her smile.

It had been busy in The Gig, with locals and holidaymakers. Noisy. As they stood to leave he had stepped quickly behind her and lifted Jane's quilted bright-orange thigh length jacket from the back of her chair and helped her on with it before he had looked over to the bar and waved goodnight to the barman and his wife. Then they were glad to be on the Christmas tree decorated ferry-boat again and on their way back. 'So, now?' he had said as they cruised past the empty pontoons just past the Yacht Club, around half way back, 'Do you want to come back to mine for a drink, or maybe go to the bar?'

He had had an enjoyable and surprisingly intriguing time in The Gig and was more than keen to avoid letting the evening go. He knew that Jane was at The Valley of the Tides for a few days to visit her nephew and his mother, Gloria, her sister, and that Gloria was angry with her husband because he was never at home and was having an affair; and that he dealt with stolen cars all over the country. He knew that Jane's nephew was at The Valley of the Tides on a court order and that if he wasn't at The Valley of the Tides he would have been in prison doing between five and ten years for pushing drugs, especially cannabis and cocaine.

He knew that Gloria's husband knew the bent police detectives in Hampshire who had arrested Jane's nephew but who had agreed to a significant quantity of the drugs that they had seized not finding its way into evidence. Her husband had also agreed to their support, even though it was the third time he had been arrested with large quantities of drugs in his possession, for the defence suggestion that he be treated leniently provided he agreed to a nine month minimum therapeutic placement at The Valley of the Tides. He also knew that Gloria thought her husband knew the said police detectives through his car related activities and that they helped oil the wheels, 'so to speak,' Jane had explained, at Southampton docks, to help the cars on their way to foreign climes.

He also knew that not long ago an Aston Martin and a Maserati had gone mysteriously missing in St Mawes just along the coast from Fowey. They had been taken from the main car park close to an upmarket boutique hotel that had no car park of its own. He knew about the thefts because they had caused great excitement on the BBC's Spotlight news programme at the time. He also knew that a friend of Mad Cam's was a potential witness if anyone should end up in court for the thefts, that he had been questioned hard by local police and had made a witness statement.

He also knew from Cam that his mate was being "leant on" by persons unknown to think very hard about what it was that he really had seen and what he could actually remember about that night. About cars being driven up ramps onto tarpaulin enclosed trailers early in the morning in the lay-by just up from St Mawes castle. 'Course 'e bloody remembered it,' Cam had said. ''e'd been on his way in 'is bloody boat past the castle to the quay to drop off fish for the same bloody 'otel the people with the cars was stayin' at. They was lit up like bloody Christmas trees so they didn't fall off the bloody ramps, 'ow could 'e NOT see? Bastards.'

He also knew that that morning when he had seen Jane she had been on her way from Gloria's room to her own, after spending the night unexpectedly on Gloria's sofa. The previous day they had been having lunch at the Trafalgar Inn in Fowey after shopping, and afterwards were on their way up the spiral staircase for a coffee on the roof of the pub when they literally bumped into two well-known middle-aged actors coming down the staircase. There had been apologies all-round, followed by an invitation from the actors, who lived locally, for Jane and Gloria to join them for dinner at the Thai restaurant in Fowey that evening.

The actors had not turned up, which fuelled Jane and Gloria's suspicions that the media was correct in the general assumption that they were gay but they had stayed and eaten anyway and really enjoyed themselves. Afterwards they reached the steps by the quay and realised that they had missed the last ferry and returned to the restaurant to ask if someone could help them back across the water. The owner made three phone calls without success and then on the advice of the maître D went across the road to The Steamer, found the off duty kitchen cleaner he was looking for and persuaded him to take the two nice ladies back across the water in the small and open, but reliable and workable, boat that he used for fishing, for a reasonable consideration.

Jane and Gloria had arrived back at Gloria's room much later than planned, their coats damp from the spray flying up from the swells made by the small boat because, Jane thought, the driver had been going much too fast because he was keen to get back to the pub before a lock-in started. An hour after getting in they were still laughing after another half bottle of vodka when Gloria had gone to bed and left Jane asleep on the sofa. Her damp coat draped over a radiator where it still was.

'Well,' that depends doesn't it,' Jane replied with a knowing smile and raised her right eyebrow. They were standing facing each other on the other side of the gently pitching and rolling boat from the Christmas tree, each holding with one hand onto the same vertical grab-pole for support. 'On whether or not you're ready to tell me a bit about you ...' The sides and front of Jane's unzipped jacket were blowing to either side of her in the chill breeze created by the forward motion of the boat, and his right hand had discovered without resistance the unsupported fullness of her breasts and the size and stiffness of her left nipple as his palm rotated over it slowly. '… and show me your hidden treasures,' as she looked him in the eyes and placed her left hand on his right hip and then ran it slowly across and then down the front of his thigh, stroking it and pressing his key ring as she moved her hand over it and between his legs and then, frustratingly, quickly back up before gently tugging downwards on his belt and pecking him lightly on the lips.

They had gone back to his room with no real debate, and once he had poured their drinks in the kitchenette corner, a large vodka tonic with ice for her and a large scotch and soda for him, Jane had been very persuasive. She put her drink on a table next to the sofa, stood in front of him and kissed him full on the mouth before he had chance to put his own drink down. Her tongue was long and warm in his mouth and it stroked slowly up and down the front of the inside of one cheek before moving across his tongue and stroking it on its way over to work on his other cheek, and then her tongue started running over and then under and then twisting seductively around his own tongue while she simultaneously rubbed the front of his jeans, hardening him even more.

Then she suddenly stopped, 'Right mister, lets see what you've got,' she said looking him square in the eyes, and knelt in front of him while continuing with her right hand to rub his erection, and then Jane squeezed the fore finger and thumb of her left hand with difficulty into his right jeans pocket, which was faded in the same place as on the jeans he had had on earlier, and hooked them round and removed the key ring and held it up triumphantly. 'Right, now we'll see,' she said with a husky laugh.

She looked at it and began walking around the living room, skirting the upholstered armchair which was facing the sofa, and in no time at all her eyes locked on to the desk in front of the window with its keyholes in each of the top drawers and walked straight up to it. She could see the lights of Fowey on the other side of the river and quickly drew the curtains closed before fitting the mid-sized of the three keys to the keyhole in the right side drawer. She unlocked it and slowly drew it open. She turned back from the desk and saw him still standing in front of the sofa, looking at her open mouthed, a small darkening stain on the front of his jeans where the erection was rapidly receding, then turned back and gently lifted out the black plastic box and set it on the desk top and turned back to look at him again, this time holding up the smallest of the three keys and raising her eyebrows.

He had nodded back to her. She turned back and unlocked the box and slowly lifted the lid and after a few seconds turned back to him with one of the tubs in her left hand, holding the label to the light and reading it. Then she smiled and looked at him, then looked back behind her at the box and then back at him and walked slowly towards him while removing the lid and then the piece of orange sponge.

By the time she was standing in front of him again she had tipped orange capsules into the palm of her left hand, scooped some of them back in, and placed the tub with its lid and the orange piece of sponge on the table by the side of the sofa next to her drink. Her right hand was rubbing him back to his former glory as he counted eight capsules in her left hand. Jane looked at him and raised her eyebrows in a question, and he separated them into two groups, each of four. 'They should keep us going for quite a while … up all night probably,' he said to her, smiling, then took four from her and swallowed them with two swigs of his drink. She raised her left hand quickly to her mouth and deftly tipped the remaining capsules from her palm into her mouth, took his drink and after two swallows and a mild grimace she smiled at him, all with her right hand in perfect motion. 'Yeuch!' She moaned, 'I hate whisky, the things we girls have to do,' she said laughing.

Then she had smiled and looked him straight in the eyes. She walked over to her own drink and picked it up with her left hand, took three good swigs, rinsed the vodka round her mouth before swallowing each time and walked back to him, then kissed him again, full on the mouth, while her right hand picked up where it had left off. Less surprised this time he responded by moving his left hand under Jane's sweatshirt, he still had the drink in his right hand, running it around and across her breasts, feeling the tautness of the nipples, now hard and stiff even without the chill, squeezing one, then the other, then twisting them with a quarter turn, and when Jane opened her mouth to gasp the first time he pushed his mouth onto hers and moved his own tongue into her mouth deeply, returning the cheek licks while her own tongue slid past his and began doing the same again to him.

They parted mutually after what seemed to him like the kind of incredible age that his early teenage kisses had seemed to last, but had really been only a minute or two at most. 'How long?' Jane asked.

'Well ... '

'Not that, idiot, 'she said, slapping his erection.

'Ow! You little bugger!,' he said, laughing, and squeezed her left nipple hard between his thumb and forefinger before quickly releasing it and then stroking one side and then the other before finger slapping the top twice. 'Depends, sometimes twenty minutes, if you're lucky, which we might not be with what we've eaten and drunk tonight, might be fifteen or even ten. Once it kicks in though, it'll last quite a while.'

'Seven, maybe eight so far,' she said looking at her watch, and finished her drink while he finished his and they walked over to the drinks bottles on the counter in the kitchenette corner and he topped up while she was opening and closing drawers, and then opening a door that opened into a full-height cupboard that had a combined washing-machine/tumble-dryer at the bottom and a shelved airing cupboard at the top, and he heard her say 'Ah.'

They took their drinks back to the sofa but he put his down on the table and went over to a matt varnished pine cupboard at the side of his large screen TV, pulled the door down from the top. An iPod music centre was mounted on it which had already been switched on automatically as the door had been pulled down to become a shelf. He selected The Beatles' White Album and the amazing sound of a passenger jet landing through the window and then passing over the sofa surprised Jane as Back in the USSR kicked in. There were tall thin speakers that ran from floor to ceiling in all four corners of the room, with smaller ones attached to each wall. 'When this starts for the second time you'll be flying in it!' he shouted over the music and laughed. 'Better turn it down a tad for now; we can turn it up again later with headphones on if you like.'

Then he walked back to the sofa, picked up his drink and they began kissing again, and one-handedly touching and rubbing and squeezing with their tongues deep in each others mouths and breathing through their noses, then stopping at the same time and taking a swig of their drinks and starting all over again and Jane suddenly drew away and said, 'OK right I think I'm nearly drugged now, I'm feeling more confident, I needed it' and laughed, 'I … hang on a second I won't be long, turn round and look at the window … the curtains.' Then she went over to the kitchenette corner and he heard the airing cupboard door open, then nothing except Dear Prudence for a while then, 'OK sit down on the sofa now and close your eyes and don't turn round … … right, open your eyes now.'

Jane was standing one metre in front of him, naked apart from her Folsom heel boots, and she had her hands behind her back. She said, 'hold up your hands,' and she slowly bought out her own hands from behind her back, with a sprung clothes peg in each. She slowly fastened one peg onto the end of his right index finger, and he winced, and the other onto his left index finger and he winced again.

'They've not been used much have they? Don't do much hanging out … with washing anyway, do you?' and she laughed.

Then she took the peg off his left index finger and, with her eyes locked onto his, slowly moved the peg towards her right breast and held it open over the nipple and allowed it to close fully onto her right nipple and she took a sharp intake of breath and he sat and stared at the peg standing proud from the nipple. Then she took the peg from his right index finger and moved it slowly until it was open over her left nipple and allowed it to fully close and she took another sharp intake of breath and then slowly breathed out again, and looked at him and smiled and said, 'Right mister, now your hands and fingers can be doing something REALLY useful, so let's go!' And she walked over to the upholstered arm-chair opposite the sofa, sat and placed one leg over each arm and used her left index finger, curling it to beckon him over and then pointed it at her hairless self.

He stood slowly, smiling, walked over and stood in front of her then took off his own clothes before kneeling in front of her and putting his fingers to good use, and then his tongue which was well fuelled and moving especially rapidly and he occasionally did move his fingers to her nipples to twist the pegs a half turn and the noises she made told him she enjoyed it, and it wasn't long before she shuddered noisily and relaxed, then opened her eyes and smiled. 'Swap?' she had asked; it was an idea he had quickly agreed with.

Twenty Six

The following morning Treloar woke early and restless. He needed air and exercise. He pulled on his jeans, boots and t-shirt and grabbed a soft apricot cotton pullover that Lucia has sent from Bel y Cia in Barcelona. Letting himself out of the back door, he walked down the drive and out onto Quay Street. Turning right he wandered along the river Fowey, stopping to gaze across at the lights of Brunel's converted engine sheds. His mind drifted back over the years.

Of his three sisters, the youngest Beatriz, Bee, had been the most affected by their father's disappearance. But she was a very different person now. She was spending half her time at Cove Farm and half in St Ives staying with her boyfriend Jory Nancarrow in the flat above Seafood on Stilts restaurant where she worked as principal chef. She was flourishing under the tutelage of Jory's father, Jowan, and had a growing reputation as a jazz musician playing double bass and piano in a band. She had her own life now, far removed from that of the quiet isolated teen who had spent all her spare time with the donkeys and goats on the farm.

When Jago had gone, middle sister Lucia had already left to study photography in Barcelona. Since, she had married, moved to Milan, had two children, separated and returned to Barcelona. She was a world renowned photographer.

Eldest sister, Eva, had stayed at home. Her life now was exactly as it had been when Jago went: unmarried, living and working on the farm with their mother. The only development was that she had built up the customer base selling and delivering vegetables, fruit and herbs to local restaurants, shops and hotels. But essentially, Eva had not moved on in any sense.

So he thought, his mother, Inés, who had always believed his father was alive, would be relieved and content. Bee would be fine, shocked but fine; she had truly moved on. Lucia was volatile: she would be furious initially, especially for her two sons, but she would then be overjoyed and forgiving. But Eva? Eva was deep and silent. Molly was right, Eva was the unknown. Had she abandoned all hope of a life beyond the farm; something glamorous like Lucia or ambitious and fulfilling like Bee? Would she be bitter and resentful at the sacrifice she had made? He hoped not.

He found himself at the end of Quay Street where the railway crosses the road. It was time to get back, time to get on. He turned and headed back towards the medieval bridge, walking fast. He felt much calmer now; he was past the initial shock. He had a plan to find his father and he knew how to set it in motion. He was back on course, moving towards the shoal. It was time to turn his focus back onto the girl. He needed to speak with Fi Sinclair but his gut told him she'd be delighted with her new permanent role in the team. Colin was something else. Something had been troubling Colin for some time. He had hoped that Winters' departure would sort it but no, he was still distant and distracted. Still, it was DCS Chamberlain's decision.

At breakfast Treloar mentioned the other issue on his mind.

'There's something else I wanted to run past you and it may be related to my father's predicament. And it could be another reason why Joe Thwaite has chosen now to speak.'

'What's that?' said Doc Tremayne through a mouthful of toast.

'I've not been directly involved in any investigation into Gideon Spargo, but I've been doing some digging.'

'Obviously,' said Molly.

'Gideon Spargo has always seemed to be one step ahead as if someone has been passing on information on raids and interceptions by the Navy and the Coastguard. But that has stopped recently and there have been a couple of small victories catching his boats with tobacco and alcohol but nothing major: no drugs, no weapons. No people.'

'So if there was a mole they've shut down?' asked Molly.

'Or moved on. We're talking high level access to know about planned operations and raids.'

'You're thinking of Detective Superintendent Winters?' asked Doc Tremayne. 'Are you sure you're not influenced by personal animosity towards the woman?'

'No. It would need to be someone at her level to be able to tip Spargo off in time. We're talking about boats docking at unplanned ports when secret inspections were scheduled; calling into Mevagissey, Porthleven or Plymouth instead of Newlyn.'

'Well you know there's a long history of tolerance towards smuggling in Cornwall; a 'watch the wall my darling' attitude; turning a blind eye. At least wrecking has gone out of fashion.'

'But surely not when it comes to drugs and firearms? *People* for God's sake!' said Molly outraged.

'I think Molly's right,' said Treloar. 'I don't think we're looking at a conspiracy; too many people to keep the secret. And from what I've gleaned about Spargo, too many people to share the profits.'

'Well if Spargo's information and protection has

gone, that would weaken his position enormously and loosen his grip on your father. But how would Joe know?'

'Oh Joe has his sources; friends in very high places,' said Treloar.

'Let me see what I can find out from him today,' said Doc Tremayne.

'How are you finding Winters' replacement?' asked Molly.

'Chamberlain? Fine. I like what I've seen so far.'

'I've put in some calls,' said Tremayne, 'and I've only had good feedback.'

'He's looking to shake up the team,' said Treloar reaching for the coffee.

'Well that's only to be expected from a new man, putting his stamp on things, said Molly.

'I'm getting promotion, so is Sam. And she's coming back from France.'

Tremayne and his wife exchanged a glance. Molly had been one of the first to spot Sam's feelings towards Treloar. She hoped fervently that something would come of it and had been rather disappointed when Sam had gone to Interpol, although she could see the career advantage.

'About bloody time. Long overdue on both counts,' Molly muttered.

'But he's thinking about moving Colin out.'

'Ah Colin. Perhaps a change would serve him well,' Tremayne said. 'He had become very stale I thought when we last worked together, lost his edge. Too much time with Winters away from the field. He needs ... refreshing. I think that's a brilliant idea actually.'

'Let's hope that's how Col sees it,' said Treloar.

As Treloar's Land Rover turned out of the gateway Molly lowered her waving him and stood deep in thought. So much potential for joy on the horizon: Jago home, Sam home, Christmas, but also a lurking fear that it could all go so horribly wrong for people she loved. What if the girls could not forgive their father? What if Sam had met a wonderful man in France? What if Phil had blown his chance? She sighed and pulled her shabby gardening coat around her chest. Inés Treloar would be telephoning soon about the almond cakes she made for all celebrations, Molly always had one from her for Christmas, it was a tradition, a gift for special friends. How could Molly speak to her, knowing what she did now about Jago? She nodded to herself, resolved: Tremayne would have to take that call.

'Molly! Come on in and shut that bloody door, you're letting the heat out woman!'

Twenty Seven

That morning had dawned with a cloudless rinsed blue sky. The air was still and the river was shining, its waters stirring gently. The sunlight formed a sparkling path across the river directly through Tulip's bedroom windows onto her face, waking her. Perhaps this Cornwall thing had some merit after all.

After a lengthy shower she headed down to breakfast. She was surprised at how busy the place seemed: phones ringing, people checking in and out, deliveries. Wasn't this the low season? She asked the waitron who delivered her Eggs Florentine. Apparently, that weekend there was a popular street market: Fowey Christmas Market. The event lasted three days and drew a lot of people to the town.

She was sitting at a window table overlooking the river but her attention was focused on her iPad screen. The previous evening she had sat in her room conducting an extensive email exchange with her contact. As a result she had been able to confirm that

Guy Masterson was indeed a resident at The Valley of the Tides where he was being treated for cocaine addiction and that the other man on the footpath, "my dear Speer" was a psychologist, a Dr Ivan Speer, acknowledged for his work with children and teenagers. Interestingly, another resident was Juliet Morrow, the daughter of Foxy Flora MP and her plastic surgeon husband. But most interestingly the girl found in the river had died of ligature strangulation and was now believed to be a European migrant, AND they believed that she had been put into the water somewhere along Seal Creek. Pay dirt big time.

Tulip decided it was time for a direct approach. She would call Sindy Cardrew the Chief Operations Officer at The Valley of the Tides for comment.

Cardrew was very charming and totally unforthcoming. When Tulip asked, very tactfully she thought, if any of The Valley of the Tides troubled residents could have been involved, she got very short shrift: "If a body were found in the River Fal just downstream from the King Harry Ferry would everyone at Trelissick, the National Trust property, fall under suspicion?" And it would be "inappropriate" for Tulip to visit Seal Hall at that time. So much for that. Still, the staff members weren't all resident; perhaps she could have a word with one of the locals?

Colin Matthews was onboard his 22 foot yacht, the *Ziggy*, brooding. Bitterness, like lemon juice dripping into warm milk, was curdling his soul.

He was like an essential appliance; a washing machine or a central heating boiler. Taken for granted unless it required maintenance and then resented for the outlay of time and money. He had never been a golden one, but he had enjoyed a certain respect for his skills, particularly in technology. But now he had been totally usurped; obliterated; first by the precious Sam with her charm and easy manner and now by the new black boy wonder, Luke Calloway. It wasn't fair.

It had culminated in the episode of the team photograph. He hadn't been around and apparently, fucking Frosty Winters, Detective Superintendent bitch, had said it didn't matter as he was not photogenic like the others and his presence would jar, spoiling the portrait of the good looking crime fighters, reducing the media impact and devaluing the entire project. To his credit, Phil had objected strongly, but everything was arranged, Frosty prevailed, and the session went ahead without Colin. Even his forename, 'Colin', was not cool like those of the others Frosty insisted. It didn't project the right image, it didn't appeal to the public, especially the younger audience.

Well fuck them, fuck them all. He'd show them.

In just a few more days he'd be gone. Then let them catch him, let them try.

Colin was sailing the *Ziggy* out of Fowey. He followed a course westwards, running parallel to the coast across St Austell and Mevagissey Bays, around Dodman Point across Veryan Bay, past St Anthony's Lighthouse and up Carrick Roads. He was heading for Mylor Yacht Harbour where his destiny awaited him in the guise of a 16 metre Beneteau Sense 55 ocean-going yacht valued at £400,000. She was not bought with his money, she was not registered in his name, but she was his. She would take him anywhere in the world, anywhere he wanted, and where he wanted was a long, long way away from Cornwall. She was his beauty: the *Serious Moonlight.*

Twenty Eight

By the time Treloar and Sinclair reached The Valley of the Tides the weather had turned, and the day could not have been more different from their first visit. As they sat in the library, gusting wind was hurling rain against the windows like handfuls of gravel. Instead of golden natural light, floor standing lamps ranged around the room were casting circles of light to the floor and ceiling. It was still a pleasant environment. And Sinclair was glowing. He had sounded her out on the permanent role in the team and she had accepted with relish.

They had made an arrangement with Sindy Cardrew to interview the residents, visitors and staff, in the library by a series of appointments. The Valley of the Tides was quiet in the run up to Christmas, although guests were expected for the Christmas party on Friday which had been timed to coincide with the Fowey Christmas Market at the end of the week. Although nothing had been said, expressly,

Treloar had gained the distinct impression that it would be appreciated if their enquiries at Seal Hall were completed before then.

Upon their arrival they had been ushered into the library by Caitlin and served with coffee and excellent tiny ginger and vanilla biscuits. Treloar thought again that they must have a good cook. After fifteen minutes the door opened and Sindy Cardrew walked across to greet them. It took Treloar a moment to recognize her. For one thing she was taller. In place of the bare feet were a pair of four inch scarlet stilettos and her hair was swept back from her face in severe no nonsense style. She was wearing a black shift dress and a cropped scarlet cashmere cardigan. All business.

'Good morning, Inspector, Constable.' They all shook hands and sat down.

'Ms Cardrew,' said Treloar.

'Right. I have here a schedule and everybody knows their time. I thought we might start with Juliet Morrow. As she is a minor I thought I might sit in with her as an appropriate adult. Would that work?'

'That would be fine. Thank you.'

'Right. I'll just fetch her.'

Four hours later Treloar and Sinclair had spoken to everyone. Nobody had seen anything, nobody had heard anything; that night or since. He was happy that most of them were not involved. Tom Palmer and his mother and aunt had been in the private cinema watching Jackson Power films with Davis Lindström, before retiring at eleven. Everyone had been in their offices or rooms or the library or sitting room. Unsurprisingly, the silken mermaid Bella Dean had been in the swimming pool.

Treloar was still bothered by her. What was with the two voices? Was she perhaps undercover press? A rival of Gregory Masterson looking for a scoop on his son or the Morrow girl? Fiona had found no trace of her before her appearance on The Valley of the Tides website. And this nebulous sensory therapist title? What did she actually do he wondered? Still, that wasn't relevant at the moment: he didn't believe she had killed the girl.

Of them all, he had doubts about Forrester, the Lindström boy, Guy Masterson and Dr Ivan Speer. Forrester's therapy had clearly not been entirely successful: the guy was on something. But other than being a cocky bastard, which he could believe of a famous chef, he couldn't see him as the murderer of a small child. He certainly had an eye for the ladies. He had spent the interview grinning at Fiona Sinclair, looking at Treloar only when answering a direct question.

He had liked Hitch Lindström but the boy was hiding something. He had admitted being down by the creek late evening "just getting some fresh air" but insisted he had seen nothing. Gut feeling: it wasn't him, but he was hiding something.

Guy Masterson he had instinctively disliked. He was an arrogant little shit who he wouldn't believe if he told him his own name, but he had been with Dr Speer who backed him up.

Speer could only be described as creepy. He had been with Masterson in his office. He had a good reputation as a psychologist specialising in children's issues: Fiona had looked him up. But there was something deeply unpleasant about the man; something sly.

But in the end there was nothing concrete. No obvious holes in their stories; nothing obvious or suspicious that anyone had seen or admitted. It was no surprise. They were talking about a remote creek in Cornwall in winter at night. But someone had dumped that girl. Killed her and dumped her.

He was getting into his Land Rover when John Forbes rang; the toxicology results were back.

'Well I can confirm what we first thought. She's probably six or seven, Caucasian, malnourished. No signs of sexual abuse, no signs of physical abuse apart from the branding and the ligature strangulation. No old broken bones or scars. No drugs. The marks I thought might have been caused by the chain were not. There are regular abrasions actually penetrating the skin and tiny embedded traces of what appears to be sheep wool survived the water. I'm thinking ...'

'Barbed wire,' said Treloar, thinking of the missing fence above the hall.

'Yes. I think someone must have fashioned some kind of garrotte, you couldn't just use a length of barbed wire with your bare hands.'

'Anything to help identify the girl?'

'Well interestingly her clothing had labels from several countries in different languages: some in Arabic, some Italian, some English, some French. Her skin was ingrained with dirt as if unwashed for days, her feet particularly were filthy and very hard skinned for someone her age.'

'You're thinking she was a refugee trailing across Europe from the South?'

'It would fit the clothing and the dirty skin. But it wouldn't explain her being in Fowey. No refugees have taken boats across The Channel down this way.'

'No John. I think we're looking at something else, something much darker.'

'You think she was snatched and trafficked?'

'Yes I do. Snatched or sold.'

'What a bloody business.'

'You're right there my friend. The bloodiest.'

Treloar was brooding on dark thoughts, convinced of a very local connection given the barbed wire coincidence. As he was turning out of the drive he noticed Bella Dean ahead of him on an ATV. She turned onto the road and headed down towards the ferry at Bodinnick. He slowed and followed; he was going that way anyway. She stopped at The Old Ferryboat Inn and walked across to enter the bar.

Intrigued and suspicious of the lovely Ms Dean, Treloar parked and followed her stopping to look through the door to see who, if anyone, she was meeting.

She slid onto a bench next to a fit looking man with short steel grey hair who resembled Ralph Fiennes. He was wearing an old brown leather jacket and jeans. He smiled at her revealing a chipped tooth.

'Well, well, well. I might have fucking known,' muttered Treloar under his breath. Stepping back into the lane he pulled his phone from his pocket and speed dialled. The phone was answered on the third ring:

'Hello mate,' said a rich accent-less male voice.

'Mine's a pint of bitter,' answered Treloar walking back to open the bar door.

The man in the leather jacket stood up, his phone in his hand. He broke into a broad grin and chuckled.

'Well I always said you were a passable detective.' He advanced across the bar hand outstretched. 'Betty Stoggs?'

Twenty Nine

That night with Jane had continued as it had started and by five o'clock he was seriously pleased that he wasn't in the kitchen again until the following day. Today he was available in The Valley Of the Tides on-line diary for the renowned Room-Chef service but no-one had booked it so he was thinking about a leisurely day; over to Fowey for lunch and a drink, maybe with Jane, who had definitely been flying when Back in the USSR came on for the second time ... and still for the third. Wow!

Jane was in the shower freshening up and he had just dressed in jeans and sweatshirt and was outside on the veranda drinking a freshly brewed coffee when she surprised him by putting her arms around his chest from the back and pulling him tight. He spilled the coffee on the sweatshirt, 'Christ! I thought you were in the shower!'

He turned and looked her up and down, saw

that she wore only the very skinny jeans, and looked her up and down again, more up than down, and raised his eyebrows and pouted his lips in a mock kiss. 'Forget it mister,' she said, 'you must be joking! Some of us are worn out; I'm surprised you can be even thinking about it! Oh sorry about the coffee, come on let's get you another one and I can get a cup of tea.'

They had started to chat about their mornings and later in the day and possibly going over to Fowey for lunch and agreed when to meet and who was going to call the ferry, and that Jane had said that she would be fine without any more caps and he had said he wasn't sure yet and would see how it went, and were talking about nothing much including the weather and what the lunchtime river crossing would be like and the state of the tide and what time they should be thinking about coming back and what they might buy and where they could go for lunch when Jane suddenly said, 'Oh NOO! Can't. Going to spend some time with my nephew this morning, forgot all about it, then I've told Glo' I'd see her later and have a chat, bugger, that would have been nice'.

Neither of them spoke for a split second, 'about the Room-Chef thing,' Jane said, 'are you sure you wouldn't want a booking, for a lunchtime session, I'm sure Glo' would love to meet you, and I just know that you would like her, she's very likable, nice, and she's really fed up at the moment, she's quite like me really, have you ever seen her? I bet you have, she's on the ground floor just round the back, got a thing about red, always wearing it, you must have noticed her, blonde hair, short, always wears red lipstick, usually on her own, well unless I'm with her or sometimes she's ….'

'STOP! Right,' he said and they both laughed. 'Just to make it official you'll need to ring the office first thing, well, when it opens at eight thirty, or actually you could ring before and leave a message thinking about it, best if you and Gloria could …'

'Oh call her Glo' I'm sure she wouldn't mind, she'd probably like it coming from you, you know, a new man in her life being friendly like that, well, you know what I mean don't you, oh, I'd better put my top on, sorry, stop looking at me like that you …'

'RIGHT!' He held up his hand and said, 'OK, Glo' it is and you'd better get your top on … quickly before you catch cold … or something.'

Jane went to find her top, then came back without it because it was still in the airing cupboard crumpled on top of the washing-machine/tumble-dryer where she had left it last night, put it on and then agreed to call the office as soon as it opened or leave a message, but she needed to speak to Glo' first but didn't know what time Glo' would wake up, and then she had asked about what they could have and he had said she could choose and there would be a menu in her room and that if she wanted anything special that wasn't on the list she would need to ask the office and they would get in touch with him and he would be able to tell them whether or not it was do-able and they would call her back and let her know then she had asked if he would be able to join them for the meal, which she thought would probably be at about one o'clock in the afternoon, and he had said he would like to but it was a bit frowned upon by the "Powers" that be and they had both laughed and then he had said that he was sure they wouldn't mind too much if he came inside for a drink or two.

Of course, before lunch, they all had to speak to the police about the ghastly murder of that poor little child. But that wouldn't take long 'cos they didn't know anything.

So, at twelve o'clock he had appeared outside Gloria's door, not long after dropping four more sousies, standing next to one of the portable smokers that he had wheeled along with him and knocked. The door opened, he wasn't sure why but he had expected Jane. 'Ah, yes, hi, I thought that was probably you. I've seen you around, you know coming and going, but we haven't met,' Gloria said as she extended her arm to shake his hand. 'Friends

call me Glo'. I feel as if I know you quite well already!'
she said with a smile then took a quick glance back
over her shoulder.

Sure enough Gloria's hair was blonde and short,
very short all over, and she wore seriously red lipstick
and understated eye makeup and he thought she
was beautiful but looked a little down, not happy,
even though she was smiling, it wasn't in her eyes. She
wore a plain white blouse buttoned up to the neck
underneath an unfastened pink denim jeans jacket, a
long red flared denim skirt with white buttons all the
way down but which were only fastened from above
the knee, and very high-heeled red pumps. Her legs
looked long and tanned.

Jane came to the door and stood just behind
Gloria, put her arms round Gloria's waist from the
back, and looking over Gloria's shoulder said, 'hi
mister, this is my Glo', come on in, she's been dying to
meet you.' He noticed that despite her makeup Jane
was looking more than a little bleary. They had all
gone inside and Gloria and Jane leaned against a
work surface in the kitchenette corner and he leaned
against what he knew was the airing cupboard door
and they looked awkwardly at one another. Breaking
the silence he said, 'Right girls, might as well get down
to it, you've ordered the smoked goats cheese starter
and then smoked mackerel with mixed leaves and
the boiled potatoes drizzled with olive oil, is that right?

Oh, I suggest if you've not had it before, oil on potato that is, you should try it first ... just one ... in case you decide you prefer them with butter, or on their own.'

'Well mister Chef, that sounds great to me, what about you Jane?' Gloria asked.

'Funnily enough that's exactly what I asked them for,' Jane said, smiling. 'Christ this is all a bit formal isn't it? Shall we get a drink to get the party going?' she asked, looking at him and then Gloria.

'Works for me,' he said, 'I'll have a ...'

'Scotch and soda?' Jane finished, 'What about you Glo', G and T?' she asked as she walked over to one of the cupboards, 'I fancy one of those too'.

'Right, brilliant. I'll be back in a few minutes. I need to get the coals lit and fetch the cheeses and fish and organise everything else,' he said. Jane and Gloria looked at each other then back at him, frowning. 'The leaves will be freshly cut so I need to get someone to go and get them, and we need the potatoes up here so that I can cook them on your stove, there,' he said pointing at the cooker. 'Brian, that's one of the chefs, will bring the leaves and potatoes across in around three quarters of an hour' he said, 'Christ, give me a bloody drink ... quickly ... this is ridiculous.'

After two drinks everyone was a lot more mellow, Brian had indeed brought the potatoes, and the leaves, and after taking the food inside and saying hello to the girls Brian had looked at him standing by the smoker on the veranda and smiled and shaken his head as he had asked, 'Anything else Chef?'

He had nearly kicked Brian up the backside instead of gritting through his teeth, 'No thanks Brian, that'll be all for now, GOODBYE!'

The girls had opened a window to chat to him and pass drinks through, despite his warnings about smoke getting into the room, and he was enjoying himself. Amy Winehouse was playing and wafting through the window, and the Back to Black album was on; when he heard Amy asking "what kind of fuckery is this?" he couldn't help looking through the window and Jane had done the same and smiled at him, and he saw Gloria playfully wag a finger at her. Treating it as a barbeque party was turning out to be a good plan.

The smoked goats cheese had gone down well and the plates were loaded with leaves in the kitchenette corner and ready to go, the potatoes were cooked and ready for a reheat in the microwave before the oil went on and he was about to put the mackerel on the grill and Amy Winehouse was still not in Rehab, for the second time, or maybe it was the third, he had been focused on food and wasn't keeping track, when the harshness of an old fashioned telephone ringing interrupted everything. 'Hold the fish,' he thought as he looked up and saw Gloria run into the kitchenette corner to grab her mobile to answer it or maybe switch it off before it woke Jane who he saw was now crashed out on the sofa.

Thirty

They had shared a drink in the bar then left. Bella had returned to Seal Hall and Treloar had taken an Orkney Longliner Pilot House boat from the ferryside in Bodinnick to Teal House in Polruan with his male companion.

Benedict Fitzroy wasn't the heir and he wasn't the spare. He was the third son and that brought a certain freedom and absence of responsibility. He had progressed from school at Ampleforth to Sandhurst and Military Intelligence; then the Metropolitan Police, Europol, back to the Met and then on to join what one of its members jokingly called the Triple S: the Secret Squirrel Squad. Sitting somewhere between the police and the intelligence services it had a 'flexible' role in law enforcement. Fitzroy, with his proven track record and creative approach, was an early recruit. He had always been ready to operate in the shady margins of the law, flexing the rules. He knew a lot of the right people, a lot of the wrong people, and where quite a few of them were buried. Treloar had worked with him the year before in London. They were kindred spirits, both believing that the rules were there for interpretation. When Sam Scott had found herself in trouble with the powers that be, it was Fitzroy who had engineered her secondment to Interpol to remove her from the line of fire.

Once aboard, it was obvious that Treloar was the more comfortable and steadier on his feet, and he had taken the boat's helm with confidence.

'Well mate, you certainly know your way around a boat,' said Fitzroy.

'Yeah, well, before I joined the forces of law and order on land I was with Marine Conservation. I know my way around boats and I'm a qualified diver.'

They motored down the river in companionable silence.

'Good boat this. What does it do – 25 knots?' Treloar asked.

'Fuck knows. It gets me around the river very nicely. Why the change of career?'

'It was when my marriage folded and I wanted something new.'

'Fair enough.'

'But I was getting disillusioned at the lack of power to punish the sheer greedy vandalism. Like scallop dredging in protected areas ruining ancient vulnerable reefs and destroying future stocks. Mindless. And our response? Slapped wrists and paltry fines. Pathetic.'

Treloar upped the speed and swung the boat with ease between the buoys and moored vessels, heading seaward.

'We were called in when the third body turned up.'

They were sitting in the kitchen at Teal House. The property boasted a private licensed frape mooring down a slipway which allowed Fitzroy faster access along the river than had he been obliged to use a car.

'Why you? Why not the usual national squad?' asked Treloar.

'Because the third body was found on a royal estate. We were handed the case and the whole business was contained. Nobody had made a connection between the first two girls, they remain unidentified, nobody reported them missing, no local publicity and the press weren't all over it. '

'So who made the connection with the third girl?'

'Well, as you can imagine, with a royal connection, some heavy resources were applied and research turned up the other two girls with the same M O.'

'And that's the same as our girl?'

'Yes. She makes four.'

'Timescale?'

'Over the last couple of years; coinciding with

academic holidays.'

'You're thinking teacher or student?'

'Indeed.'

'And you're here, you and "Bella Dean", because you're watching someone, and since it's you here, it must be a strong suspicion.'

'Yes. We're watching ...'

'Guy Masterson.'

'I always said you were a bright lad. If you'd joined the Met back when you had the chance Christ knows where you'd be now. It's not too late.'

'Yeah well. I had my reasons, you know that. With my father gone, I felt I needed to stay close to home. Anyway why Masterson apart from the fact that he's an arrogant obnoxious little shit?'

'Opportunity. He was in the right places at the right time, and with the third body, well that location limited the possibilities considerably. Masterson had been staying on the estate. One of his old school and university chums is a minor royal, as is his mother by the way.'

'Aren't you?' Treloar asked with a grin.

'Actually no. Not quite.'

'That can't be all.'

'No. It turns out that Masterson has a link to the M O. The barbed ligature used in all the cases. With the first three it was still in place. With our latest girl it must have been lost in the water. We discovered that Masterson had a younger sister, Christabel, something of a miracle baby much younger than her siblings who were all boys. She died when she was five. It was ruled an accident, well it was an accident: she ran into a barbed wire fence whilst on holiday. The tension in the fence was too tight and it snapped and lashed back around her neck. She bled out at the scene.'

'Coincidence?'

'It might well have been, if it weren't for the fact that our boy was with her. He waited for an hour before raising the alarm, claimed he was in shock. We think he watched her die. Our shrinks think he enjoyed it; got off on it. That was the trigger and now he likes to recreate that rush. That's the theory. Before Christabel came along he was the baby of the family. The ultimate sibling rivalry.'

'How does a twenty year old student at the London School of Economics get access to pre-pubescent girls? I assume they were all about the same age as his sister.'

'Yes, well, that's something else about the M O. There are no signs of any physical or sexual abuse, just the violent strangulation. Bella ...'

'Yeah Bella. How the hell did you wangle that, getting her inside?'

'A discreet word with the efficient Ms Cardrew. She was encouraged to see our point of view and that her cooperation was in the interests of everyone. So she created a ... new vacancy for an alternative therapist, her name's Hannah Rose between you and me, and she doesn't think Masterson's a paedophile, but like one, he needs a source and that's the other reason we're down here. We think he's buying them from a Cornish fish ...'

'Gideon Spargo.'

'Oh yeah. That is going to be one expensive purchase and our boy has no problems there. We know these guys operate by word of mouth and with photographs, usual paedophile behaviour, but we know Spargo has a more sophisticated, global operation. We know he has links with a nasty piece of work, Ukrainian, called Roman Rotan, who in turn has links with some very dodgy Russians. Lots of guns floating around that part of Europe; lots of people smuggling and trafficking. But we think our boy has expanded his business online. We think Spargo has a site on the deep web, like a club, but we haven't been able to find it. I wondered if your pal ...?'

'Jamie will be able to find it if anyone can.'

'I hoped you'd say that, and tell him not to worry about ... legalities. We'll cover him.'

Treloar had come across Jamie Deverell several years previously during a series of nasty killings on the south coast. Jamie had gone from suspect to covert asset and over the subsequent years had proved invaluable to Treloar, and indeed to Fitzroy on their joint operation in London the previous year. Now in his early twenties, Jamie lived at Linton

Crucis Abbey in Hampshire, which he had inherited along with a substantial fortune. From here, he operated a company with his childhood friend Alisdair Frobisher offering Internet consultancy services. Both were super-skilled masters at accessing other people's hidden information.

'Has Masterson really got access to the kind of money we're talking here, without having to explain himself in some way to his father?'

'A very good question. We know he's down here on the pretence of a cocaine addiction but Hannah tells me nobody there in the know is buying that. He just doesn't behave like a cokehead. I have no idea how much his father knows. People like Guy Masterson grow up with the privilege of privilege; limitless money, limitless freedom, boundless resources; literally spoiled rotten by years of indulgence and parental indifference. Trust me on this, I went to school and Sandhurst with the Guy Mastersons of this world.'

'I take it you're excluding yourself here?'

'But of course. I am the exception that proves the rule.' Fitzroy grinned.

'OK. I see it. But how did he get his hands on the latest girl? The Valley of the Tides is remote and not easily accessed. She must have been brought in by water. That would fit with Spargo.'

'We're ahead of you there. Two days before the girl was found, the *St Senara*, one of the smaller vessels in Spargo's fleet, came into Fowey with a reported engine problem. Stayed overnight.'

Thirty One

'You can't you bastard,' Gloria hissed into her mobile phone. 'It's just not right'... 'Don't be stupid, 'course he doesn't, he only came in the first place so he didn't go to prison.' ... 'No thanks to you he's doing great, wants to, now anyway, so NO, it's not a good idea, and why don't you ever try and get down here to ... Oh ... WHAT, WHEN? You're fucking crazy' ...' Oh for fuck's sake if you bring one of those cars' ... 'Look I'm not an idiot you know ... you bastard, I do actually know what you do, doesn't take a rocket surgeon to figure it bloody well out.'

'It's not exactly Kensington here you know' ... 'Yeah .. Christmas, bloody well remembered, but it'll stand out like a polar bear at a ...' ... ...'And what if some-one recognises it? What ... different kind of paint job?' ... 'Christ, what about the guy your bloody mates have been squeezing, he only lives ...'

'What is it Glo'?' he heard Jane ask, 'was that

209

your favourite man?'

'Christ he's only going to give Tom one of those fucking cars for Christmas, bringing it Sunday, driving it down him bloody self. Can't believe it. Present for all Tom's efforts while he's been in here'.

'Cars. What cars? What's up with a car for Christmas? Christ he's got enough of them ... Ah ... one of THOSE cars ... Sunday. Jesus.'

'Yeah, Jesus. Talk about the wrong thing at the wrong time, Tom's doing so well, I'm sure it won't do him any good.'

'Well, we could always try and head him off, stop him, where's he stopping, when's he arriving?'

'Well, he's not staying here that's for sure, bastard. Sunday. The Old Station Yard up at the old docks, with a mate. He'll be bringing his own car down to go back in. Christ he wants it to be a surprise. Well it'll be that alright, Tom hasn't even spoken to him for months. Fuck. What am I supposed to tell him? What about the doctors, you know, the people here ... Beckermann. Christ Jane, what am I supposed to do? Bastard!'

Well what abou ....'

'Right ladies we'll be about forty minutes now, the mackerel's just gone on ... any chance of another drink? There's people dying of thirst out here. Hang on, I'll come in for it, just got to make a quick call, only be a sec. Just going to push this window to, smoked mackerel's great but you don't want it hanging in there with you for the next couple of days.'

He had pushed the window closed and walked round to the end of the veranda and switched on his phone, then touched re-dial. 'Voicemail, bollocks … … It's Harry from The Tides. Got an early Christmas prezzie for you. Call me back as soon as you get this, sooner, it's urgent.'

Thirty Two

Just along the road from Teal House, Hitch and Georgie were sitting in The Gig in Polruan eating fish and chips. Hitch had told her about the visits from the police investigating the dead girl. She had confirmed that she, too, had seen nothing that night. He said he knew that, had kept her name out of it, and saw no reason for her to become involved. If there were an appeal for witnesses she wouldn't come forward would she? They knew nothing that could help. Georgie was concerned that they should at least confirm that they were down on the creek in case someone had seen them but Hitch was adamant. They didn't want her father to find out. Keep it zipped.

The Gig was a good place for them to meet. Hitch would ride over on his bike and Georgie would take the ferry from Town Quay. As Bella Dean had pointed out to Benedict Fitzroy, Polruan was virtually deserted during the day at that time of year. Opposite Fowey at the river's mouth it is a smaller isolated community with many second homes and rental properties accessed by a single narrow road or by the water. Other than some activity at the boatyard and the occasional lone visitor that still gray lunchtime the streets were quiet.

Just after one o'clock, a tall slender girl with cropped black hair and striking sapphire eyes walked into the bar pulling off a mustard yellow waterproof jacket. She was wearing a striped Breton top and seriously distressed jeans with tan suede ankle boots. She bought a glass of cider at the bar and crossed to the table by the fire. One person who did know about their relationship was Hitch's sister, Davis.

Davis had really taken to the British pub. She loved the feeling of age from the worn furniture and the trodden flagstones, the feeling that if she had walked in a century earlier it would all have been virtually the same. She could just picture her mother's face looking at the dark wood and the dark still beer, the open fires with real logs, the people sitting at the bar; Christ she would so hate it all. Erin Lindström was a fan of outdoor eating and the modern light cuisine of Los Angeles. She liked the Polo Lounge at the Beverley Hills hotel, Yamashiro Hollywood: sushi, tofu, sprouts ... air food. The thought of earthy grub like steak and kidney pie, black pudding, bangers and mash, stew and dumplings, fish and chips ... anathema. She had put her poor Bronx upbringing firmly behind her when she got of the plane at LAX as a hopeful teenager. Davis couldn't blame her but she wished her mother would "chillax" to use her term. God she was gonna hate this place.

'Hey,' said Davis sliding along the seat next to Georgie, sneaking a chip off her brother's plate, 'you ain't gonna believe this bro.'

'Oh yeah?'

'Mom and Posy are coming over for Christmas.'

'Jeez! I thought they were visiting with Gramps in New York.'

'Not anymore.'

'Pops'll be pissed.'

'You betcha.'

'So they'll be here for the pre-Christmas family party when the inmates nearest and dearest join us,' said Hitch glumly.

'Mom won't go to a party, you know that.'

'Posy will. She'll be in her element, you know what a total show off she is.'

'Well Pops will need our support even more bro.'

'I know,' said Hitch sadly turning to Georgie, 'sorry Babe.'

'When is it again?' asked Georgie.

'Friday, before the Christmas market. It was Sindy's idea, she thought it might hold more appeal for the folks, more reason for them to come down.'

'Well I couldn't see you that night anyway. I'll be at the lantern parade with my family. Dad sponsors something or other and we always go: family tradition. They switch the Christmas lights on and there's a hog roast and mulled wine and singing in the streets. My stepmother adores it. It's very much a friends and family evening.'

'It sounds like fun,' said Davis, 'we don't have much of a Christmas family tradition, unless you count ...' she whistled a tune.

'Oh no,' Hitch sighed putting his head in his hands, 'Posy's special song.'

'Which song is that?' asked Georgie.

'Oh girl, it's the one from that Snowman cartoon,' said Davis shaking her head.

'You mean *Walking in the Air*?'

'Oh yeah,' Hitch moaned.

'I like that song,' Georgie said indignantly.

'Me too, once,' said Davis grinning, 'played just once. But our darlin' baby sister has it on repeat for hours. After the tenth time it sucks. See if you still like it then.'

'Maybe she's grown out of it,' said Georgie.

'You wanna bet Sis?' said Hitch glumly.

'No ways. Posy's fifteen goin' on ten.'

'But you two are so ... well, mature and normal,' said Georgie

'Posy ain't. Go figure,' said Davis, stealing another chip.

'Ah well,' said Georgie smiling sweetly, 'ding dong merrily.'

Meanwhile Tulip was getting absolutely nowhere. Nobody, absolutely nobody was prepared to even talk to her let alone go on the record. What was it with these wretched people? Even her main source seemed to have gone AWOL; unreturned calls, texts and emails. Perhaps she should give up and go home. But then she wouldn't be able to claim the expenses for the trip and this hotel was not cheap. Jackson Power must be something special to command this much loyalty. Either that or a right litigious bastard. The only sniff she'd got was that apparently, there was a ditzy therapist, into aromatherapy and "colour harmony" whatever that was, who came into Fowey to visit the galleries. Perhaps she should stake out Fore Street? Or try for a tip off from one of the shop owners?

Thirty Three

'Right ladies, not long now,' he had called through the window after re-opening it for a minute, 'I'll be in in a second to get the potatoes going and plate up the leaves.' It had all seemed quiet inside. Then he had pulled the window closed again, lifted the smoker lid and decided the mackerel would take another twenty minutes, pulled the lid back down then knocked on the door and walked in and straight over and into the kitchenette area to get to work.

'Yes ...... thanks, that's great,' Gloria said. She was standing by a table next to the sofa using a cordless phone, and then she started pacing up and down between the sofa and the window. Jane was sitting on the sofa. Amy Winehouse was still going, quietly, her tears were drying on their own before she segued into Back to Black, 'must be shuffling,' he thought as he put the potatoes that were already in a saucepan onto a hot ring on the cooker. 'Are you sure though? .... well thanks ... yes ... on the number I just gave you ... thanks, thanks again.'

'Sorted?' asked Jane.

'Yep, they reckon he won't be able to get in. They think it will definitely be bad for Tom if he get's the car, not right at all, so best to persuade the bastard to give it to him, if he has to at all, when this is all finished and he's back at home. Hopefully by then he'll have decided to get rid of it anyway. They're going to make sure the gate at the top of the lane's locked from now, and they'll only open it using the security systems, and if the bastard turns up they'll only open the pedestrian gate so he'll have to walk in and leave the car at the top. Sindy Cardrew will speak to him herself if she has to. I doubt he'll have brought his wellies so I reckon he'll be pissing back off and not seeing anybody. I'm going to ring now and let him know; see if he'll change his fucking mind. Christ what a hassle!'

'Well, not so bad now though eh? I'll top you up.' Jane said sounding relieved, and walked over to the drinks' bottles next to the cooker. 'Hey mister Chef, do you want topping up as well?'

'Great, cheers,' he had replied, 'these potatoes will be ready in a few minutes, do you want to try one with oil first or are you going to risk it?'

'Oh me and Glo have always been adventurous HAVEN'T WE GLO?' she shouted across the room, but Gloria was glaring at her mobile and did not reply.

'Fucking idiot, bastard,' Gloria said as she put the phone back into a jacket pocket, 'he's still coming, made plans, reckons he'll be able to sweet talk Sindy round and get it done and dusted anyway. Idiot doesn't know what he's got coming. He'll be here Sunday afternoon, late. Stupid arsehole ... oh sorry Harry Chef, 'scuse my French. Bloody hell give me that drink ... I'm starving, when are we going to eat?'

The girls had loved the mackerel and surprised him by genuinely liking the potatoes with just the drizzle of extra virgin and a sprinkle of salt. Then Jane told him she wanted to stay with Gloria so that she could provide moral support if it was needed, and catch up on sleep. He had smiled and said, 'OK,' and spent the rest of the afternoon planning and the evening catching up on recorded episodes of Game of Thrones. Then he had an early night.

Thirty Four

Flora Morrow had really not wanted to attend the Christmas party at The Valley of the Tides but as ever when it came to daughter Juliet, guilt won out. Of course, her husband Michael wasn't with her. Guilt over Juliet no longer touched him; he had written her off after the episode in his study. That was what had led to Juliet's referral: setting fire to her father's study. As far as he was concerned his responsibility to his daughter ended with finding this place.

The only redeeming aspect of the visit was that she had managed to hitch a ride with Gregory Masterson on his helicopter. She knew Masterson through her role as MP; one of Masterson's two London residences was in her constituency. His son was also at The Valley of the Tides. Given its select clientele and specialism in troubled youth it was an obvious choice.

They had arrived mid afternoon and landed in a field behind Seal Hall. There they had been met in a

Range Rover by a tiresomely bright and beaming American girl called Caitlin. She had driven them to a converted stable block which accommodated visitors. Flora had been shown to a suite named *Sweet Cicely*. All suites were named after herbs for some pretentious reason. Her door held a wooden plaque with a painting of what looked like cow parley. She remembered Juliet's room was called *Cerulean*, its door painted the colour of a glorious summer sky; the key fob matching. All the room doors were painted in different colours. What was wrong with numbers? Must be the idea of the "Sensory Therapist". And what the hell was a seaweed infinity pool and who the hell would want to set foot in one? God she was in a foul mood. Time for a bath, a drink, and a "show-time" face.

After a long soak in a claw foot bath Flora did in fact feel much better. She checked her watch: it was 18:55. On a sideboard was a tray bearing bottles of spirits and glasses. The hall itself was dry but the guest accommodation offered alcohol. She located Tarquin's Gin. In a small fridge concealed beneath she discovered tonic water. She made herself a stiff drink and took a seat on one of the two soft green sofas in her sitting area facing the window.

Looking out she could see a huge Christmas tree covered in tiny white lights standing by the portico of Seal Hall. Further light was seeping from the rooms on the ground floor, presumably through gaps in curtains. On upper floors she could see a dull glow from curtained rooms and some brighter squares where the windows were not covered. A lantern burned above the front door. Otherwise it was pitch black. She shuddered, unaccustomed to the lack of streetlight glow and struck by the strangely disturbing thought that if she could see, she could be seen. She drew the heavy cotton curtains.

It was party time. Flora checked her makeup in the bathroom mirror, donned her little black dress and Jimmy Choos and draped a magenta pashmina around her shoulders. She grabbed her satin clutch and her door key and headed out to face the music.

The entrance hall was dominated by a second giant Christmas tree, but this one was very different from the traditional pine outside. It was constructed from pieces of driftwood and decked with shells: oyster, mussel, razor clam, all sprayed in silver and gold. Cuttlefish shells, coated in sparkling white, looked like angels' wings. There were feathers, shards of plastic and fragments of rope, smooth dull sea glass pieces and strands of seaweed. Tiny pale sea green lights lent the impression of an underwater cave. The whole effect was wondrous. Flora was transfixed.

'Good evening Mrs Morrow,' said Sindy Cardrew suddenly at her elbow. Flora recognised her from Juliet's interview. 'Quite something isn't it?'

'It's marvellous,' Flora replied. 'Who made it?'

'A prominent local artist, Ochre Pengelly. She's

enormously talented. We have several of her works. You'll see her paintings in the drawing room.'

'It's quite stunning.'

'Did you have a good journey?'

'Well I can't say that I'm a great fan of helicopter flights but they are enormously convenient of course. I was surprised that Lady Isobel wasn't joining us.'

'Ah yes. Prior commitments I believe.'

'Yes it's such a busy time of year,' Prior commitments my arse thought Flora who knew that Lady Isobel Masterson was "fragile". It was common knowledge in London that she hadn't been right since her daughter's death. Probably half the problem with the son Flora thought. Flora had little sympathy with people who didn't "man up". The Lindström wife, Erin, was another one she had little time for. What did these powerful men see in them?

'Come, let me take you through,' said Cardrew taking her arm rather forcefully she thought.

She led the way across the hall. They passed the seal water feature Flora had admired on her first visit and entered a large room which opened onto a lit patio and lawns. A log fire was burning in a marble fireplace and a further traditional Christmas tree stood to one side. On the wall opposite the fireplace were two large acrylic canvases of underwater seascapes in vivid blues and greens. There was a pervasive subtle scent of orange and pine and vanilla. Large pillar candles stood on iron candelabra and vases filled with holly and bay were scattered around the room surrounded by tea lights in clear glass holders. There was flame in every direction. *Jesus, they do know about Juliet don't they?* Flora thought. Groups of people were clustered around the room amid the bright modern furniture. Flora looked around for Juliet but couldn't see her. Sensing this Sindy spoke.

'Juliet hasn't come down yet. Let me see what's keeping her,' with that she turned and left the room, leaving Flora alone to face the music, which was a subtle orchestral medley of traditional Christmas carols. Oh *Joy to the world*, thought Flora.

Yeah it had been a fuck up. But really? Really? He was supposed to know the little bitch would get tangled up in that anchor chain or whatever the fuck it was? He was at the London School of Economics not Dartmouth Naval College for fuck's sake. And he was a fucking good customer, paid good fucking money, cash money. She should have been taken out to sea by the tide: he'd even fucking checked the tide tables. Now he was in the shit. Still, he had been given a way "to make amends", "to wipe the slate clean" and it would be a piece of piss.

As Guy stood smiling his 'fabulous smile' at the people assembling in the room, his father approached.

'I hope you're behaving yourself Guy. I've spent

a fortune on your mental ... rehabilitation. This place was recommended by your "psychologist" and he, and it, is costing me. I have much better things to do than to come down here and offer "family support at this special time of year". I hope that ghastly little prick shrink is doing more for you than he does for me, the money he charges. How many years is it now since your sister died? How much have I paid that prick? I don't know how you can stand to be in the same room as him. Another ... incident and you're on your own. No more money, no more protection, no more "therapy", you hear me boy?'

'Yes father.'

'Your mother is expecting you home on Christmas Eve. I truly hope you will not disappoint her this year. It would certainly go ill with me if you did. Do I make myself clear boy?'

'Yes father.'

'Now I want to speak to the luscious Ms Morrow. What a fine pair of tits that woman has. I wonder if they came courtesy of her husband? Remember what I have said tonight boy.'

'Yes father,' under his breath as Gregory Masterson walked away, 'fucking bastard,' Guy spat. He was thinking about his mother, a session he had had with Dr Ivan Speer years ago:

'You said that people leave emotionally long before they leave physically. My mother left us years ago when my sister died. That's the big irony. I thought I'd get my mother back, get that closeness back. All that happened was that I lost her altogether.'

That afternoon Erin Lindström had arrived from Los Angeles with younger daughter Posy. Erin had commandeered the largest suite in the stable block, *Angelica*. She did not want to stay in the main house with her husband and other children. Whilst the family was fractured rather than broken, everyone agreed that it was best that the two parents maintained a distance, and whilst Jackson Power thought the width of the Atlantic Ocean and the mainland American continent was ideal, well, it was Christmas so the width of the courtyard would have to suffice.

In the early evening Erin and the children caught up over pizza in *Angelica's* sitting room. Erin was not attending the party, claiming jet lag, but Posy, who had encountered a "lush guy" in Seal Hall library, was up for it. She had spent the early evening on her phone updating her Facebook page and texting the gals back home about him. From her description, Hitch and Posy had concluded she was describing Guy Masterson. Masterson was purportedly battling a cocaine addiction, hence his presence at The Valley of the Tides. But Hitch, who had watched his brother Ford's decline, was not convinced. The dude was too calm, too balanced, too normal. He was also devious, obnoxious and a slime ball: gut instinct. Hitch had warned Posy and he and Davis had agreed to keep an eye on baby sis. But, hey, this was Cornwall, England. What could happen?

Tulip was licking her wounds in the hotel bar, ordering her third large gin and tonic. Christ! What a nightmare, what a witch! Tulip had been in the street chatting with the Aussie barman when he pointed out this stunning woman on the opposite pavement. "That's Bella Dean from The Valley." So she had chased after the vision in the long green velvet coat and accosted her. She'd been told Bella was a rather vague, insipid creature. Huh! When Tulip confronted her, explaining who she was, the luminous smile had tuned into a snarl and the most "if looks could kill" glare Tulip had ever seen, and being in her profession she'd seen a fair few. The only comment was a deep guttural "Go away RIGHT NOW." And Tulip, although not a shy and retiring individual, had turned on her heel and fled.

So that was that. Enough of these bloody people. She would stay 'til the weekend and the famed Christmas Market and see if she could milk something out of that to get her expenses past the editor. And when she finally got hold of her contact she would offer a piece of her mind and no mistake.

At Seal Hall the room filled with more people and the evening wore on. With "wore on" being the operative phrase for Flora Morrow. Juliet had finally graced them with her presence but had decided not to stay because she was unsettled by all the naked flames. The creepy Dr Speer had thought that the exposure might be a good test of her progress but had accepted that she should be excused. He had then mercifully moved on from Flora and seemed to hover around Masterson's son for the duration. Something unhealthy about that relationship thought Flora but she had never liked psychiatrists and apparently the man had been Guy's therapist for years. He had brought the boy here when he joined the team and Guy had suffered a setback. It seemed he was doing something right because, whilst not an attractive personality, too fond of his own reflection, too Dorian Gray, Flora mused, he did appear fairly stable to her. Not hyper, not sniffy, not at all like the addicts of her acquaintance. Though he was somewhat fixated on the youngest Lindström girl for some reason. Flora thought she seemed like a classic American brat.

She had liked the other Lindström kids though: Hitch and Davis. Both had been polite and attentive in their brief conversations with her, perhaps their time in Cornwall had smoothed some of their American brashness. And they were that bit more mature. Perhaps she was being unfair to Posy, comparing her to the quiet, withdrawn Juliet because they were similar in age. She drained her glass of sparkling water – Seal Hall itself was dry, no alcohol to tempt the inmates. Enough. Juliet had long since gone to bed and she, Flora, had stayed on for the requisite period of time to be polite and friendly. Bed.

As she crossed the courtyard towards the stable block her eye was caught by a figure emerging around the side of the building and heading to the rear of the hall; just a glimpse of black shiny leather and a mane of long blonde hair.

As Posy skipped back across the courtyard to *Angelica* she was on cloud nine. Guy Masterson had spent all evening talking to her, fetching her drinks, admiring her dress, loving her accent, and he had invited her to join him on the trip to the Fowey Christmas Market the next day. It was going to be the best Christmas ever!

Tulip Khan was totally disillusioned. Her plan had been to get in fast and get a scoop. It was going to be her ticket to the big time. And it had started so well. She had to have been one of the first, if not *the* first journalist to get the word that the child's body had been found and to link it with The Valley of the Tides and thereby Jackson Power. She had her source. She had an exclusive. Hah. Now her source had run dry, run dry and bloody well disappeared without a trace. She had hoped that she could use Sindy Cardrew to get her into Seal Hall; Christ, she had written a very flattering piece about the place singling the woman out for special praise, virtually a profile, she should have been able to get some comment, at least get some photos.. Hah. Should have known better. Closed ranks. At this rate all she'd have was a hideously enormous expenses claim which nobody would pay.

Still there was always the man in charge of the investigation: Detective Inspector Félipe Treloar. The man looked like a fit Australian surfer dude; hunky and brooding, all muscled body and blonde blue-eyed intensity. She could picture him striding from the waves, dripping wet, steaming in the sun, shaking the water from his blonde mane: Wow.

She had done some research and he had an interesting back story: Cornish father, missing presumed dead, Spanish mother. Before the police he'd had one of those sexy environmental jobs; Surfers against Sewage or something like that, something really cool. She wondered why he'd jumped ship and joined the establishment? There must be something there. And then there was the early marriage, the child bride who went on to become the supermodel Lamorna Rain and how that had all ended recently so tragically and under suspicious circumstances. He'd make a great profile piece. But her source had warned her off. The man was intensely private and fiercely protective of his family. Wasn't one of the sisters some kind of media celebrity? Yeah, that was it, a photographer, Lucia something or other exotic. Hell it would be so saleable. Perhaps she would put out some more feelers whilst she was here.

And if push came to shove there was always this poxy market. Perhaps she could get some interesting photos and a piece out of it for one of the lifestyle sections or a web slot what with Christmas coming. The label "Cornish" always sold for some unknown reason. It worked with all those Tory ministers following Dave and Sam Cam down here for their holidays. Bloody politicians. Tulip Khan was not a happy bunny. Time for a nice cocktail from that lush Aussie barman. Maybe some moules marinière with frites and mayonnaise? At least the food was delish. And she should be able to pick up some unusual presents at this market, maybe even something cool to wear. Was she Tulip not an optimist? There was always a slant, always a silver lining. Courage!

Thirty Five

When Posy woke up she had no idea where she was or how she had got here. Was this a bad joke or what? Was this Davis messing with her? And where the hell was her phone?

All her life people had underestimated her, doubted her abilities, and then after Ford's death her mother had smothered her with excessive security. Well, she was going to prove them all wrong. She was not going to panic. She was going to suss this and get herself out of it. She had been on the studio course on kidnapping run by an ex FBI guy. They all had. She knew to keep calm and pay attention to detail. So – what had happened and where was she now?

Posy had been pushing her way through the Christmas Market crowds in the marquee on Town Quay. It was very busy, warm and noisy. She had been tasting some really neat preserves when she noticed that Guy dude beckoning to her from the side of a stall selling colourful jute bags so she walked over to him. Then what? Just sensations really. There had been something soft and dark over her head. She recalled an unpleasant smell like the seafood market in Santa Monica, a bumpy ride in some kinda truck. Then nothing until she woke up in this room.

So first things first, how was she? Well she still had all her clothes on, she wasn't sore or injured or violated in any way she could tell. So, she had been taken but not assaulted. Now, where was she? She was in a bedroom which was warm and smelled of fresh paint. It was lit by two freestanding lamps with cream shades. She surveyed and noted the contents. Everything looked clean and new and good quality. There was a pine double bed with matching table and two ladder-back chairs. The bedding was white seersucker. There were two windows with closed curtains of blue and white striped thick cotton. There was a small cream sofa with blue and cream cushions with a fish pattern. The walls were sponge washed white.

She swung her feet to the floor and looked down at polished wood boards. Standing, she went to the door opposite the windows. It was locked. She moved around the bed and tried a second door. It opened on a blue and white tiled wet room with walk-in monsoon shower, toilet and basin. There was a heated towel rail with thick fluffy white towels and beneath a large white wooden rimmed mirror, a shelf holding a selection of *Zennor Aromatic* toiletries in small plastic bottles: shampoo, body lotion, shower gel and hand wash; scented of cardamom and orange blossom, seaweed, lavender and mown summer meadow. A large white fluffy towelling robe was hanging on the back of the door. She turned back into the bedroom, walked to the windows and drew the curtains. She looked out onto darkness, a distant sparkle from moonlight on water. Jeez what time was it? She looked at her watch: 18:20. She had lost hours!

So to sum it up: she had been abducted by the Guy dude or his pals six hours ago and now she was being held in an upmarket Pacific Coast style hotel room. What is wrong with this picture? Did ruthless kidnappers bent on ransom usual provide luxury accommodation? Hell no. Not in her Pop's movies.

*

The only sounds were the bird cries, and on the edge of hearing, the distant buzz of a small boat motor muffled by the swirling mist. How different from L A where the drone from the freeway was a constant and the fog was a heavy tangible layer of felt-like smog. Here it was allusive; a living, moving presence. It was just like the scene in *Raiders* when they finally open the Ark. Hitch kinda liked it.

And the roads. In California there was a fucking great freeway all along the coast: the Pacific Coast

Highway. Here there wasn't space for two small European cars to pass once you got near the sea and no bridges over the water. It was neat. And people walked. Hell, down in Polruan you *had* to walk. Cool. All things considered Hitch liked it here. You wouldn't catch him bitching like little sis Posy who couldn't get her head around a place with no streets with stores like on Melrose or Rodeo Drive, and where the sky was grey for days on end. For Posy England sucked. But at least Seal Hall had an awesome swimming pool and Posy loved to swim.

And best of all for Hitch, here lived Georgie; the incomparable, fearless, beautiful Georgiana Spargo. Hitch was smitten.

He fired up his Kawasaki dirt bike. He was off to Fowey and his beloved.

He could have gone to the market with his sisters in the Range Rover but Hitch liked to be independent and Posy didn't know about Georgie. By the time he reached the river the fog had dispersed. From his place at the front of the Bodinnick ferry as it made the passage across the river he could see Georgie in Caffa Mill car park standing beside a beautiful old car. She was talking to a very strange looking man. He was standing by the open rear passenger door of the car and weirdly for December in England, he was dressed entirely in white: white trousers, white polo neck, white shoes, not trainers, but shoes. He was tall and thin with pale blonde hair. Sitting next to him was a small white and brown dog, its head cocked as if following the conversation.

As the ferry floated closer Hitch watched as the driver got out of the car. He could not have been more different from the other man: shorter, hugely muscled, shaven headed, he was dressed entirely in black: black jeans, black shoes, black leather jacket. Hitch watched in fascination as the hulking man moved around the back of the car to gently pick up the dog, walk to the front passenger door, open it and place the animal on a white blanket, close the door softly, and return to his position behind the steering wheel. As the ferry docked the passenger climbed into the rear of the car and it drove away out of the car park and up past the library out of Fowey.

Hitch fired up the bike and rode over to where Georgie was waiting smiling and waving.

'Who in the name of God was that?'

'Oh that's my uncle, Gideon. He's off to see my father.'

'Jeez, he's kinda creepy.'

'Yeah. As you would say, he has a "bad rep".'

'Oh yeah?' he grinned.

'Well my love you will find that Cornwall has a history of illegal trade; basically smuggling though there used to be wrecking where the locals would entice ships onto the rocks, murder the crews and loot the cargoes.'

Hitch looked horrified and she laughed.

'Don't worry that's mostly died out now ... Joking! Joking! Anyway, let's just say that my uncle has been rumoured to land more than just fish in his time.'

'Wow ... bad dude. Has he been banged up?'

'No. he has never been to prison. Never been arrested. Like most of these things I expect the story's been vastly exaggerated down the years.'

'What about your Pop?'

'Jeez no. Dad has so totally nothing whatsoever to do with Gwavas Fish. I remember he went ape-shit when he found out there was a photo of me on the website. You know a "the latest three generations in a centuries' old family business" kinda thing. Dad was furious. I think he's a director, he has to sign papers and stuff, that's what Uncle Gideon's doing here today, but Dad has nothing to do with the fishing. He hates fish; won't touch it, won't have it in the house.'

'So that's why you're always eating fish and chips.'

'You can talk my 'ansome!'

She lifted her hand to brush hair from where it had fallen across his face.

'Woah, what's that God awful smell?' he asked.

'Oh it's violet. My uncle has this thing for the smell of violets. He has this special French soap and cologne. I've always thought it was to counteract the smell of fish, but anyway it does linger.'

'Creepier and creepier. Neat dog mind.'

'Perish is a darling but a rascal. He's a rough-coated Jack Russell terrier.'

'Neat car too.'

'Oh yeah, that's uncle's precious car, his pride and joy.'

'What is it? It's sure a beaut.'

'It's a 1968 Rover P5 Mark III with a V8 3500 cc engine in Burgundy Red with black leather interior,' Georgie said in a sing song voice as if reading from a car magazine ad.

'And the heavy dude in the driving seat? Chief henchman? Sidekick? Bodyguard?'

'No silly,' she punched his arm, 'that's Todd Vickery. He's my uncle's chauffeur and chief mate.'

'Christ, what do they do, run casinos?'

Georgie laughed out loud. 'No! Uncle Gideon runs Gwavas Fish, the family trawling business in Newlyn. He took over from my grandfather.'

'Oh right. Wow. Cool looking dude.'

'Come on. Let's not talk about him. Lock up and we can get along to the market. We could go up to the Leisure Centre first, there are stalls up there, or we could walk into town.'

'Town.'

And with that he grabbed her and kissed her. They pulled apart after several minutes and a round of applause from a group getting out of a people carrier. Georgie blushed and Hitch bowed. Everybody laughed. Then they all set off in straggling groups to join the flow of people heading along Passage Street towards the town centre and the market on Town Quay.

Thirty Six

Gideon arrived at Corsica House that morning on the pretext that he needed brother Christian's signature on a contract for the purchase of a new boat for the Gwavas Fish fleet. Set high above the west bank of the River Fowey, Corsica House was a Georgian stone house set in mature gardens dotted with towering evergreen trees. Gideon admired it. Todd Vickery drove the Rover through the gate and parked on the gravel drive. He would be staying with the car.

Gideon entered the open front door and was greeted by the glorious smell of baking bread. He knew it would be rye and caraway sourdough and considered asking for a loaf. He could hear *Hark the Herald Angels Sing* accompanied by a tuneless "la-la-la-ing". He followed the sound to the dining room where he found Svetlana, Christian's wife. The large mahogany table was strewn with lengths of evergreen foliage, dried fruits and berries, small silver stars and baubles and coils of wire. She was making wreaths and garlands for Christmas. Through the french windows Gideon could see that every tree and shrub in the substantial garden was smothered in nets of tiny fairy lights; he shuddered at the thought of the upcoming electricity bill.

Svetlana, known to all as Lana, was Christian's second wife. He had met her at one of his less salubrious bars where she was working as a dancer and waitress. She was a leggy blonde twenty something from Belarus and Christian's children loved her. She was a warm, happy person and a skilled creative gardener, a far cry from the bimbo envisaged by Christian's local detractors before they met her. Lana was a demonstrative affectionate person who hugged and kissed spontaneously, but she new instinctively not to touch Gideon.

'Is he upstairs?'

'Yes darlink, he is in front office.'

Standing in the marble floored hall, Gideon gazed up to the glass cupola. The second floor's circular gallery was railed in mahogany like the staircase. There was a generous balanced feel to the house and Gideon loitered to enjoy the space before heading up to find his brother.

Christian was in the smaller of his two offices, a former bedroom on the second storey where his desk was set in the bay window with wide views along the river from up towards Golant down to the sea. It was a comfortable environment, housing his Napoleon memorabilia, his books and the plans and drawings of his latest project: Megrims, a small boutique hotel in a converted farmhouse upstream from Fowey towards Lostwithiel.

'Jesus Christ Gideon!'

Gideon had entered the room and was standing silently behind his chair when Christian looked up and caught his brother's reflection in the window. Gideon shared with their father the unnerving ability to move silently and suddenly appear without warning. It had spooked Christian since childhood.

'I have the contract for the St Ia.'

'Right, give it here,' said Christian reaching back to take the papers.'

'This Megrims?' Gideon pointed to the drawings spread across an old pine long table against the wall.

'That's right,' Christian answered distractedly. He was reading the contract. He wanted rid of his brother.

The fact that Christian had little involvement in Gwavas Fish and none whatsoever in any of Gideon's nefarious business activities did not spare him from the opprobrium heaped upon the Spargos, despite his protestations that he was not his brother's keeper. Christian was tarred with the Spargo brush and he hated his brother for it.

Gideon had read all about Megrims in a feature in the latest edition of Cornwall Today. It was the latest offering in Christian Spargo's growing empire of holiday facilities. Over the last few years he had been moving determinedly upmarket intent on capturing his share of the burgeoning market of rich tourists, and eager to leave behind the caravan parks and holiday camps of his past. Megrims was almost fully refurbished, ready for opening at Easter. There was still some work to be done in the gardens but the rooms were finished. It was in an isolated location upstream from Fowey above the river and its forested bank. It was perfect for Gideon's purposes. As Christian scrutinised the paperwork, his back to the room, Gideon lifted one of the sets of keys out of a wooden box on the table and pocketed them.

When Gideon left Lana turned back to the task of making the Christmas garlands. Christmas had been a big deal in her home town of Minsk. She had decorated the garden trees with lights just like the public squares at home. Back then she had been working in Gambrinus Pub, a huge bierkeller in the city centre, when she was approached by a man who was offering passage to the UK.

Looking back, that time in her life seemed like a distant dream. On a cold April evening she had been collected by a minibus at the colonnaded entrance to Gorky Park. It was a new minibus, no airless container or back of a dirty lorry for Lana and her companions. They could have been a group of students on a cultural tour of northern Europe. From Minsk they had been driven to Lithuania where she had acquired a Lithuanian EU passport. Then a ferry from Klaipeda to Karslhamn and the E22 road to Malmo. She recalled the majesty of the Øresund Bridge as they crossed the strait into Denmark. Then an endless succession of numbered roads: E45, 1, E40 taking her through low uninspiring countryside to the coast at Dunkirk and the ferry to England.

They had crossed to Dover on a still, blue-skied day with the promise of summer and hope for a new life. The white cliffs had in fact been gloriously white, glinting in the sun. Then more roads: M20, M25, M5, A38 until they had finally arrived in Plymouth late on a cold damp evening and she found herself deposited on a wet pavement in a wide straight urban street filled with staggering drunken people. It was as if she had come full circle; had never left Minsk.

As she knelt on the pavement sobbing she heard a soft deep voice and through her blurred vision saw a dark haired hand stretched down to her:

'Come on my 'ansome. Let's get you inside.'

She was pulled to her feet and found herself towering over a dark haired man who looked exactly like pictures of Napoleon Bonaparte.

'Nap-o-lay-on,' she blurted without thinking. She could have bitten her tongue. Surely the English like the Russians had hated Napoleon. This man might be hugely insulted and angry. But to her amazement he smiled broadly and roared with laughter.

'You and I are going to get on just fine,' he said leading her into the cavernous club. And he was right. Within a year they were married. Christian and Lana Spargo were truly very happy together.

Thirty Seven

Mid afternoon Hitch and Georgie had wrangled a table in Sam's and were enjoying burger and fries. They had spent the day wandering along Fore Street and around the market. Georgie had bought Raw Chocolate Pie, fudge and toffee for her siblings. She had found a leather wallet for her father and a tall ceramic vase decorated with butterflies for her stepmother. Unbeknownst to her, Hitch had bought a lovely sea glass and shell necklace on a delicate silver chain. They were laughing at a joke they had heard at the counter when Hitch's phone rang.

'It's Mom,' Hitch took the call walking outside.

'Hi Mom, hang on a sec.'

Georgie watched through the window as his face turned grim.

'Calm down, calm down. When? Where? OK, OK, leave it with me and I'll check around. It's a small place but it's packed with folks here for the market. I'll get back to you. Yes, yes. I know Mom. Leave it with me.' He pocketed the phone and walked back into the boisterous restaurant.

'What's wrong?' Georgie asked, touching his arm.

'Posy is AWOL and Mom's frantic. She was in the tent on the quay at about half eleven when Davis last saw her. She assumed she'd got a water taxi back.' He checked his watch. 'She's been gone around four hours.'

'Maybe she went up to the rest of the market at the Leisure Centre.'

'Four hours ago?' he asked bewildered, 'Trust me babe, she wouldn't have gone anywhere on her own. She ain't like you and Davis, and since Ford died Mom's smothered her. '

'Come on,' she said waving to the staff behind the bar, 'I've got a tab, I can settle up later. Let's go look for her this minute.'

Hitch smiled in relief. They gathered up their bags, coats and helmets and headed out into the darkening street.

At 15:08 the last of the party from The Valley of the Tides had arrived back from the Fowey Christmas Market and it was confirmed that Posy Lindström was not with them. Nobody had seen her since she had been in the marquee on Town Quay. Everyone had assumed she was with someone else. When Erin had angrily questioned her daughter Davis as to why she hadn't kept her sister with her, Davis had told their mother to chill, explaining that this was small-town England, not the Hollywood Boulevard. Erin had glared at her elder daughter and phoned her son. Hitch, who was also in Fowey independent of the Christmas Market party, had been despatched by his mother to walk the streets in search of his sister. Now Erin was raising the roof, demanding the police and shouting at anyone who crossed her path.

At 17:00 Sindy Cardrew, satisfied that Posy was not on the premises or in the grounds, was not answering her cell phone and had not been in contact, decided that, given the recent discovery of the dead child, and with no positive word from Hitch, the police should indeed be informed. She went to her office, retrieved the business card of DI Félipe Treloar and dialled the mobile number he had scrawled on the back.

At 18:21, just after Posy checked her watch in the strange hotel room, Treloar parked his Land Rover alongside an enormous Christmas tree bedecked with thousands of tiny white lights, and entered Seal Hall for the fourth time.

Sindy Cardrew was standing in the hall. She was dressed in jeans and a pale yellow cashmere V neck sweater, barefoot again, and she looked worried. She was talking to a thin tanned female also dressed in jeans but in a baggy denim shirt and red flip flops. Her long black hair was hanging in a ponytail. As she turned to face them Treloar was struck by her beautiful large blue eyes, the image of Hitchcock's. This must be Erin. Beside her was the tall rugged unmistakeable figure of Jackson Power.

'Oh my God, oh my God, are you the police?' said Erin Lindström rushing forward to grasp Treloar's arm.

'Thank you for coming personally Inspector,' said Power extending his hand for a firm handshake.

Treloar was struck by the absence of an American accent in the deep voice, just the slightest hint, so unlike the Californian twang of his wife and children. Presumably the years spent playing a medieval English knight and his rural Minnesota upbringing explained the difference.

'Sindy has told me you are in charge of this bad business with the little girl.'

'Indeed Sir.'

'Well we appreciate it even more that you would come here now.'

'Is there somewhere we could talk?'

'Yes come upstairs, you too Sindy,' and with that he took his wife's hand and led the way up the mahogany staircase.

Flora Morrow was sitting in the library in a large armchair, her stockinged feet curled beneath her. It had been a long day. That morning they had assembled for the trip to the famed Fowey Christmas Market. Flora and Juliet had left in the first group with the Lindström children and Guy Masterson. They had been driven down to the river at Bodinnick and then across on a chain ferry. From there they walked into town along a narrow street with glimpses of the river. To be fair she had actually enjoyed herself. Juliet had been in a good mood, talkative and upbeat, and they had bought some unusual Christmas decorations, local chocolates and fudge and even a scented candle as a special treat for Juliet.

The Fowey shops from Lostwithiel Street to Fore Street were joining in; their doors open; wares displayed on the pavements; carols drifting into the streets; people milling everywhere. The market stalls had been divided between a modern Leisure Centre and a big marquee on the quayside and there had been a town bus minivan ferrying people between the two. Alternatively, you could walk up from Town Quay; up Lostwithiel Street and then left up the steep steps crossing Hanson Drive through the car park to emerge on Windmill. It had been cool, crisp and sunny and Flora had chosen to walk. Now her feet were questioning that decision.

Flora and Juliet had returned with Sindy Cardrew and two other staff at half past two. Lunch had been a wonderful bouillabaisse. She had spent the afternoon in the drawing room by the fire reading with Juliet. Juliet had been absolutely fine, not at all distracted by the fire, and they had had hot chocolate with marshmallows and played Cluedo. It had been idyllic. A Victorian Christmas. All they had needed was the gentle falling of snow in the garden. Then all hell broke loose.

Now it was more like something *out of* Cluedo. Everybody who had been on the market trip, with the exception of Posy, who was missing, had been summoned to the library to talk to the police. The two staff members were sitting on a sofa by one of the shuttered windows, Juliet and Flora on their seats by the fire, Davis was standing by the Christmas tree and Guy Masterson was studying the seascape canvases, his hands behind his back like a male member of the Royal family. In fact, it was more like an Agatha Christie novel with the guests of the country house assembled in the library.

Juliet had not liked Posy. When they got back from the market, just before lunch, she had been talking to Jenna Mellin about it in the graveyard.

'Honestly Jenna she is a total drama queen. You would hate her. Last night at that dreadful party she was drooling over that creep Masterson. She was so obviously gagging for it. It was totally disgusting. I wouldn't be surprised if she didn't do it with him over in Fowey and now she's ashamed to come home. She's so transparent everybody would be able to see it. And she's got the most irritating drawling twangy voice. She must put it on because the other two don't talk like that. I like Davis, she's cool and Hitch is gorgeous.'

Juliet had enjoyed herself at the market. They hadn't stayed too long because it was very busy but she had bought some neat ear studs and a huge jute bag patterned with dolphins with a shoulder strap. Mother had even bought her a scented candle in a glass jar; the wax was marbled in sea shades of blue, turquoise and green and it smelled fresh and clean. It would be a reminder of Cornwall when she was back home in Surrey Mother said.

She was just telling Jenna about the yummy fudge stall when she heard someone calling her name: lunch was ready.

As an awkward atmosphere pervaded the library, upstairs Treloar was sitting in a warm private sitting room decorated in autumn colours with a french window opening onto a veranda. He could make out the lighter night sky over Polruan and beyond, where the moon was reflecting off the sea. Matching sofas covered in apricot canvas faced each other either side of a coal fire. Edward Hopper paintings of sailboats and lighthouses lined the walls. Treloar wondered if they were originals. He would ask Ochre Pengelly, she would know. She had been here: he had recognised her handiwork in the gigantic driftwood tree in the hall.

'From what I understand from Ms Cardrew, your younger daughter Gardner left this morning with a group to visit Fowey. They were dropped off at Caffa Mill and expected to return from there when they called for collection. Various groups have returned, not in the same groups as went out, but Gardner was not with any of them'

'We call her Posy, she's Posy,' Erin was wringing her hands and rocking gently.

'Posy it is,' said Treloar gently. She acknowledged his comment with a sad but stunning smile.

'The last time anyone can remember seeing her is at around 11:30 in the marquee on Town Quay. That was her sister Davis.' Treloar continued.

'Yes. That was our other daughter, Davis, Inspector,' said Power.

'I understand that Posy only arrived here yesterday with you Mrs Lindström and that she has not been here before.'

'It's her first visit to England,' Power confirmed as his wife nodded bleakly.

'Does she know anyone other than the family and the residents here?'

'No! No of course not!' wailed Erin.

'No friends of your other children? I understand they have been here on several occasions.'

'I don't think so, but you could ask them Inspector. Davis is in the library with the others, Hitchcock is still in Fowey looking.'

'She wouldn't have run off, she wouldn't,' Erin cried. 'I know she's not that keen so far, but we had plans, were going ice skating at Eden Park tomorrow and then, on Monday, to an Xmas tree show at somewhere ...' she faltered.

'Eden Project and then the annual Christmas tree exhibition at Polgwynn in Porthaven,' said Sindy Cardrew softly.

'And she had the pool, that glorious pool,' Erin continued.

'The swimming pool here Inspector. Posy is a great swimmer,' Power confirmed.

'OK. Well let me speak to the others downstairs. Can you find me a recent photograph?'

'I have loads,' said Erin leaping up from the sofa, 'I'll fetch my phone,' and with that she rushed from the room.

'My wife is very upset Inspector. Since our son Ford ...' he trailed off gazing into the fire.

'I understand perfectly Sir.'

'Please call me Rolf.'

'Perhaps you could also give me the number for your son.'

'Of course.'

As it transpired this would not be needed. As they made their way back down the staircase Hitch Lindström was bursting through the front door like Aragorn entering Helm's Deep in the Lord of the Rings' film *The Two Towers*. Looking up he caught his father's expression and slowly shook his head. Close on his heels was a beautiful pale girl with cascading red curls.

Flora Morrow was considering how it would look if she were to ask for a whisky, when a gorgeous tall blonde guy, nothing like Hércule Poirot, walked into the library; he could have been Jackson Power's younger brother. Sindy Cardrew introduced him as Inspector Treloar.

'Inspector Treloar has a few questions for you.'

Treloar went over the events of the day confirming with the others what he had been told. It stuck him that Davis Lindström should be here in the library rather than upstairs with the family. When he spoke to her it became clear that her mother held her responsible for the fate of her sister. He sympathised with her belief that Posy should have been perfectly safe in a small Cornish town on a crowded market day at midday.

Hitch and his companion joined the group in the library and confirmed that they had found no trace of his sister in Fowey. They had checked with people in both market locations and in the shops and galleries. Nobody had seen her after noon.

'By the way,' Hitch said, 'this is Georgie. She's been awesome. She knows everyone in Fowey.'

The name triggered a synapse in Treloar's brain and he recalled a photograph on the Gwavas Fish website: Georgie; Georgiana Spargo. Interesting.

Treloar also thought, although he did not express this, that it was highly bizarre that Posy should disappear less than thirty six hours after her unannounced arrival at Seal Hall. Somebody at The Valley of the Tides was involved in this and Treloar had his eyes fixed firmly on Guy Masterson. It also worried him that Posy must have been about the same age as Christabel Masterson had the latter survived.

Having gained nothing further of interest and collecting several excellent photographs of Posy, he left Seal Hall.

Outside it was a glorious winter's evening. It was a night that could have been in any age but only in this one place. Last year, last decade, last century, but only here. Cornwall was like that. Standing on the high point of his land above his converted barn with two coasts in view or on the cliffs at his family's farm he felt it. But never elsewhere. The tiny lights on the giant Christmas tree were mirrored in the sky where countless stars and a bright moon cast a soft grey light over the wooded valleys and the river. He was thinking about his father. Tomorrow was Sunday, a sacrosanct day for family lunch at Cove Farm. He was not expected given the investigation, his mother content that he would spend some time with the Tremaynes in Lostwithiel. It was a huge relief. He could not bear the thought of facing his mother and sisters. Joe Thwaite had taken a turn for the worse and Doc Tremayne had not been able to see him. The prognosis was not good. There was no news.

He was still sitting in his Land Rover in the courtyard. He had sent the photographs of Posy to DS Nicky

Chamberlain who was organising the response. He had also sent one to Benedict Fitzroy who had promised help. When his phone rang with a number he rarely saw on an incoming call he knew it was bad news. Jamie Deverell.

'Ben. I've just had a call from Jamie Deverell.'

'Right ...'

'Well in itself that unnerved me. Jamie doesn't instigate communication; he calls when he's found something for me. So I knew it must be serious. He's been monitoring activity on Spargo's deep site and he's come across something and I think it concerns Posy Lindström.'

'Shit.'

'Indeed. There's nothing specific: no new photographs or entries in the main body of the site, but he's picked up a new private chat room with a flurry of activity between Gideon and two IP addresses. No details on the content yet, Jamie's working on it, but he's got the title – *Hollywood Cherry*.

'Anything on the IP addresses?

'Just that one is in Nigeria and the other in Pakistan.'

'Fuck. I'm thinking bidding war.'

'My thought exactly.'

'Anything useful from Seal Hall?'

'Nada. Nobody saw her after the marquee on Town Quay late morning. But one interesting point;

Hitchcock turned up with Georgiana Spargo. Could she have the tipped off her uncle that Posy was here?'

'Nah. They're screwing; been an item since the summer. Young love eh?'

'Jesus Ben is no secret safe from you?'

'Nah mate, nobody at all.'

Thirty Eight

Sunday had dawned clear and bright, a glorious red sky giving way to the palest of blues, a soft sunlight - and no wind. Gideon had told Roman Rotan that using the *Taras* for this operation was an indulgence, a vanity, fine for messing about, cruising The Channel, but useless for a critical mission. She was a beautiful boat: a wooden sailing trawler from the 20s, but she was slow and difficult to manoeuvre. Most of all she stuck out like a sore thumb. But he, Gideon, was as ever prepared. He was sending the *St Minver* the newest in his fleet, small but fast. She would get into Fowey mid afternoon, probably before the *Taras*. If the wind didn't pick up *she* could stand in and deliver the goods. But he was still uneasy. Things were slipping, moving beyond his control and now he had that wretched Masterson brat to deal with. God knows he, Gideon, loved cash but this boy was a liability.

Gideon had taken the call before dawn. The

police had found CCTV of the Lindstrom girl's abduction clearly implicating Guy Masterson. He had been caught on two different cameras. There was no doubt. Luckily, the police officer who had found the footage was *his* police officer. He had been forewarned. The discovery could be delayed for a couple of hours before it became general knowledge in the investigation, but no longer than that.

Gideon had phoned Masterson, told him to get on the move and stay on the move, to get the money to him and wait for instructions. Then he had sought advice, made arrangements and called up his best team, and he himself was going along this time. Still the bidding war for the girl had been phenomenal, the outcome beyond his wildest dreams. He would need to keep an eye on the sister; potential there. Admittedly she was older and probably not a virgin but she was still Hollywood royalty and she would fetch a good price.

Posy was getting seriously pissed. If this was a joke Davis, it just wasn't funny anymore. Eventually she had fallen asleep: it was a really comfortable bed. Then this morning when she woke up someone had been into the room. On the table were a plastic bottle of freshly squeezed orange juice, a basket of bananas and apples, two sweet roll kinda things, a paper plate of sliced cold meat and some brioche. There was also a plastic knife and fork and a bunch of paper napkins. Weird.

She had a shower and dressed again. It was kinda yucky putting on the same clothes. She was so gonna tell on Davis. She ate the fruit and the sweet rolls: they were good. She drank half the juice. Then she looked out of the window again. It was light now but all she could see was a bunch of fields and trees and then the water. Didn't anybody live around here? She tried the window again but it was still locked, she tried the door, also locked. She put an ear to the door and listened: nothing. She hammered with her fist.

'HEY! HEY! My Pop is so going to sue your asses!'

Nothing.

Luckily, Posy had not been blessed with her sister's wit and imagination. She sat on the bed and braided her wet hair. Hours later she heard footsteps and a key turning in the lock.

In the end Treloar had not stayed with the Tremaynes. He had taken up Fitzroy's offer of the spare room at Teal House. Uniforms had completed the door to door in Fowey and found nothing. Nobody remembered the girl. They had gathered as much CCTV as they could and were looking through it. They were thinking of calling in divers at first light. They were organising a TV appeal for Sunday evening; they anticipated a huge viewing audience. But nobody really thought anything other than abduction. Those beyond the core team were waiting for a substantial ransom demand: all the equipment was in place at

Seal Hall and Fiona Sinclair, an experienced Family Liaison Officer as well as bright detective, had spent the night.

Treloar and Fitzroy had sat at the kitchen table with a bottle of Laphroaig. Treloar was amazed at his friend's capacity for alcohol. At 02:00 Treloar had told the story of his father's presumed drowning and Joe Thwaite's recent revelation. Fitzroy had thought it eminently possible that Jago was still alive. He had experience of "causing people to disappear for their own good" and witness protection. He told Treloar that he agreed that he should hold fire until he knew something concrete before saying a word to his family, hard as he knew that must be. But as well as offering sympathy he also offered his considerable resources in the search. At 03:20 Treloar retired to bed. Fitzroy was on the phone checking in.

At 06:25 Treloar woke and made his way to the kitchen for coffee. To his amazement Fitzroy was up, obviously showered and dressed in clean clothes, coffee brewed, bread rolls in the oven and bacon in the skillet.

'Jesus,' Treloar groaned, 'must be the military training.'

'Catholic boarding school,' Fitzroy replied, grinning and pouring coffee.

'Anything?'

'Nada.'

Treloar checked in and confirmed that there was

no news. The men ate a hearty breakfast. Treloar showered and put on his dirty clothes. The men checked in again.

Tulip was manic. She was playing catch up. When the story had broken in the early hours she was AWOL. She had missed the calls from her editor and she owed him big time. After a boring trawl around the Christmas market jostling with the sweaty, noisy masses she had enjoyed a long evening in the hotel bar finally adjourning to bed with the Aussie barman. When she returned to her room and her iPhone she had 12 missed calls. Deep doo-doo.

Now she was in her room chasing leads, trawling the newsfeeds, calling in favours. She had her phone, Brett the barman's phone, her laptop and his iPad. She was on top of the story but she had one infuriating issue: she couldn't get hold of her local police contact. They weren't picking up and they were ignoring her texts.

At 08:00 Fiona Sinclair reported that Guy Masterson was missing. He had not appeared for breakfast. They had searched his room and all the facilities. Some of his clothes and an overnight bag were gone along with a valuable art deco vase from the drawing room. Nobody had heard or seen him leave. In the bottom of his wardrobe under a pile of discarded dirty washing was a barbed wire garrotte. He hadn't even tried to hide it or dispose of it. He really was a cocky bastard

Fi thought. He could have tossed it in the river, buried it in the grounds, they would never have found it. Perhaps he was saving it for his next victim? Perhaps he had panicked and not had time to get rid? Perhaps it would damn him.

An alert was put out to all patrols.

At 09:24 Colin Matthews had found CCTV footage from inside the marquee on Town Quay showing Guy Masterson shepherding a smiling Posy Lindström from a side opening. Outside coverage then showed him escorting her to an unmarked van with an obscured number plate and being bundled into the back by a large man in a baseball cap and dark clothing. Masterson returned to the marquee. The van pulled off and was tracked along Fore Street and picked up again near Caffa Mill. There was no further coverage. Nobody could explain why it had taken so long for the footage to be checked.

An all ports warning went out.

At 10:15 Jamie Deverell confirmed a series of phone calls between one of Gideon Spargo's mobiles and Guy Masterson's. Masterson was still in Fowey.

Then nothing.

The watchers watched.

At 13:09 the Spargo trawler *St Minver* left Mevagissey on the ebbing tide heading east across St Austell Bay towards the red and white striped daymark on Gribbin Head as cover for Roman Rotan's Taras. An unusual visitor, she had arrived the day before, and her departure was noted by local fishermen and Fitzroy's trackers.

At 14:30 Guy Masterson's credit card was used to hire a Zar Formenti Well-Deck Rigid Inflatable Boat (RIB) from a boat hire company in Fowey. Jamie Deverell picked it up. He called Treloar.

Treloar and Fitzroy were sitting in the kitchen at Teal House. They had agreed that basing themselves there gave them the greatest flexibility: they had immediate access to the boat and the boat gave them the flexibility to reach both sides of the river and Seal Hall fast. They agreed to get aboard and position themselves down river mid channel so they could pick up Masterson as he made his way seawards. They thought it most likely he would be making for a rendezvous with a Spargo boat. The only issue was that his boat would be a hell of a lot faster. They had time. They were downstream of the boat hire company and there would be a delay while Masterson underwent the mandatory safety drill and handling instructions. They'd see him.

Thirty Nine

It was all going to be so easy and for once it wasn't going to cost him cash. The bitch was already drooling over him. Christ she'd hardly set foot in the place with her Mommy before she had cornered him in the library. And what's more, she was a spoiled precious princess just like his sister. In fact it was perfect; poetic fucking justice. How could it go so wrong?

Shit. Who would have thought it: CCTV coverage in a fucking tent? Apparently he had been caught on camera taking the precious princess out of the Christmas Market and bundling her into the back of that van. Shit. Shit. Shit. Luckily Gideon Spargo had found out and got word to him. Now he had to hide, hide and then run. Fuck his father would disown him for this. There would be no more help. He knew that. Still. There were always his pals.

Guy had a close band of friends. They had mostly met at LSE, although Simeon had been at school with Guy. They had formed a 'society' with rules and secrets. They shared indiscretions, petty crimes and as their bond grew; admission, confession, betrayal became inconceivable and intolerable. Shared guilt covers many a sin. Guy would not be short of help. They knew his secrets; Simeon knew how it had started, he knew about Christabel.

He, Guy, had been the darling baby; he had been the youngest by five years. Then, eight years later along comes another, greater miracle: another baby and a fucking girl. A fucking girl! The only girl. The precious poxy princess. A total culture shock when you're used to being the little prince. It just wasn't fair. And now this! What had he ever done to deserve any of this?

Yes his pals would help him. But what to do now, right now, right this fucking minute? He needed help.

He was reluctant to make the call but he was in so deep now what the hell. It was a staggeringly exorbitant amount of money but what choice did he have? He had left Seal Hall early that morning before dawn and hidden out in one of the roundhouses down by the creek waiting for instructions. Then he had taken one of the quad bikes and headed down to Bodinnick. It seemed an eternity waiting for the first ferry. Finally he had arrived at Caffa Mill car park on the Fowey side.

Normally on an early Sunday morning in December the streets of a Cornish town would have been deserted and everything would have been shut if not shuttered for the winter. But luckily this was the weekend of the Fowey Christmas Market and the place was surprisingly busy so Guy did not look out of place wandering along Fore Street. He grabbed a coffee and sat outside a pub watching the streets fill up with busy people laden with boxes rushing to restock their stalls in the marquees on Town Quay, dodging the drifting aimless tourists waiting for the event to start. He now had instructions, directions and a plan. He had cash, he had a new untraceable phone, he had arranged transport. He had a few more calls to make but things were looking up. Magic.

So that afternoon found him bouncing over the water in a powerful RIB. It was a blast. Perhaps everything was going to be OK after all. He was getting away with it ... again. Life was totally cool. He had gotten hold of Simmy. They were going to meet up in St Malo and head for Simmy's folks' place in Avignon. Christmas in the South of France: way cool. Father would be pissed off that he'd "let your mother down again", but Guy knew that was just not true; she wouldn't even notice he wasn't there.

As usual Guy Masterson had paid in advance. This time that was a huge mistake. As he pulled the RIB alongside the *St Morwenna* at the rendezvous near Gribbin Hole, Todd Vickery lowered a rope ladder. The plan was to abandon the RIB running, as if he had fallen overboard. It was a good plan. As Guy reached the deck Vickery took his hand, pulled him away from the rope ladder and hurled him out to sea where he landed with a loud splash.

'Wait! Stop! What are you doing? I can't swim!'

'Shouldn't have come to Cornwall then,' said Gideon emerging on deck. It was an opinion he had held for some time.

Vickery's aim had been good. Soon Guy Masterson was caught in the current and pulled towards the Hole where he disappeared beneath the water dragged down by the undertow. As the *St Morwenna* turned to cruise west, the RIB powered into the rocks at the mouth of Polridmouth Cove, exploding on impact. Guy Masterson's body would never be found.

Holding off some distance from the Fowey river mouth, Treloar watched through binoculars and Fitzroy filmed, as events unfolded.

'I don't believe in the death penalty, state sponsored killing, but I do believe in the death opportunity, as do you my friend,' Fitzroy said with a smile, alluding to an incident that occurred in London when they first met.

'Right,' Treloar said quietly.

'There can be no doubt, reasonable or otherwise, that Guy Masterson was a nasty, vicious, murdering bastard and now the world is rid of him. You know as well as I do that he would never have stopped and with all that money he would always have found victims. You also know that we would never have got him for it, too much influence, too many dirty secrets on people in high places held by his father. This is a righteous thing mate, no doubts, no qualms.'

'Now we just need to get Spargo.'

'Well a video posted on the deep web would be a warning to others and crippling to Gideon's business. Not good to be seen killing the clients. I'm sure we could get someone to post it.'

As they motored back to Polruan Treloar was thoughtful.

'Won't Gregory Masterson make a fucking stink about his precious boy?'

'Accidental death in a boating incident? Tragic, but he was known to be an impetuous, foolhardy youth afraid of nothing, searching for the missing girl, brave and selfless.'

Treloar stared at him incredulous. 'He knows. He did a deal with Spargo to kill his son?'

'Put it this way. Masterson had harboured suspicions since his daughter's death and we have "shared" some evidence with him. If it ends like this? No trial, no costly lawyers, no shame.'

'Jesus Ben, what about the little girls? What about their families?'

'We don't know their families Phil. Trust me, we've searched. We do know Masterson. It may not be justice but it is retribution.'

'And public opinion? What will people think

when the police fail to solve the murder of a little girl, for Christ's sake?'

'Ah well, I think it's going down as a tragic boating incident.'

'John Forbes will never agree to that. I won't and nor will my team.'

'Well I'm only saying that's the official line as far as Gregory Masterson is concerned. Of course, should something leak before then, well, we'd have no choice but to corroborate the true version of events. Obviously, Masterson would understand that leaks do occur, given his line of business.'

Treloar was grinning.

'You're a devious bastard Fitzroy. No wonder your family's been powerful since the Norman Conquest. You have no scruples.'

'Way of the world mate, way of the world.'

Back at Teal House Treloar had been checking in with the team. Fitzroy had been upstairs on the phone for some time when he walked into the kitchen. He was grim faced.

'We've found your leak. It's not Winters. I'm so sorry mate; it's Colin Matthews.'

'Colin?' Treloar was dumbfounded. 'Where is he?'

'You know we've been watching the waters around the coast. This morning we tracked Matthews coming out of Fowey on the *Ziggy*. Treloar went to speak but Fitzroy held up his hand to stop him.

'I know, I know that's normal, nothing strange about it. But it's what happened next. He sailed down to Carrick Roads and up to Mylor where he boarded a very different boat, a 16 metre brand new Beneteau worth almost half a million.'

'So? He sails; he knows people who sail.'

'There was nobody else onboard. The boat's registered to a Russian Black Sea fish processing magnate, Anatoly Petrov, a known close associate of Gideon Spargo. Matthews was loading up supplies, lots of supplies. And the boat's name: *Serious Moonlight*.'

'Col was always a great Bowie fan.'

'He's getting ready mate; he's going to run.'

'Shit. Shit, shit, shit.'

'I'm so sorry. I know you thought it was Winters. But with her gone, this explains how Masterson got word we were on to him. Matthews was reviewing the CCTV coverage. It also explains the delay in discovering the right footage.'

'I wanted it to be Winters. I let that blind me. I was too close.'

The two men waited, working their phones. Fitzroy was making yet more coffee when his phone rang again. He listened nodding, saying nothing. Then he ended the call.

'Spargo's back in Penryn. We're watching him and Todd Vickery. They're going nowhere.'

'Yeah well I know that Spargo's phone's not moved; Jamie's been monitoring. And there's more: a lot of activity between Spargo and one of Roman Rotan's mobiles. It seems he's coming from France.'

Fitzroy's phone rang again and he answered. It was one of his watchers.

'Hang on. Let me put you on speaker.'

'I'm in Fowey on Town Quay. You know we've been tracking unusual movements of the Spargo fleet. One boat, the *St Minver* came in earlier this afternoon and it just so happens that a lovely wooden sailing trawler has also just come in. I'm looking at her now: the *Taras*, registered in St Malo to Roman Rotan.'

'OK. Thanks mate. Keep watching.'

Treloar was frowning. 'We know they transfer just offshore but I wouldn't have chosen to come into Fowey; it's too busy: too many web cams, too many idle watching eyes. Plus it's a traffic nightmare at Christmas. We know it's nothing to do with Masterson. That was a panic job arranged today. If it's not a coincidence, it's got to be some special delivery.'

'Or collection?'

'Yeah. A special Christmas present, a specific order: the Lindström girl.'

'It would explain Fowey, if they've kept her close by.'

'Christ this is a wretched trade.'

'You're not wrong there mate, but we're watching and I've called in reinforcements holding

273

just off Lantic Bay. If we're right, they won't get her out of our waters. We just have to wait. Watch and wait.

'

Forty

This morning had gone well. He had been up early for just four sorrel omelettes which he'd agreed to cook because they had all wanted to try his lightly cooked breakfast special 'O's. 'Very handy that,' he had thought to himself when he found out there had been some takers, because he refused to cook any omelette for longer than thirty seconds. "Slightly runny under the folds and bright yellow or sometimes lightly browned only, from your choice of cooking in regular or goats' butter," said the note on the special 'O's menu.

Lunch had gone well because all the specials today had been extra special specials, self cooked - they had pan fried their own cod after filleting it themselves in the morning's therapy session. They had been loudly applauded by the other diners as they carried their own plates into the restaurant, still wearing their aprons. They had also made their own tartare sauce. 'Always fun that one,' he thought, 'they can't believe the taste of the mayonnaise and how easy it is, and the looks on their faces when they've added the mustard! .... and they'd all said they'd start growing their own chives and parsley, some of them might even do it. Brilliant.'

'You can't beat it ... well OK ... maybe apart from salsa verde,' he had said to the therapy group, laughing, just before they began frying the cod. 'Hey Jimmie, you've missed some of your chunks!!' he remembered shouting at Jimmie as he had smiled and pointed to the chopped olives and capers that were hiding on the board behind the bowl after he had stirred in the chopped parsley and chives. He had even had the same himself and eaten in the restaurant with them. Great.

And here he was, waiting. In the trees behind the parking space at the back of Shed 5, the biggest of the Sheds in The Old Station Yard, behind and down towards the river from the main car park that was mostly filled with over-wintering boats at this time of year. It was the last but one in the line. There were only six altogether and he knew that the only other shed occupied was Shed 1. They were old storage sheds with small offices that had been recently refurbished and converted to luxury accommodation. The lane running in front of the Sheds was a private road accessed from Station Road on the eastern edge of Fowey, next to the library; close to the Caffa Mill car park, just up the road from the ferry slipway. It ran along to the docks, and it was rarely used. He could sometimes hear the wind rattling cables against yacht masts in the car park.

On the other side of the lane was a nicely kept wide grass verge with a bench table for each Shed, and then a steep rocky bank sloped down to the river. There was a refurbished jetty just opposite Shed 4. It was dark apart from around Shed 1 and all the buildings had their boarded window covers pulled down and locked apart from Shed 1 which had its outside lights on. He had not seen anyone through the windows and there was no-one outside. Nor was there a car there. Shed 1 was more than a hundred metres away.

The cars drew into the parking spaces in front of him and the lights of a 4 x 4 illuminated the Aston Martin as it drew in, and he saw that its driver was the only person inside and then the lights of both cars were turned off.

He had known when they were coming because Jack from security had rung him on his silenced mobile as he had asked, and told him about the fuss at the gate, that none of them had come in even after being invited personally to meet with Sindy, even after the personnel gate had been opened, and that the two cars outside had turned round and gone back, presumably towards the Bodinnick ferry, after the ten minute stand-off. And then he had called the others to let them know.

When the driver of the Aston Martin got out he made sure that the number plate at the front of the car and the driver were both in the shot and pressed the shutter button on his phone, and there was suddenly a bright flash of light that seemed like a bolt of lightning and then everything kicked off. All at once.

'What the fuck?' shouted the driver.

At the same time a deep voice from the side of Shed 5 shouted, 'Oi, little bastard, fuck off,' and he heard heavy footsteps running towards him from the side of the building.

Just after that there was a whirring, whistling sound and a thud, and a voice from the ground next to where he knew the 4 x 4 was said, 'what the fu...' just before another thud.

Next was the very welcome sound of Mad Cam saying, 'roight moi lovely fuckin' 'ansomes, let's see how fuckin' scary you really are!!' and then more thuds, but the heavy footsteps belonging to "Oi little bastard fuck off" were getting closer and still coming in his direction. He picked up an old tree branch that he had found lying in some nearby trees and put next to him for later, switched on his phone's torch app and pointed the light towards the voice guy just before swinging the branch at the voice's stomach. "Oi little bastard" stopped suddenly and bent double, and then he gave him a hard karate chop to the back of his neck. "Oi little bastard" remained standing and didn't move.

Forty One

Treloar took a call on his mobile. It was Tulip Khan. He remembered her from the Porthaven case.

'Inspector, I have something I need to give you, urgently.'

'Really Ms Khan,' he commented acidly.

'Look. I know what you probably think of me, but this is information critical to your case and it will damn some bloke called Gideon Spargo. I have hard copy and thumb drives. I'm staying at the Old Custom House in Fowey. Can you come here, now?'

'Very well.'

'Ms Khan?' Fitzroy asked.

'Journalist. Says she has something "critical" on the case that'll nail Spargo. Want to come? I think you'll like her; she's ballsy.'

'But is she hot?'

'Oh yeah.'

The two men and Tulip Khan were in her room at the Old Custom House Hotel. The bed was covered in papers, photographs and photocopies.

'This was waiting for me at reception when I got in yesterday evening,' she showed them a large jiffy bag addressed to "Tulip Khan Room 12". Treloar glanced at Fitzroy. He had recognized the handwriting.

'Colin Matthews,' he said quietly.

'Yes,' she looked surprised. 'I didn't pay him anything. He didn't want money. He knew it was wrong but he didn't know who was involved, who he could trust.'

'So what was in it for you?'

'An early exclusive and a means to get the information to you. Obviously I'll have to bide my time 'til you get the bad guys, but then I'll have a scoop.

'Is there any mention of Gardner Lindström?

'No. Nothing. This material is older.'

'So Matthews was working undercover?' Fitzroy asked disingenuously. He wanted to find out what she knew. He had been introduced as an interested party from the National Crime Agency.

'Hell no. Colin was totally disillusioned. He felt that he had been overlooked, underestimated and sidelined and he wanted payback. I've been up all night looking through this. Colin documented all his dealings with Gideon Spargo. At first it was just advance warning of boat and catch inspections. Colin thought it was just booze, tobacco and drugs. He didn't realise that Spargo had moved onto bigger fish, excuse the pun.'

'It's been happening for some time then?' Fitzroy asked.

'Several years now. He was in it for the money; well, the promise of some boat he wanted. It was when Spargo moved into trafficking people Colin couldn't go along anymore. So as well as making notes, he started to collect evidence.'

'How long have you known about all this?' Treloar asked.

'Since last night, I swear.'

'So why are you here?' Fitzroy.

'Look. I've been in contact with Colin since those murders in Porthaven but he told me nothing about this, nothing. He rang me when the little girl was found and told me to get down here. It's a story that sells papers, you know that. But this other stuff. He left it for me with a note to pass it on to you,' she pointed at Treloar. 'He was my friend, a source agreed, but still my friend.'

'What got him started?' Fitzroy asked.

'I've no idea. He doesn't say.'

Treloar and Fitzroy exchanged a look.

'Really. I have no idea. Look, fundamentally he was a decent bloke. He could have been saved but he was abused and exploited beyond endurance by that bitch you all worked for. I remember her from Porthaven, couldn't keep the cow away from the cameras as I recall. And anyway, in the end, he tried to do the right thing, hence all this,' she swept her arm across the papers on the bed.

'Why didn't he come to me directly?' Treloar asked, although it was a rhetorical question.

'You would have stopped him. He just wanted to make things better … and get away.'

'And you've had no contact today?' Fitzroy again.

'No and I don't expect to have, not anytime soon anyway.'

'Well thank you for bringing all this to us,' said Treloar rousing himself from his thoughts. He had been staring at the papers strewn across the bed.

'I did it for Colin, not for you. Your people destroyed him. I made him a promise.'

'And you'll keep that; you'll hold fire on your article?' Fitzroy.

'Yes. I don't betray the people who trust me.'

'Why now? Why has he gone now? What tipped the balance?' asked Treloar.

'You. Colin says in his note that Spargo was getting out of control. The dead girl was a huge mistake. Once you Inspector were brought in Colin knew that you would move fast and bring in resources that would track Spargo's deep web dealings.'

'What resources?' Treloar asked, again knowing

the answer.

'He doesn't say. Just that they were better than him, and Colin was one of the best I've come across.'

Treloar stood and held out his hand. Tulip collected the papers and thumb drives and stuffed them back in the jiffy bag, then handed it to him.

'All this came in the one envelope from Colin?'

'Yes, as I've said.'

'But there are copies of invoices here, spreadsheets, internal company documents. How did Colin get hold of these?'

'Oh he had a mole of his own; an insider. It was a two way street. Colin was gathering information as well as passing it on.'

'Who?'

'He wouldn't say. If there's nothing else, I've a story to write.'

'Well thank you for your prompt call Ms Khan.'

'Oh, one last thing Inspector. When this is all over I'd be very interested in getting an interview with you, perhaps exploring your personal take on the case, what drives you. The public is always interested in the man behind the job.'

'I don't think so Ms Khan, but thank you again.' Treloar said with his iciest smile. Fitzroy nodded. The two men left the room.

Having left the hotel Treloar and Fitzroy walked along Fore Street to Fowey Town Quay where they had left the boat. Bella Dean was coming over from Polruan to join them with an update from Seal Hall. They saw that the orange ferry boat had just set off from Fowey so they had time to kill and a discussion to hold.

'Beer?' Treloar asked.

They walked back to the King of Prussia pub and up the steps. The bar was on the first floor of the building and from a window table they could watch for the returning ferry. Fitzroy took a window table and Treloar fetched two pints of Tribute bitter.

'Did Matthews know about Jamie Deverell?'

'No. He knew the name from the Porthaven case but he didn't know we were still in touch. Only Sam knows that, apart from you, and Bella Dean.'

'Hannah.'

'Yeah, Hannah.'

'So, what do we do about the lovely Ms Khan?'

'Well I suppose you could get her for something, conspiracy, perverting the course of justice, conspiracy to pervert the course of justice. No journalist is absolutely clean in my experience.'

'Yes, or I could always make her disappear? Still mate, I think she took a distinct liking to you.' Fitzroy said with a grin.

Treloar snorted. 'Yeah, or we could just bank her as a useful contact and let her write her story'

'It is positively Shakespearean. A noble man brought down by a manipulative exploitative woman.'

'You know what makes it worse? Colin was the most decent, honest man; a real stickler for the rules.

Why didn't he say something? Why didn't he tell me? Winters must have worn him into the ground. I could have saved him if I'd known. Poor bloody sod. Do you think the lovely Tulip might be encouraged to mention that the woman has been moved on to a new posting on the East Coast?'

'So that she can be easily identified and pursued by any angry press on behalf of an outraged public? Why not?' I never liked Winters either.'

'You only met her once.'

'Once was enough.'

'What about this insider? It would be a brave minion who'd betray Gideon Spargo.'

'Well mate I've been thinking about that and my money's on the father or the brother. From what I could make out of this stuff it has to be someone high enough up the tree to get hold of anything they wanted.'

Treloar took a swig of beer. 'Christian. It's got to be. Old man Spargo's too powerless now, too out to pasture to lay his hands on all this without arousing suspicion. Christian is well known to have nothing but contempt for the fishing business but he's still on the board. I reckon Colin approached Christian with an offer to bring down his brother. Colin would have known that Christian could provide evidence he himself couldn't get hold off. Gideon's dark business dealings were casting a pall over Christian's brave new world of upmarket tourism, tarnishing his hard won clean image.'

'No love lost there then; should have named them Cain and Abel.'

'There already was an Abel: the grandfather.'

'Still it's good news from Matthews' perspective. When all this comes out Gideon and his pals will know there's a whistleblower; they won't think insider and outsider. They'll work out the betrayer and go after Christian. Good news for Matthews bad news for him.'

'Christian will have a plan.'

'The only plan that would truly work, leave him safe, would be Gideon's death. No bitter incarcerated brother planning revenge.'

As it turned out Colin had operated as Winters' personal technical support, accessing all systems for her unbeknownst to the others because she lacked skills, didn't want to make the time to learn, and she didn't want anyone to know. Then when she was transferred Colin saw his opportunity to cast suspicion on her. Suddenly the raids were getting results; cigarettes and alcohol, low level drugs. Gideon was willing to sacrifice some profit for the bigger picture. There was no direct tie back to him just the odd fine and warning to a captain who received a handsome backhander for taking one for the team.

All those years being suborned by Winters into doing "little jobs" for her with no reward and no respect; concealing his activities from his friends and colleagues, betraying himself. Then along comes Gideon Spargo with much the same request but he is offering the Holy Grail: Colin's dream boat. Winters had eroded his resistance to corruption.

As Doc Tremayne would say:

'Corruption is like an illness. It's a slippery slope and once you start down it, it becomes increasingly difficult to gain purchase, to secure even the slightest foothold. Winters made Colin her creature; she has much to answer for in this.'

*

There was an unusual amount of traffic that night on the river Fowey. It was a still, overcast night, damp but not cold.

Running without lights, a small fishing boat set out from upstream of the china clay docks. On board were two men and a struggling girl, her hands tied. They headed downstream toward the sea.

In the channel, opposite the Royal Fowey Yacht Club the wooden sailing trawler *Taras* was waiting to set sail on the ebbing tide. Just upstream was the trawler *St Minver*. Unbeknownst to either crew they were being watched.

Forty Two

'I've got 'im, don't worry, just get on,' Mad Cam's mate said, just before his rubber mallet thudded into the back of "Oi little bastard's" left leg at the back of the knee. "Oi little bastard" collapsed onto the ground on his left side.

"Oi little bastard" slurred 'you fuckin' bast..' just before one of the cloths they had soaked in fish guts for most of the day was stuffed into his mouth; a rope securing it when Cam's mate pulled it sharply over the cloth between his lips and teeth, and then tied it tightly behind his neck. Then Cam's mate thudded the mallet into the top of the back of "Oi little bastard's" right thigh.

The Aston Martin driver had been netted and dragged to the ground by another of Cam's mates, and he had also been gagged. Mad Cam had brought down the 4 x 4 driver with a brilliantly thrown net that had spun and whistled its way over its target, courtesy of six small buoys that had been fixed at intervals around the net's edge. He was still tangled in the net, but Cam had freed his head to gag him like the others, before wrapping the net back round his head.

'So, 'ansome,' Mad Cam said quietly into 4 x 4's ear before thudding his rubber mallet into the top of 4 x 4's right thigh. 'Y'all 'r' stain' away from down 'ere now eh?' and the mallet thudded into 4 x 4's left thigh, then his right buttock, then his left buttock. 'See, the poleece round 'ere 'r' nosey enough without smart bastards like you 'n' your mates from up-country ...' and he thudded the mallet into the back of 4 x 4's right thigh and then his left, 'coming down 'ere to make 'em even nosier. See what oi mean 'ansome? ... Just nod your 'ed if you see what oi mean. Agreein' are you?' Mad Cam asked.

4 x 4 nodded and his eyes pleaded, and a throttled grunting noise came from his mouth, and Mad Cam thudded the mallet into his right buttock, then his left buttock and said, 'Well that be bloody marvellous that be, 'cos, if we see you bastards down 'ere again, you'll be absolutely fuckin' sure that this is us lettin' you bastards off lightly.' And Mad Cam smashed the mallet into 4 x 4's right buttock and then his left buttock as hard as he could.

They had agreed on no broken bones if possible, or visible injuries, to reduce the chances of a need for local hospital treatment and with it the possibility of discussions with the local police. It took a while but when Cam's mate had said that Kim, the fishmonger with the wet fish stall on the harbour wall in Mevagissey, swore blind by the rubber mallet she kept for cracking spider crab shells and claws without damaging the meat, they knew he was onto something.

Cam's other mate had made a trip to B & Q in St Austell to buy three large-headed rubber mallets and they were in business. Soaking the gags in fish guts had been Cam's idea, and Harry had mentioned that photographs would probably come in useful. Making them as uncomfortable as possible for as long as possible, including the long drive back to wherever they were going was top of the agenda for the rest of their discussion.

'Now, just so you and your pals understand,' said Harry, nodding at Cam's other mate, who smashed his rubber mallet into the side of the Aston Martin driver's right thigh, 'if the local plods happen to be successful and catch you bastards you're just going to have to fucking take what's coming,' and nodded at Cam's other mate again, who smashed his mallet into the front of the drivers left thigh. 'So it's tough fucking shit, right? Nod if you understand.' The driver nodded. Harry nodded again at Cam's other mate and he rolled the driver over and smashed his mallet into the driver's right buttock and then his left buttock before rolling him over again. 'AND, don't forget I've got your picture with the car. If anything untoward should happen to me, that means bad, any kind of fucking bad, the copies of it I'm going to leave with some pretty reliable people will find their way to all sorts of people you wouldn't want to be seeing them.' Then he stood back and the flash lit the driver, net, gag and all, as another picture was taken. 'And Mr Smart Arse, don't forget the people you wouldn't want to see you looking like you do right now!'

Then he had walked back towards "Oi little bastard" and picked up the old branch then back to the car and used the thick end of the branch to smash the driver's side window, then round the back of the car to the other side and smashed the passenger window. Then he walked, hearing occasional mallet thuds and grunts, over to the bench table where Cam and his mates had left two buckets filled with water. He picked them up, walked back to the car, put one down and emptied the other one slowly through the broken passenger window down the seat back and onto the seat before putting the empty bucket down. Then he picked up the other bucket, walked round to the driver's side and emptied it slowly down the seat back and over the driver's seat like its twin before stepping over to the driver, kicking him in the stomach and saying, 'now fuck off, right off ...... right now.'

They had retrieved the nets without incident, taken them and the buckets back to Cam's boat which was just up the lane at the deserted docks, and removed their balaclavas before looking at each other, breathing quite hard, and smiled, and then laughed and triple high fived. 'Brilliant guys, thanks, really 'preciate it,' said Mad Cam's mate. Cam looked through his night vision scope towards Shed 5 and saw that the three were struggling to untie the ropes holding their gags in place, but they were now at least on their feet.

By the time the boat had been unmoored and was silently running on the strong outgoing tide past Shed 5 Harry was using the night scope. He saw "Oi little bastard" locking the door of Shed 5 with a hold-all in his hand, and the 4 x 4 and Aston Martin drivers in a heated discussion. The Aston Martin driver was pointing at the 4 x 4 and the 4 x 4 driver was pointing at the broken windows of the Aston Martin and shaking his head. The Aston Martin driver slapped the 4 x 4 driver hard across his face and held his hand out. The 4 x 4 driver handed over what Harry thought must have been car keys and the Aston Martin driver got into the 4 x 4 and drove off.

'Looks like it worked' thought Harry. 'Rush or

what? Got the pics, they're out of here, probably not coming back, brilliant ...... what a rush, Christ!' He watched as the 4 x 4 driver used his hand to try to sweep the remaining water from the driver's seat of the Aston Martin before sitting and "Oi little bastard" got in the passenger side before the beautiful looking car glided up the lane and out of their lives.

A few seconds later Mad Cam fired up the engine and they were about to cruise past the ferry slips, close to the Bodinnick side and Harry said, 'just drop me at the Tides slip mate, thanks.'

'OK boy, and thanks.'

'Hey .... what ... what the fuck's that! ...... down there,' Harry said, pointing towards the gloom under the trees on the Bodinnick side of the river. He picked up the night scope and carried on pointing.

'Can't rightly see,' said Cam's mate.

'Fuck knows, might be a fight,' said Cam's other mate.

Then he saw a figure jump off a boat close to the bank and eventually resurface. Harry saw through the night scope that the figure was only using its legs to swim, no arms, and that it was struggling to make progress and was drifting down the river at the same pace as the boat, moving only slowly away from it. One of the two people on deck was using a boat hook to try and grab it and pull it back to the boat.

They got closer. 'Christ ....,' he said as he

threw the scope at Cam's mate and dived over the side.

Forty Three

As the unlit boat had steered close to the riverbank past the ferry landing at Bodinnick, Posy had made a decision. Clearly her situation was deteriorating as the FBI would say and she needed to make a move. She was a strong swimmer and even with her hands tied she thought she could make the bank. She was going to jump.

The water temperature in the river Fowey that night was 13.9° C. Harry had reached Posy quickly, the boat she had jumped from had powered away as its occupants saw mad Cam's boat approaching at speed. Having been in the water for fewer than ten minutes, she was cold, shaken and frightened but she was unharmed and uninjured.

By the time she was sitting by the fire in the drawing room with an attentive audience the whole episode was already turning into an adventure. Just wait till she got home, she would tell her pals about this like you wouldn't believe. She had already decided that frat-boy Masterson was a creep. This guy Harry who had rescued her was strong and handsome and so much *older* and he had this sexy British accent. As he handed her a specially made hot chocolate with a dash of Armagnac she gazed up at him adoringly. Happily for Harry, Erin had already declared the visit a total car wreck and made the decision that she and Posy would be leaving for New York the following morning.

Todd Vickery had driven the van and kept watch at Megrims. He had been in the small fishing boat delivering Posy to the *Taras*. He was arrested along with the other man in that boat. The *Taras* set sail for France as planned and the *St Minver* returned to Newlyn. Just without a catch.

The police moved quickly. They swooped on Gwavas Fish and rounded up Todd Vickery and the senior crews. Colin had provided names. French police tracked Roman Rotan to a bar in Granville where he was found out of his head on cocaine and Calvados.

But they missed Gideon Spargo.

Christian had heard what had happened from his father. He was incandescent about his brother's abuse of Megrims. It had been essential that the police get hold of Gideon fast but he'd slipped the net. They would have all the information from Matthews and when Gideon discovered that, he would know where most of it had come from. Then there'd be his grubby pals. They'd be fingered and they'd be after blood, his blood. Really Gideon needed to get out of the country taking the whole sorry story with him.

Then again maybe it was time to make some calls, call in a few favours from some old acquaintances from his Union Street club days; hard men who would get the job done. Something had to be done about Gideon. Maybe something final, something permanent. To be rid of Gideon at last would be the best Christmas present ever.

What was certain was that he'd never listen to Christian but perhaps their father could make him see he had to get out. He'd persuade the old man to go talk to him. He'd be at the Captain's House.

Forty Four

Gideon was in a foul mood. Everything was falling apart and it was all down to that total fucking dickhead Masterson boy. He had always known he was bad news. Should have cut him off months ago. Now Todd Vickery was in custody but Todd would keep his mouth shut. Roman had been taken in after the debacle with the bloody Lindström girl. They had nothing on him for fuck's sake but Roman wouldn't be able to keep his mouth shut. Weak, weak, weak. What a fucking mess. Roman and his absurd ideas; like that fucking insane branding of the girls. Needless, senseless. He, Gideon, should have put a stop to that at the outset. No, Roman would drop him in it without a moment's hesitation and with Todd – guilt by association. He needed to finish up here fast, get over to The Captain's House, grab some gold and get across to Ireland. Shit. It had all been going so well. Christ, he could just picture Christian's grinning face when he found out. Bastard brother. He hated it but he needed help; he needed the Russians.

Gideon was counting money and his phone was on speaker. A gruff eastern European voice came over the crackling line:

'Yes we help.'

'Thank you Anatoly, thank you.'

'But it cost. Jacov want girl in photo.'

'What photo?'

'You with brother and girl on Gwavas Fish website. Jacov like girl.'

'You mean Georgie ... but she's family, she's my niece, my blood!'

'You want live?'

'There must be another way. I'll give you exclusivity on routes, money, gold.'

'Plenty money, gold, plenty routes. Jacov want girl, want *this* girl. You want live Gideon?'

'OK. OK. I'll sort it.'

Gideon was concentrating on the task in hand and was unaware that his father was standing in the open doorway. Abraham never came to The Captain's House. He was not expected, certainly not invited. But he was there that day and he had overheard the conversation and grasped its meaning. Suddenly conscious of the soft tread behind him and recognizing the gentle wheezing, Gideon spoke:

'What the hell are *you* doing here?'

Abraham said nothing.

'What do you want?'

As always, at his father's approach, he didn't turn his head to acknowledge the old man, so he never saw his father pick up a 25cm French Seanox stainless steel gaff hook which was lying on a pile of unopened cartons waiting to shear through the packing tape and shrink wrap. He never saw it swing through the air before embedding in his neck with considerable force, piercing his carotid artery. He bled out in a matter of 10 minutes.

As Gideon lay twitching on the floor with Abraham standing motionless over him, Perish the terrier trotted into the room and approached his master. Confused, he looked up at the old man and whined, then turned back to Gideon, sniffed his face, and started licking the blood as it seeped across the floor.

Afterwards many said they never would have thought that the old man had it in him. What they didn't know was that since childhood and the keelhauling incident which had mangled his left arm, he had been forced to favour his right arm, increasing its strength disproportionately. He was more than capable of a powerful swing. And the threat to his beloved Georgie was the final straw.

Everyone agreed that spending the rest of his life in prison would be an improvement on a home life with Gideon.

Perish wasn't bothered. He had been taken in by

Christian Spargo and was relishing his new life at Corsica House with a big garden and lovely ladies to take him for walks.

The Exchequer was delighted. The confiscation of Gideon Spargo's assets brought in millions, especially when they discovered the treasure haul at The Captain's House.

And Christian was quietly delighted. He could finally rid himself of the family legacy. Christian hated fish. He sold his father's house in Newlyn and the Gwavas Fish business. Gideon had legally held no interest in either and they were not subject to the confiscation. Just before Christmas Christian Spargo drove out of Newlyn for the last time, without a backward glance, vowing never to return.

Forty Five

'How's it going with your father?' asked Fitzroy. 'My guys are on it but there's nothing yet. You getting anywhere?'

Treloar sighed deeply and dragged his hands through his hair. He was sitting in the kitchen at Teal House with Fitzroy. Fitzroy was finishing his packing before heading back to London. He was running late. He was supposed to meet Bella/Hannah at St David's railway station in Exeter for the onward journey to London.

'Jamie's on the case.'

'Well you couldn't do better mate. He's a fucking great asset. Talking of assets, you know that Sam Scott's secondment finishes next week? She'll be back here for the new year.'

'So I hear from Chamberlain.'

'You need to sort that out. You can't leave the girl dangling. Either tell her it's not going to happen or get on with it.'

It had been abundantly clear to everyone but Treloar for months that Sam Scott was in love with him. But with a failed marriage and a troubled past with women, not to mention the fact that she was a key member of his team and a subordinate, he was very wary of taking their relationship down that road. Yet, he had to admit, if only to himself, that he was really missing her and not just for her professional contributions.

'Tell me something I don't know. Christ you sound like my sister Lucia.'

'Clearly a woman of great sense. Is she hot?' shouting over his shoulder as he headed for the bedroom.

Treloar couldn't help but smile. Fitzroy was incorrigible. Lucia was indeed considered "hot", plus she was intelligent, volatile, fierce and funny. Note to self: avoid all contact between Fitzroy and second sister. The thought of that pairing was terrifying.

'There's still something bothering me about Masterson,' he said sipping a glass of mulled wine as Fitzroy returned stuffing a pair of sheer sea green satin knickers into a packed rucksack which he dumped on the table. Mislaid mermaidwear Treloar presumed.

'What's that then?'

'Well, we know that he was sourcing the girls from Spargo.'

'Agreed. Jamie found their photos on the

Lovechild website. They obviously operate like estate agents; they don't take the photos down, they just upload a 'SOLD' banner across the image. Oh and by the way, Jackson Power has offered to bury the Fowey girl in his creekside graveyard.'

'Right. Good ... But how did Masterson find the website? You know as well as I do how secretive these people are. How did a rich privileged LSE student get the link? He doesn't mix in the right circles, Christ he's a guest of the royals.'

'Very minor royals.'

'Even so. I don't see it.'

'Well these people work by word of mouth. He must have come across somebody who knew the site.'

'Right,' said Treloar in a sarcastic tone, 'somebody with similar interests, he just happened to meet, who just happened to trust him - even though his father owns half the Internet and numerous publications who'd just relish exposing the whole sordid business - and someone he was happy to trust with his past and his specific ... needs.'

'Well, when you put it like that.'

'No. There's something here we're not seeing, or more to the point, someone.'

'Mate. The nasty little bastard's toast, we've smashed a major trafficking ring and we've cut off the serpent's head, or more to the point its father has, so take solace from that. We'll never stop them all, especially the really clever ones.'

'Yeah. I know. One at a time.'

Tulip Khan was just passing the northbound Sedgemoor services on the M5 when she took a call from the Daily Mail. She had already been approached by two other national dailies, a Sunday broadsheet and an international agent. As she told the man from the Mail, she was intending to spend Christmas considering her options but would be sure to get back to him.

Juliet was also preparing to leave Cornwall. At The Valley of the Tides she was gathering her belongings and saying her goodbyes. Those like Tom who were subject to a residency court order were staying over Christmas but most people, residents staff and guests, were leaving for the holiday. Jane was staying, ostensibly to be with her nephew, her sister Gloria having gone to Chamonix to ski, but the fact that Harry Forrester was to be there to cook for the Lindström family might have had some bearing on her decision.

Juliet had already visited Jenna Mellin in the graveyard and was now back at Seal Hall upstairs in her room. Flora was in the library waiting for a taxi, chatting with Sindy Cardrew. Sindy had offered to drive them to St Austell railway station but Flora felt an irrational but powerful desire to break free from The Valley of the Tides and rejoin the real world. The impossibly wholesome all-American girl had brought them coffee.

'Well I hope we will be seeing Juliet back with us in January,' said Sindy cheerfully.

Flora put down her coffee mug. 'I don't like to speak ill of the dead but I can't pretend that I will not be a lot happier for her to be here, knowing that the Masterson boy will not be.'

'So unfortunate, particularly for his mother; to lose two children...'

'I had the most extraordinary email from her,' said Flora lowering her voice, never one to miss an opportunity for a little light gossip. 'God knows how she got hold of my private email address. It seems to be from the content that she is almost ... well I have to say this is how I read it ... glad that they boy is dead. There's a distinct tone of ... relief. Most bizarre. I scarcely know the woman. Why she should choose to unburden herself to me ...? But I must say it only served to reinforce my belief that Juliet will be safer with that boy gone.'

Sindy nodded noncommittal and inscrutable as ever. Flora was on a roll.

'There was something deeply unpleasant, even menacing about him, a burgeoning evil. I felt something of it in the father; an odious man,' she suddenly fell silent realizing she was being indiscreet and almost certainly saying too much. Sindy smiled benignly.

'Forgive me. I lose all sense of proportion when

it comes to Juliet; overactive maternal instinct.'

'Not at all. Children with difficulties do evoke strong protective emotions in their family members. We see it all the time. In fact Dr Speer has written extensively on the subject; the role of the family dynamic.'

There was a lull in the conversation then Flora ever alert to an atmosphere spoke to dispel any awkwardness.

'Something of a coup to secure the services of Harry Forrester. How did that come about?'

'A referral actually; Harry was referred by his therapist. He had completed a stint at The Priory and wanted something of a halfway house. Here he can always get help if he feels the need for it whilst getting back on the horse so to speak. He seems very happy here and we very much hope he will stay on.'

'Well he must be flavour of the month with the Lindströms, please excuse the pun, after the business with the daughter I mean; hunk and hero irresistible combo'.

'Obviously we were all grateful for his actions that night.'

'We visited The Rock in Brighton when he was there you know, before that dreadful business with the Michelin inspectors. Michael, my husband, had a particular fondness for some kind of fish burger; I don't recall the type of fish.'

'Monkfish. Monkfish cheek to be precise. Yes he

still makes those here; they're very popular, particularly with the younger residents.'

'Really? I wonder if Juliet has tried them?'

'They also form the basis for one of his classes. He teaches classes as well as doing some of the chef work. He's very successful at it actually.'

'Really? One always thinks of these super chefs as egomaniacs; scarcely the type to be willing to share their knowledge, let alone good at it. How interesting. I expect his classes go down well with the ladies. After all he is rather delish.'

'Shall I see what's keeping Juliet?'

Before Sindy could move, the door opened and Little Miss Sunshine approached the women.

'Your cab is here Ma'am.'

'Thank you Caitlin. I'll fetch Juliet,' said Sindy Cardrew standing, pleased to be released from her tiresome mother.

'Here. I have something for you. Close your eyes and hold out your hand. Think of it as an early Christmas present.'

Juliet placed her rucksack on the bed and complied. She felt the cold metal presence in her palm and curled her fingers around the rectangular object.

'Open your eyes.'

She opened them and gasped in utter delight. There, in her hand, in her possession, in her very grasp, was a beautiful shiny golden Zippo lighter engraved with a dragon.

'Thank you! Thank you so much! It's the best ever ...'

'Merry Christmas Juliet,' said Dr Ivan Speer.

Epilogue

In the end it was Jamie Deverell who tracked him down. From a complex search for the term "Jago" he had found a reference to a Jago Penhallow on the Lost Gardens of Heligan website with a picture. The man was in the background but he thought it looked like Treloar's father and sent him a link.

Christmas Eve was a cold grey day. The gardens were open – every day but Christmas Day – but a bitter wind was blowing up from the sea as Treloar walked across the car park at ten o'clock. The landscape was bleached of colour like a fading black and white photograph and he imagined he might almost come across one of the gardeners lost in the First World War.

The car park was almost empty, unlike the neighbouring farm shop car park which was overflowing with locals collecting their Christmas orders. People would be doing their last minute shopping or decorating their trees and wrapping their presents. At home at Cove Farm his mother and sister Eva would be preparing food for the Nochebuena feast. There would be prawns in garlic followed by besugo – baked bream with potatoes. Lucia was arriving from Barcelona that afternoon with her boys Cesare and Angelo. She would bring Cava and turrón – a nougat made from toasted almonds. He loved it. He loved it all. He had responsibility for the lights and the tree. He had made a start before dawn but there was still work to do before his nephews descended. He wanted everything perfect for them. He had adored Christmas from childhood.

Treloar knew he could ask but something stopped him. With 200 acres he knew it was extremely unlikely that he would just come across his father, but that's exactly what happened. He paid his entrance fee and followed a small group of visitors towards Flora's Green with its giant rhododendrons. On a whim, he turned right and walked through the gate into the walled vegetable garden. There, hoe in hand was his father.

Jago Treloar had been living in a small flat in a house on Tregoney Hill in Mevagissey and working at the Lost Gardens of Heligan under the name Jago Penhallow, a false identity provided by an associate of Joe Thwaite. He had chosen Mevagissey because, being on the south coast, he was unlikely to come across friends and family who mostly lived on the north coat west of St Ives. He had chosen Heligan because, being an arable farmer, he had appropriate skills and he liked to work the land.

The only people from his past life who knew for sure he was still alive, were Joe Thwaite and a friend and neighbouring farmer from the north coast, Edmund Maddox. Maddox had helped him on that fateful day when he had swum out from the cove, had provided him with his first sanctuary, a six month position on a sheep farm near Abergavenny in mid Wales, and continued to keep him reassured and informed about his family.

Now sitting with his son in the Heligan Tearoom he told his story, wiping tears from his eyes.

'When I came out of the water I felt an overwhelming sadness, like I was the last man standing on the earth. I knew my life, and yours, all our lives, were changed forever. I thought I might never see any of you again.'

Treloar took his father's hand across the table but said nothing. Their coffees were untouched.

'I turned a blind eye to Abraham's petty activities: smuggling booze and cigarettes, and he knew better than to ask me to use our land or the cove. But Gideon. Gideon with his guns and drugs and God knows what else. Poor wretches no doubt.' His son nodded.

'I said no when he called me. Next thing I knew there was a threatening letter in the post. Then - you never knew this, I never told your mother - I came across one of the goats with a slit throat. Joe Thwaite called me. Word was there was a contract out on me or mine. Then to confirm it, I got a call from Abraham; man was in tears. Joe said if I was gone that would be an end to it. So I went. There was no other way. Joe said I had to stay gone until he got Gideon. He never did.'

'He's dead. Gideon is dead.'

'I know son, but it's too late ... surely it's too late? Too many years, too much pain,' as he spoke tears still trickled down his face.

'Never, never. I know there'll be some anger at first and I know it'll take time to heal the wounds, but all the girls will be overjoyed. Mamá never believed you were gone. You have to come home for her. Come home Papá, come home for Christmas.'

Acknowledgements

Thanks to Kim, and of course Phil. for all the brain food. The first hand background information about fish, fish markets and fish distribution, and the fishing fraternity and the way it is all policed was very useful and helped bring thoughts and ideas to life.

And also for running the brilliant wet fish stall on the Mevagissey harbour wall; and of course not forgetting the Fowey and Lostwithiel fresh fish rounds and local delivery services to restaurants and hotels.

Any inaccuracies in representation have been caused by misunderstanding or of course artistic licence and lay entirely at the writer's door.

About the authors

A story crafting wordsmith met a psychologist and L A Kent was born.

L A Kent is the pen name of Louise Harrington and Andy Sinden. Having lived in Cornwall for more than 20 years L A Kent writes not only about the dark, evil, obsessed, and sometimes plain mad and bad characters appearing on the dark side of their books, but also empathetically about the county, its people and their lifestyle. And bring to life Cornwall and the visitors that descend from the UK, mainland Europe and further afield, as the villains wreak havoc.

Prior to writing, both travelled extensively in their corporate lives, and have travelled extensively across the world. They lived and worked in South Africa and visited Namibia and Zimbabwe, and draw on time spent in these and other amazing locations visited for their stories.

More can be read about L A Kent and Treloar's team at www.lakent.co.uk where many photographs of the books' settings can also be found.

Preview of Sad Pelican, the Padstow murders. The next Treloar novel

Read on for the beginning of Sad Pelican, next in
the DI Treloar series, starting over the page.

One

They had arrived on Midsummer's Day. Since retirement, they came every summer on that day, travelling down from their home in Wallingford near Oxford. This year Myles and Francesca Westgarth were staying at one of the Pilots' Cottages in Hawker's Cove which overlooked the Camel estuary north west of Padstow.

They always stayed somewhere on the north coast. Francesca's maternal grandparents had been Chenoweths, tenant farmers from Holywell just along the coast towards Newquay, and she had spent every childhood summer holiday at their farm cottage. It had been a magical idyllic time, not just the usual story of fond memories through rose tinted lenses, but truly glorious summer days of blue skies, flower

1

strewn meadows and warm azure seas. So now, freed from the tyranny of the nine to five she was back again, revisiting.

Early summer in Cornwall, before the school holidays, before the hordes of visitors, when everything was clean and new, freshly refurbished for the long high season. It was the time for young families with pre-school children, retired couples, older caravanners and northern Europeans seeking the Cornwall of their television screens.

That morning promised warmth and cloudless skies. The faintest soft breeze caressed her face as she carried a tray of tea out to the terrace overlooking the Old Lifeboat Station across the small bay. At five o'clock the world was quiet and calm; it was her favourite time of day, even in the deepest of winters. Myles came out to join her at the table bringing Pickles, their five year old Airdale terrier, at his master's heel as ever. After tea they were off along the coastal path to walk the mile and a half into Padstow for the morning papers and fresh bread. It was a morning full of childlike hope.

The path ran beside the estuary passing Harbour's Cove and St George's Cove. Normally they would walk along the sand as far as St George's Cove, the nearest beach to Padstow where the 'No Dogs on Beach' ban applied between Easter and October and Pickles would be dutifully leashed, but that morning the tide was in. It was a perfect morning. Across the water the east facing walls of the white-washed houses above Daymer Bay and St Endoc were glowing soft gold in the reflected light of the rising sun.

It was Pickles who made the discovery. As usual he was running on ahead and out of sight as they approached St George's Well. But far from usual, when Myles made his customary short whistle nothing happened, no dog appeared.

'Goddamit, what's wrong with that dog. PICKLES!' Myles was annoyed. He was proud of the dog's obedience and his ability to control him. He hated to be obliged to shout, especially so early in the day.

'I expect he's over-excited. It must be the sea air,' said Francesca in a mollifying tone. But then a thought crossed her mind. Pickles was a keen hunter, true to his breed originally created in the Aire Valley of Yorkshire to catch otters and rats between the Aire and Wharfe rivers. Had he come across something dead?

The first member of the serious crime team to arrive was DI Samantha Scott. This was hardly surprising since she was living just outside Porthcothan only five miles away. Sam had been back in the UK for three weeks. Although an established member of the major incident team she had just returned from an extended secondment to Interpol in Lyon in the south of

France. During her absence she had sold her house in Truro and had taken an extended let on a privately owned holiday cottage on the north coast whilst she considered her options.

'My first thought was it was like the opening of an episode of *Midsomer Murders*. If we were at home in Oxfordshire I'd be looking for the camera crew. They were always in Wallingford filming the town centre,' said Francesca Westgarth. She was talking very quickly, probably in shock Sam thought.

'Well I suppose it must be a coincidence with it being six months exactly from 23rd December, but it struck me at once,' said Myles.

Met with enquiring faces he continued, 'You know, Tom Bawcock's Eve? Mousehole? During a lull in the storms - which were so bad the boats hadn't been able to go out – Tom Bawcock, a fisherman, caught enough fish to stop Mousehole starving. It was 23 June yesterday that's six months from Tom Bawcock's Eve. Though I thought the tradition was specific to Mousehole.' The others continued to stare at him.

'Look,' Westgarth pointed towards the sand. 'Look from this standpoint. That unfortunate fellow has his feet sticking out of the sand sculpture like a pilchard.

Sam turned and looked at the scene again. The sand was indeed shaped into a huge pie with crimped pastry. The pie dish formed from a circle of slatted wooden fencing.

'Of course, Stargazy pie!'

The next arrivals on the scene were from the local policing team, Sergeant Digory Keast and Police Community Support Officer (PCSO) Christopher "Kitto" Betties.

'How the hell could you build something like that overnight in the dark?' It must have taken a crew of people. What the hell are we dealing with here, some kind of murder club?' asked Keast.

'Maybe it's a new kind of activity holiday: Estuary exterminations? Camel carnage?' said Betties with a grin.

'Seaside slaughter?' said Keast joining in.

'Enough already!' barked Sam. 'We need to get it covered over better than this or it'll be all over the Internet by lunchtime.'

'They're bringing up a marquee from Wadebridge. It should be here any minute,' said Keast. The Royal Cornwall Show had taken place earlier in the month and there were some tents still left at the showground on the A39 some eight miles from where they stood.

'Good initiative Sergeant,' said Sam with a smile. She needed these guys onboard. Local support was critical.

'And the doctor's been called. He's a local GP, Dr Zac Jordan. He's on his way,' said Betties.

'Excellent,' said Sam meaning it. These guys were no slouches.

With the Westgarths having cancelled their plans for Padstow and returned to Hawker's Cove, Sam and the two local policemen had taken a closer look at the strange construction on the high water mark in St George's Cove. A sand embankment some four metres long and a metre high had been surrounded by the slatted fence to form a giant pie. The sand had been crimped like pastry crust around the edges and half buried in it, poking out from the crust, were four surfboards and one body, presumed male from the size of the feet, to represent the pilchards.

'Could it just be a coincidence? The killer comes across the sand sculpture and sees a convenient disposal site?' asked Betties.

'Nah,' said Keast,' well I suppose it's just possible but highly unlikely. There's been no competition along here. This has been built around him. You couldn't just force a body in without destroying the sculpture.'

'I agree,' said Sam, 'and it's a strange subject matter for a sand sculpture: wrong coast, wrong time of year.'

'That Westgarth knew about it though didn't he? Worth a look?'

'Yes Sergeant. Definitely. Unlikely I think, but we need to eliminate the Westgarths. I don't suppose there's any CCTV coverage of this beach, no handy webcams?'

'I'll ask over in Daymer Bay, but I doubt there's anything pointing over this way. Long time since we kept a watch for Vikings around these parts.'

As they stood gazing over the Camel towards the white buildings across the water they heard voices approaching and tuned back to greet the newcomers. A dark haired man of about thirty five dressed in cut-off Levis, a washed out pink T-shirt and boat shoes, carrying a medical bag was heading towards them from St Saviour's Point. Loping along beside him was a taller man, forty something, with thick blonde hair, dressed in khaki Chinos and a plain white shirt, sleeves rolled to the elbow. He carried a small rucksack slung over one shoulder. Sam Scott felt her heart lurch and her pulse quicken despite herself. It was her boss and the unrequited love of her life: Detective Chief Inspector Félipe Treloar.

Also by L A Kent

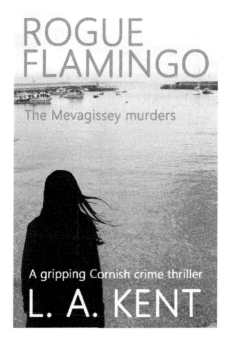

Rogue Flamingo launched the DI Treloar series:

A lawyer's body is found on the beach in the small
Cornish village of Porthaven, staked out with a tarred
bag over its head, just as the peak summer season gets
underway. When a second body is found bizarrely
fixed to the floor of a building not long afterwards, the

laconic police surgeon remarks 'Well, psychopaths need holidays too'; and DI Treloar, a maverick to some bosses but a driven, committed investigator to his fellow officers, takes charge. When more bodies turn up, Treloar and his team are at first unsure - accident or murder?

There seems to be no connection between the victims whose murders are violent, with escalating viciousness and sexuality. What is going on? Could they have brought their fates with them, festering secrets from the past? Could either of the two mysterious men staying at the camp site be involved?

Is it one or more doing the killing? What about the rabble of students in the big house or the local recluse and his enigmatic brother? What about embittered locals resentful of incomers buying up their village?

And who is the extraordinary female, obsessed with birds, institutionalised in the South of France as a child, who reflects on her past as the story unfolds?

Then a brutal attack on one of their own shocks Treloar's team and their focus switches in an unexpected direction when a heartfelt injustice surfaces.

Broken Dove, the St Ives murders
No. 2 in series

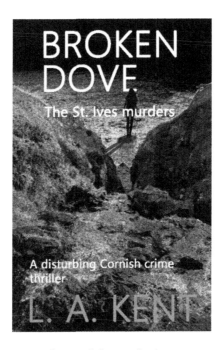

It's May Day, a day celebrated since pagan times to welcome in the summer.

In the wild countryside of west Cornwall, it is also the famed annual Treloar family party, being hosted for the first time by DI Félipe Treloar at Lost Farm Barn. The Treloar clan, friends and colleagues from the major crime team will all be there.

But a ghost from summers past is also coming, and unbeknownst to all, bringing madness and violence in her wake.

And whilst the early guests are revelling, in nearby St Ives two young girls disappear from a holiday park swimming pool.

Who is tormenting the beautiful Amy? Is it a demented fan or someone much closer to home?

And what is wrong with the parents of one of the missing girls; what are they hiding?

And as the story unfolds, after a tragedy in Amsterdam, a troubled soul is falling deeper and deeper into a personal hell, following his demons across the country from his home in Islington.

Treloar and his Sergeant chase answers from the wilds of Cornwall to the busy streets and leafy lanes of London, and as events bring back forgotten memories and long buried emotions they are both challenged to the core. But Treloar meets a kindred spirit. And the rules are left behind.

**And by Beatriz Treloar,
chef at Seafood on Stilts restaurant in St Ives,
and youngest sister of DI Treloar:**

Including mains, soups and salads, sauces and sides, from the grill, early bird breakfasts, and gluten free baking. There are a few non-fishy meals in this 19cm x 23cm kitchen friendly paperback with wipeable cover!

For more about the Treloar series, the characters and the authors, and beautiful photographs of Cornwall take a look at www.lakent.co.uk